Freeman's

Family

Previous Issues

Freeman's: Arrival

Freeman's
Family

Est. 2015

Edited by

John Freeman

Grove Press
New York

Published simultaneously in Canada
Printed in the United States of America

First published by Grove Atlantic, August 2016

FIRST EDITION

ISBN 978-0-8021-2526-2
eISBN 978-0-8021-9044-4

Grove Press
an imprint of Grove Atlantic
154 West 14th Street
New York, NY 10011

Published in collaboration with the MFA in Creative Writing at The New School

THE NEW SCHOOL
CREATIVE WRITING

Cover and interior design by Michael Salu

Distributed by Publishers Group West

groveatlantic.com

16 17 18 19   10 9 8 7 6 5 4 3 2 1

Contents

Introduction
John Freeman...................... vii

Seven Shorts
Sunjeev Sahota........................1
Angela Flournoy......................4
Adania Shibli 7
Colin Robinson 9
Heather O'Neill.....................15
Édouard Louis 19
Nadifa Mohamed...................24

Crossroads
Aminatta Forna 31

Lost Letter #1: From Phillis Wheatley, of Boston, to Arbour Tanner, of Newport

Lost Letter #2: From Obour Tanner, Newport, to Phillis Wheatley, Boston
Honorée Fanonne Jeffers 55

A Family Name
Garnette Cadogan 61

Little Jewel
Patrick Modiano..........................73

Nola
Amanda Rea 87

Ode to My Sister
Amaryllis Ode
Victuals Dream Ode
Sharon Olds 95

A Tomb for Uncle Julius
Aleksandar Hemon 101

Tunnel
Mo Yan 119

One Day I Will Write About My Mother
Marlon James........................... 131

Tell Me How It Ends (An Essay in Forty Questions)
Valeria Luiselli 141

The Selected Works of Abdullah (The Cossack)
H. M. Naqvi............................ 185

Letter to a Warrior
Athena Farrokhzad 217

CONTENTS

When Living Is a Protest
Ruddy Roye .... Insert

Ema
César Aira 229

10-Item Edinburgh Post-partum Depression Scale
Claire Vaye Watkins 233

Wild
Tracy K. Smith........................ 243

If There Was No Moon
Joanna Kavenna 245

You Better Not Put Me in a Poem
Sandra Cisneros...................... 257

Going to the Dogs
Claire Messud 269

Rich Children
Alexander Chee 279

Inside Voices
David Kirby 287

This Old Self
Helen Garner........................... 291

Contributor Notes.................... 297

Introduction

JOHN FREEMAN

I come from a family of story collectors, rather than storytellers. My parents were social workers and they listened for a living. They heard private stories, hard-won stories. The kind that people polish and protect because it is all they have left. Say the words "talking therapy" and jokes quickly follow; but this was no laughing matter. This was early AIDS patients dying in terror. This was mothers losing children to foster care. This was men going to jail for life for minor marijuana possession. This was children left behind, lonely and angry.

I knew these details only through inference as a child. I had ears and they caught and assembled things heard from several rooms away. To know more would have been a violation. My mother would even cover her patient notes if I stood behind her while she was working. She often sat at our dining room table, late at night, transcribing her counseling notes from a legal pad onto hospital forms so her clients could be reimbursed by their HMOs. She was creating a record of a life. My mother never wanted to be a writer, but at nights she became a narrative abacus.

Growing up in the vibration of such stories was a strange thing. To know that stories conveyed and possessed such power, the ability to save your life, when my own life did not need saving, was like being prepared for an earthquake that happened everywhere but here. It created a kind of free-floating dread and a sense of intense good fortune. My brothers and I developed highly tuned Geiger counters. We tapped the ground and picked at fault lines. All of us sought out stories. All of us practiced for the future. And when the earthquake came, as it must, in all families—either through biology, or bad decisions, or simply bad luck—we took the tools my parents had demonstrated as being of such great value, and we went to work.

When people die—if they are known—their bodies are transformed into stories. He used to, she was like, he helped me, he was a, that one time she visited, remember? In this way a family's stories are as important as its DNA. In remembering the dead, they say where a family is from, and by marking time they give us consolation against loss. From the sacred to the profane, family stories convey love and they ask for it. In this sense, stories are as important to family life as water and food and shelter. A family without stories is no longer a family.

From the beginning of time, family has been one of the richest threads within literature. Whether it is *The Odyssey*, a poem about a father's trip home; or *Hamlet*, a play about a son's battle with his father; or *Beloved*, a novel regarding a mother's terrible act of protection for her daughter, great works often entangle us in the moral and emotional dilemmas of families. Through families, we have seen the history of nations refracted, as in Naguib Mahfouz's *Cairo Trilogy*, and in families it's been possible to watch a people fight over and preserve their past, as in Louise Erdrich's *Love Medicine*. Even to be born without a family—like the orphan narrators of Dickens—becomes a drama. These books are written out of a loss that cannot be repaired but insists on being mapped.

Even as social convention attempts in much of the world to view difference as a threat, or through some kind of hierarchy, difference in family life enriches literature. The kinds of families people come from vary intensely. Some have two parents, some have none; some are biologically related, others become related by choice. Some have long histories; some peer into a past and find a shallow well—be it stopped by enslavement, holocaust, or simply a lack of data. What all these shapes of family life share is not so much the so-called family unit, but rather the need to narrativize experience—to mythologize it, to think on it, to show it back to itself in the form of a story. And in this sense, we are always just at the beginning of our world's culture of family stories.

This issue of *Freeman's* is an attempt to give space to the variety of family stories out there, for in that breadth one can glimpse how the world presses down—with urgency—on family matters. During the summer that 80,000 children turned up in the United States, fleeing difficult circumstances, Valeria Luiselli goes on a road trip to the Southwest with her husband and two children as their own green card paperwork hangs in suspension. The juxtaposition of such fates compels her to volunteer as a translator in New York City for a legal aid concern, helping some of these children answer a questionnaire that tries, in big ways and small, to categorize their stories.

There is a search at the heart of many of these pieces. Sometimes it is to make sense of the past. Aleksandar Hemon remembers his Uncle Julius, a committed communist who spent great portions of his life in the Soviet gulag, losing his job and his family in the years he spent away, but for some reason never forsaking his beliefs. Meanwhile, Aminatta Forna meditates on the profound differences between how a family of mixed race is perceived in Britain and how it is perceived in America; and how the past, which informs that social construction, bears down on her own family in both places.

Very often, there is a missing person at the heart of this search. Joanna Kavenna's short story conjures a woman grown wild from the disappearance of her father. In his essay, Garnette Cadogan explains why he has three names, and what his father has to do with the shell game he plays among them. In an excerpt from Patrick Modiano's novel *Little Jewel*, a woman recalls babysitting for a couple who seem to have little concern for the whereabouts of their young daughter, a situation into which she thrusts herself for reasons at the heart of her own experience. We pass on our concerns, from family to family, whether we know it or not, Tracy K. Smith observes in her poem.

In some cases, the past is not knowable, creating a vacuum in which stories develop. Sunjeev Sahota comes from a family in which birth years are vague, and even lineage too; while the poet Honorée Fanonne Jeffers looks into the lunar eclipse of antebellum America, giving voice to a woman who writes to the early African-American poet Phillis Wheatley. Writing a letter to an unborn daughter, the Swedish-Iranian poet Athena Farrokhzad explains the world into which her own child comes, and why she has no official past to give her.

Nations loom into view here as überfamilies, demanding loyalty but sometimes not returning it with love. In Palestine, the novelist Adania Shibli gets a voice mail from the Israeli Defense Forces on a borrowed cell phone informing her that the house to which the phone belongs is about to be bombed; only she doesn't know whose phone it is. In Mo Yan's feverish short story, a father attempts to outsmart the enforcer of China's one-child policy by digging a tunnel under the family house. In Italy, a vacationing David Kirby cringes with recognition at fellow Americans the way one does at family members behaving badly: "American tourists, American tourists!" he cries. "Hold it down, will you?"

Sometimes, in family life, you have to laugh to keep from crying. Amanda Rea writes of a woman who came to live with her family, not telling her own family she had annexed another. Alexander Chee recalls the time he catered for a wealthy New York clan that treated a statue better than its own matriarch. Entering the burying years of middle age, Claire Messud and her husband cling to a pair of mangy, cantankerous, half-blind and deaf dogs who rule their house. In a humorous essay, Colin Robinson describes how he and his younger brother have become notable among the local barbershop patrons for the way they approach the idiosyncratic style of a stylist they call Edward Scissorhands.

To write about family is to love it, and several writers here have written portraits of fathers, mothers, aunts, even—in the case of Sandra Cisneros's poem—the extended family of one's lovers. These are the people who made me, their stories tell us. Marlon James rejects the urge to once again write about his father, and pays tribute to his detective mother, the woman who kept his house going and whose opinion he holds dear today. Angela Flournoy thinks back on the period when her grandfather came to live with her family, leaving behind a mysterious object. Nadifa Mohamed tells the Odyssean tale of her uncle, who wore sharp suits, worked in Saudi Arabia and Yemen, and lived hard until the day he died.

How we depict family, Ruddy Roye reminds us in his photo essay, says a lot about what we feel matters, and who matters, what is officially of value in society. Heather O'Neill recalls her gangster father, and all the wisdom he dispensed before age and infirmity made him feel unnecessary. Similarly, in her diaries, Helen Garner describes her days and hours in the grandmothering years, when the freedom to be overlooked is at once exhilarating and full of sting.

Even when left behind, family still retains the power to wound. In odes to her mother and sister and father, Sharon Olds recalls this power, and lays waste to the assumption that it is denatured with time. Sometimes, when under threat, the only thing to do is to escape, which Édouard Louis did as a young boy, in the wake of an incident he describes in these pages with intensity and horror.

In starting a new family, the possibility of this moment—to begin again—can be overwhelming. The narrator of Claire Vaye Watkins's short story reels under this pressure, as does the overweight bachelor at the heart of H. M. Naqvi's tale, who, entering his seventieth year, diabetic and disheveled, is given a ward to keep safe. There is a grace moment, before that responsibility kicks in, and César Aira captures it in a brief and lovely passage from his upcoming novel, *Ema*, as a husband and wife chat in the falling dark, after a large meal.

Now, when my family gets together, for meals and for holidays, my brothers and I invariably wind up telling stories. My mother has been dead six years and my father is now remarried with a new family of his own. He has never been a good storyteller, but he generates stories faster than Joe Gould. What about the time a sprinkler closed around his finger and he ran into the house with it on, afraid his finger would be cut off? How about when he took up ballet at age seventy and performed in *The Nutcracker*? What about the time he stepped in front of our neighbor's car as he was doing a burnout on the street, then yanked him through the window and threatened to pull his eyeballs out if he ever did that again?

My father listens to these stories with laughter and bewilderment that he gave birth to three NSA-like recording devices. It is a reaction, no doubt, that many family members have had upon learning that they have a writer in their midst. To have their deeds and words remembered, imprinted on paper, perhaps, and shared with anyone who reads. It has always been thought of as a kind of betrayal, this telling of stories. Perhaps it is, but I have always thought the opposite, and the pieces here only confirm that feeling. That to write is to narrate experience, to describe how it feels, to tell how it was lived, to say who was there; in other words, it is to treat the reader like an extended member of one's family, the one—as humans—to which we all belong.

Freeman's
Family

Seven Shorts

My family doesn't know a lot of stuff that, to be honest, they should. Hardly anyone knows their real date of birth. Mum's passport says April 1960, but following a bit of sleuthing she's adamant it's far more likely to be July 1961. Officially, Dad was born in 1954.

'That's definite,' my uncle says, half-rising towards my book-shelves, as if the spines enacted their own magnetism. 'Nine years after me. Exactly 10 years after the troubles.'

'But that would make it 1957,' I reply. 'And it'd mean your seventieth bash last month was a bit premature.' I turn to my grandmother. 'You, Biji?'

'1928.'

'Sure?'

'Give or take five years.'

'It must be July,' Mum says. 'I'm much more of a Cancer.'

'Give or take *five* years? So you might be 83 or, equally, 92?'

'I was married at 13. I had other things to worry about.'

'Sure you were 13?'

'Don't be clever,' Biji says, pointing her walking-cane at me.

I figure this elastic relationship with time isn't surprising, given a surrounding culture that uses the same word ('kal') to mean both yesterday and tomorrow, and another ('bharson') to mean all three of: the day after tomorrow; the day before yesterday; and, my favourite: a very long time ago.

The conversation drifts to other things our family hasn't always known. I point out that until the age of six I was under the impression that I had five siblings. We lived in a 'joint-family' set-up, typical in the villages of Punjab (less so the estates of Derby), with grandparents, uncles, aunts and cousins all under one roof. There'd never been a distinction made between who was whose brother or sister and it wasn't until the lead up to my first trip to India, where I was to be accompanied by only one of those siblings, that I began to realise that my immediate family, and my idea of it, was a lot smaller than I'd thought.

'You think that's bad?' Biji says. 'My mother-in-law didn't even know who her husband was until after her first child was born.'

My grandmother explained that in those days . . .

('Which days would that be?'

'I said don't be clever.')

. . . in those days, women like Preetam Kaur, my great-grandmother, had to keep their faces screened from all men inside the house and out. The only time she could pull back the deep hood of her chunni in the presence of a man was on the evenings her husband fancied her company. But, even then, on a farmstead in those pre-electricity nights, it'd be far too dark for her to see anything beyond the general outline of my great-grandfather's face. In other families, the woman would gain a surreptitious glance during the day, perhaps under the pretext of a sneeze, and see who she had ended up with. The problem for Preetam Kaur was that her husband had three brothers, and all four siblings had married within a few days of each other. So there were now four new brides in the house, none of whom was sure which of the brothers was her husband.

'But, Biji, surely—at night . . . they'd *know*.'

'What difference would it have made to them to know?' Mum says

2

(bitterly? I wonder). 'They didn't marry a man; they were chained to a family.'

'An idea of a family,' my uncle says, not looking back from my bookshelves.

'What difference would it have made to you to know that you had not five but just one sibling? Would it have made your childhood better or worse?'

'He already said knowing made things smaller,' my uncle reminds us.

'Anyway,' Biji goes on . . .

Every evening, after chasing the bats out from under the veranda, Preetam Kaur and her three sisters-in-law would gather a few feet from the window in a room at the rear of the courtyard, waiting to be summoned to collect the dishes, staring through the wooden slats at the four men eating, all bearded, all turbaned.

Maybe him on the left? His gold chain looks familiar.

Do you think I could put a candle in my room next time?

Don't, pehnji—Mother-in-law won't tolerate it.

The one with the collar up looks strong.

Oh, what does it matter? Let's not find out. Let it just be us while it can.

'And they didn't find out until they had kids?' I ask.

'So the story goes. Until they saw who held which child.'

I don't know how much of the story is true, but reckon that, like all stories, it probably contains truth enough. The farmstead remains in our family and the former women's room now stores giant blue barrels of grain. I don't have cause to enter it very often, but whenever I do I'll think of the four new brides made to hide their faces from the world, peering through the slatted window to the men enjoying the courtyard. Except these days the wooden slats are no more, replaced—what else?—by iron bars.

—Sunjeev Sahota

3

What we found looked like leather wrapped in plastic. Nearly the same color as my skin, about the size of a coaster. Square. It was under a pile of neckties in the bottom of my granddaddy's dresser drawer.

My granddaddy learned he had emphysema—a surprise to no one considering his pack-a-day habit—and was gone a month later. Died to preserve his idea of dignity, I thought. He did not want incapacitation, dreaded immobility, could not bear the thought of being a burden on his family, so he willed himself gone. But before he was gone there was a hospital bed to set up, a room to break down. And after he was gone there was a minor mystery to solve.

Granddaddy had called my mother seven years prior to say he thought his girlfriend in Oakland was slowly poisoning him, that he'd lost a lot of weight, so my mother invited him to live with us. Our first house. With a grandparent living with us I felt we had more in common with our immigrant neighbors: three generations under one roof. Granddaddy would sit in the garage and say hello to whoever walked by. Who knows how long it took the people on our block to accept that he was our blood. He had a big, bridge-heavy nose, jowly cheeks, wavy black hair and light blue eyes. Not much phenotypically in common with the rest of us, except for my mother's dimpled chin. He was paler than Mr. Reyes, our neighbor from Puebla who brought us tamales on Christmas. He sat with his thin legs crossed at their delicate knees—knees that bent deliberately when he walked, like Pinocchio's—an unfiltered cigarette dangling from his lips. He used to tell me that none of his people back in Louisiana had ever been slaves. That if I had slave blood it was from my father's side, or maybe my mother's mother's people in Oklahoma, not from him. It sounded like a lie, but an important one to him, so I kept quiet.

He had sent his bedroom furniture down from Oakland with my cousin Leon, who seemed to be in permanent possession of a U-Haul truck. Judging from the piles of clothes and the extra mattress in the cab, Leon and his girlfriend were living in that truck. But that was none of our nor Granddaddy's business.

In high school I sold vacuum cleaners at Sears and sneaked sweets to Granddaddy for extra money. Jelly doughnuts were his favorite. Sometimes he'd slide me a few dollars, sometimes he'd cut me a check for a few hundred. He never offered the money while asking me to go on a run for him. Usually it showed up in his shirt-front pocket days later. I still felt the two were connected, and I was aware that giving a diabetic a box of Krispy Kremes was akin to giving a drunk a fifth of cognac. I saved the money for college.

He fell down. This was a week or so after we learned about the emphysema. I was upstairs, doing whatever a nineteen-year-old does in the morning, when I heard a pile of books crash to the floor. The only piles of books were in my room. It had to be him. I ran. His body, all 120 pounds of him, was crumpled in a corner between the bathroom and his bed. I screamed for my sister and we got him to the couch. He made jokes in our arms, complained about my morning breath, advised us to never get old.

What we found looked like a camel-colored pocket square wrapped in cellophane and pressed into a tile by the decades. I imagined him buying such a square to complement his favorite tan suit and gold-accented suspenders, but never finding an occasion special enough to warrant pulling it out of its plastic.

After his fall, my mother came home and did forensics. She tried to figure out what, outside of general old age and feebleness, had gone wrong. Granddaddy's bed was too tall, she decided. It had to go. She took him to a doctor's appointment and tasked my sister and me with breaking it down before they returned. We set upon the frame with hammers, an aluminum bat and our weak biceps. The wood was brittle from decades of absorbing cigarette smoke. Black-brown splinters flew in my face. We worked in silence, sweating in the dry heat of August. I cried. Granddaddy's room had been a Southern

Californian suburban replica of his room in Oakland, a reminder of his independent life. All of us had made formal visits to his room over the previous seven years, asked to sit with him at the foot of his bed while he watched TV, left without protest when it seemed he wanted to be alone. With his own bed gone and a mechanical one from the hospital in its place, the room more closely resembled its true purpose: a comfortable place for him to pass on.

He passed on when I was at my new job at Ikea. I was putting together a coffee table when my manager pulled me aside. It had seemed easiest and quickest to break Granddaddy's bed into pieces, but now that I knew a thing or two about how furniture was made, I realized we could have disassembled it.

After the funeral and the repast, my sister and I sorted his clothes for relatives to claim. We found the square there under his neckties. Plastic, inorganic, unreadable, square. Was it candy? Clothing? Some ancient hair product melted and hardened over? My mother held the square close to her face, ran her thumb along its flat front. She laughed.

"It's processed cheese," she said. "For sandwiches. Look at this flap where you're supposed to peel it open."

It could have been cousin Leon's, ferreted away and forgotten during that six-hour drive south with Granddaddy's furniture. That would mean the slice of cheese was exactly as old as Granddaddy's time with us, a marker of his final years. Or Granddaddy could have hid the cheese over a decade prior, maybe two decades, even. We would have needed carbon-14 dating to find out. I like to think it was the latter, that the story of how a slice of indestructible cheese product ended up in a dresser drawer began when its owner was much younger, and his world was much bigger. Either way, Granddaddy took that secret, along with many others, to his grave.

—Angela Flournoy

To be clear, I don't like mobile phones at all. But when my family and I arrived in Ramallah, a friend gave me one in case of emergencies. Even so, when it starts to ring, suddenly, at 8:29 on this morning in mid-July, I let it go until my partner picks it up. He goes quiet and holds the phone out to me, pressing it to my left ear. It's a recorded message, delivered in a booming voice speaking in formal Arabic. I catch only a few words: ". . . You have been duly warned. The Israeli Defense Forces . . ." Then the message ends and the line goes dead. I freeze.

This is the kind of call made by the Israeli Army when it is about to bombard a residential building. The moment someone answers the call, they relinquish their right to accuse the army of war crimes, as they have been "duly warned." The strike can take place within a half hour of the call.

Just yesterday I heard about a young man receiving a warning call like this, informing him that the building where he lived in the north of Gaza would be bombed. The young man was at work in the south at the time. He tried to call his family but could not reach them. He left work and rushed home, but found the building destroyed. Some of his family members were wounded; others had been killed.

I don't know whether this incident really took place. One hears a lot of stories these days, some too awful to believe. But here it is, at 8:29 a.m., pouncing on me like my destiny.

I'm not sure who this phone belongs to exactly, or who the Israeli Army thinks it belongs to. I wonder if my friend might be part of some political group. I doubt it. I make a quick mental survey of the neighbors, trying to guess which of them might be "wanted." The only people I've encountered since we arrived two weeks ago in Ramallah are annoying children aged four to eleven; two middle-aged women and an elderly one; and a man in his late fifties. None of this puts my fears to rest. Their profiles do not differ much from those of the victims of recent air strikes. And then I realize, with dread, that

I've become a replica of an Israeli Army officer, pondering which of these Palestinians might represent a "security threat."

My partner is still standing in front of me, and behind him our eight-year-old daughter has now appeared. Our son, three months old, is sleeping in the next room. My partner, who has limited Arabic, asks me what the call was about. I look at him, then at our curious daughter. I try to find something to say, but I am overcome by a feeling of helplessness.

I look at the number again. I could press a button and call the "Israeli Defence Forces" back. Or I could send a text message. I could at least voice my objection to this planned attack. But when I try to think of what I could say or write, I feel numb, knowing that the words that will pour out of me will be useless. This realization, that words cannot hold and that they are wholly feeble when I need them the most, is crushing. The Israeli Army can now call my mobile phone to inform me of its intention to bomb my house, but my tongue is struck dumb.

After telling our daughter to get ready I go to the room where our three-month-old is sleeping. We have less than a half hour to leave the house. I walk into the darkness of the room and stare at the wall. I begin to notice a strange, intensely black cube high up on the wall. I don't understand what that cube is doing there. I am sure that the wall is white; it's not possible that a part of it has suddenly turned black. I scan the room for other dark cubes that might have crept into it while I was outside. Finally my eyes fall on a dot of green light at the end of the computer adapter, in front of which a pile of books stands. The light emanating from that tiny dot has cast the shadow of the books on the opposite wall, creating that black cube.

That tiny green dot of light, as faint as it seems, barely visible, was able to throw me into another abyss of fear. Perhaps my terror following that phone call is also exaggerated. Before my daughter and

I leave the house as we do every day—she to her summer camp, and I to the university to my students—I look at my partner and our three-month-old child. Will this be the last time I see them? We go down the stairs, without meeting any of the neighbors or their children, so I stall in the hope of picking up some noises from behind their closed doors. I hesitate for a moment, wondering whether I should ring one of their doorbells to ask if they received a similar call. But I keep walking behind my daughter until we leave the building. Then I look at the fifth floor and at the sky, trying to detect any sound or movement of drones or fighter jets. So far, nothing. We continue down the road to catch a cab from the main street.

As we reach it, the morning bustle of the main street embraces me. I calm down slightly, thinking it might have been a mistaken call, or one intended as a general warning to everyone, and not specifically to me and my family. But once we get inside the cab, fear overtakes me again. I ask the driver to turn the radio on.

For the next half hour, there will only be news about bombings of buildings in Gaza, with none in Ramallah.

—Adania Shibli
Translated from the Arabic by Wiam El-Tamami

Salon Habana, the barbershop in Chelsea, New York City, where my brother and I get our hair cut, is a hole-in-the-wall sort of place. Run by Dominicans, it has a big window facing onto Seventh Avenue and an array of ceiling-mounted neon tubes which reflect starkly from wallpaper that might originally have been cream-colored but more likely has just yellowed with age. The shop accommodates six black plastic upholstered barber's chairs along one wall, and a couple of benches for waiting customers against the other. In a back corner, bright pink and fitted slightly askew, are the establishment's only washbasin and, opposite that, a small enclosed booth where an elderly lady sits. Her job is to collect the tokens that the haircutters give to their customers so that track can be kept of their earnings. At $11.50 per haircut it seems unlikely that these add up to very much, even on a busy day. But we live in a world where the accounting of small sums has become more fastidious than that of large ones, and the financial system at the Habana is evidently quite rigorous.

The same people, five men and one woman, cut hair at the salon every day. They offer a wide variety of tonsorial techniques and chair-side mien. The third chair back is tended by a tall, elderly gentleman whose dignified bearing and immaculately laundered nylon smock give him a demeanor more typical of a consultant surgeon than a barber. This impression is reinforced by the extraordinary dexterity with which he wields his scissors. His cutting style, consisting of rapid snips applied evenly and with breathtaking speed across the customer's head, has led my brother and me to christen him "Edward Scissorhands."

The chair at the very back of the shop is worked by a corpulent gay man with a close-cropped head and a worried face. Roughly taped on the wall next to him are large autographed photographs of Paris Hilton. It's not clear how they came to be there but it seems unlikely that they were signed by the star during a haircut at the Habana. The same might be said for the photograph of the newscaster Kaity Tong, also autographed, that is stuck in the corner of the mirror facing the next chair. However, here the provenance is known: Ms. Tong is a denizen of the area and can occasionally be seen eating a late lunch in the Italian restaurant two doors away. Her husband comes in to get his hair cut and gave the picture to Akram, the barber for whom, more by chance than judgment, I have become a regular customer over recent years.

Akram's own hairstyle, an untidy Beatles mop worn with a Zapata mustache, is not much of an advertisement for his trade. But I enjoy his relaxed, genial manner and he now knows, better than anyone else at any rate, how I like my hair cut. "Good and choppy," he says, riffling the top of my head with a vigorous carelessness. Akram, of Uzbek origin, doesn't speak much English so the haircut takes place largely in silence. That's another reason why I prefer him to the other barbers, who evidently regard chair-side chat, however banal, as an essential part of the service. About two-thirds of the way through the session, Akram will reach for a pair of scissors that have large, square gaps along the length of their blades, producing the uneven cut I like. "My secret weapon," he'll declaim, brandishing them ostentatiously in front of my face. "Ah, the killer punch," I say, nodding at the scissors, but with care because they are only inches from my nose. "Yes professor," he beams into the mirror, "tequila punch."

The system employed at the Habana means that, unless you make it clear you want a particular hairdresser, you will be taken from the bench by whoever has finished with his or her customer when your turn comes. It's not easy to express a preference for a particular chair in front of the other cutters, especially for an easily embarrassed Englishman like myself, and I remember the awkwardness that accompanied my original decision to pick Akram. My brother, still more diffident than I, has never felt able to negotiate this hurdle and consequently, despite a lengthy patronage of the Habana, does not have a regular barber. This would not be a problem except for the fact that, after an unfortunate visit some years ago when the technique of a thousand tiny cuts rendered him pretty much hairless, he never wants to return to the chair of Edward Scissorhands. To avoid this he has developed a strategy where he will stroll with the studied insouciance of the flaneur up and down the sidewalk outside the Habana until he sees Scissorhands seat a new customer. He then nips smartly into the line on the benches, confident that when his turn comes it will be with one of the other hairdressers. I've seen my brother patrolling the window of the Habana in this manner for up to fifteen minutes at a time and, though I've never had the heart to tell him, I'm pretty certain that everyone in the salon, including Edward S., knows exactly what he's up to.

One Thursday morning I was comfortably ensconced in Akram's chair, my eyes closed, enjoying the sensation of the electric clippers around my ears. This is a part of the haircut which, for men of my age with silver sideburns, is apparently known in the trade as the "whiteoff." I was drifting away to the salsa music on the Latin radio station that plays continuously in the salon when my reverie was interrupted by a loud voice directly behind me.

"I couldn't get no bananas today so I brought you some grapes."

The woman's voice had a rough edge, like sandpaper on brick, and carried a strong Bronx accent.

"Hi Marianne, how's it with you?" The weary resignation of the guy working the chair next to Akram's was undisguised.

I opened my eyes and looked in the mirror. Standing behind me, proffering a small bunch of white grapes in a piece of tissue, was an elderly lady, wiry and erect, wearing a headscarf and sunglasses.

"The price of bananas is ridiculous," she complained, "but I think these grapes are OK, maybe they need a wash. Try one; they're fresh . . . aren't they?" The way her voice trailed off suggested the fruit might be anything but fresh.

The big guy took the grapes and laid them carefully on the narrow ledge under the mirror, next to his scissors and combs.

"OK. OK. Here's your cigarette Marianne. See you tomorrow." There was an unmistakable testiness in his voice as he opened the packet, withdrew a single smoke, and passed it to her.

"Thank you dear." Marianne put the cigarette behind her ear, rather jauntily for a woman of her age I thought, and began to walk out of the shop.

"Have a good one guys," she called, waving at the other hairdressers from the door in the manner of a movie star acknowledging her fans before departing the red carpet. As soon as she had left, the guy next to us turned to Akram, looking even more unhappy than usual.

"Marianne is really beginning to piss me off," he snarled venomously.

"What is your problem, my friend?" Akram's query was solicitous.

"She comes in here every day and for a piece of stinking fruit I have to give her a cigarette. That's a pack and a half of cigarettes a month . . . nearly two cartons a year." His forehead furrowed with the effort of the mental calculation. "It's killing me."

In the mirror I could see Akram cast a sympathetic look in the direction of his neighbor. He had stopped cutting my hair and, along with the rest of the shop, was waiting to see what would happen next.

"She's not just getting the cigarettes from me you know. She's working the whole street. The guy next door in the shoe store gives, and the woman in the launderette too. She can't be smoking all these cigarettes. She must be hoarding them." He was in full flow now, his voice rising to a plaintive wail.

"And what's this crap about bananas being too expensive? I mean, how expensive can a banana be? She must have lots of money. She has her own apartment on Twenty-Fourth Street. Even if it's rent controlled that can't be cheap. And look at these grapes." He picked them up and dangled them disdainfully in Akram's direction, letting the tissue paper flutter to the hair-strewn floor. "Filthy, rotten, they must have come out of the garbage. Well they can go back there." This latter was announced with triumphal bitterness as the grapes dropped into the trash can.

Akram went over to his fellow barber and placed a hand, still holding the comb with which he had been tending my hair, on his shoulder.

"If she is getting to you, my friend, why you no do something about it?"

"Yeah, like what?" The question was indignant and forlorn in equal parts.

"Just tell her you no want any more of her stinking fruit and you no want to give her any more cigarette. Then she no come in again. That's it." Akram shrugged, his arms apart in a gesture designed to show how simple it all was.

"You're right Akram, that's what I'm going to do." This was said with such a lack of conviction that an unending future of unwashed grapes and other sundry fruit seemed inevitable. The big guy placed an unlit cigarette in his mouth and headed for the door, evidently planning to cool down outside with a smoke of his own.

Akram turned back to me, lost in thought. His hands plied idly through my still damp locks as he tried to collect himself. He reached for the jar that contained his scissors and pulled out the pair with the serrated blades. "And now for the secret weapon," he announced.

I returned home, still marveling at the rich oddness of life on Seventh Avenue, with its old-fruit-for-cigarettes trade. My back was prickly from the hair that had fallen into my shirt and so I leaned over the bath and showered my head and shoulders. Toweling off in front of the mirror I noticed small but prominent wings sticking out from each side of the back of my neck. I looked like Elizabeth Montgomery in an early episode of *Bewitched*. Akram had evidently been so distracted by the Marianne business that he had failed to finish my haircut. I tried to pat the wings flat but they just sprang back. There was no choice but to return to the shop.

Akram greeted me with evident concern. "You right professor. That's not natural." He referred here to the style of the cut around the back of the neck, which in a sophisticated salon like the Habana, comes as a choice between square, round, and, my preference, natural.

"Two minutes," he said, pointing with his scissors at the new customer in his chair. I took a seat on the bench and picked up a copy of the *Daily News*. It wasn't long before he was carefully snipping off the offending protuberances. As he held up the hand mirror to show me the restoration work he nodded towards the window. I caught a glimpse of a familiar figure walking quickly past, peering sideways into the shop.

"Looks like your brother's coming in," he said, tousling my hair. "You want gel on this?"

—Colin Robinson

My mother sent me on an airplane to live with my dad in Montreal when I was seven years old. I only had to my name a wool coat and a little burgundy suitcase that contained some clothes and a few favorite storybooks I had packed. I hadn't seen my dad in years and couldn't picture what he looked like. When I stepped out of the arrival gate, a stocky man dressed in a sheepskin hat and a black pea coat grabbed me in his arms, and crushed me like crazy and wept.

My dad was a big weeper. That's because he was otherwise so preposterously masculine that he never had to worry about how it would make him look. My dad had left school in grade three. As a child he had worked with older hardened criminals, climbing into windows and the like for them. Now he worked as a janitor, but he was self-conscious about it. When he enrolled me in school, he told one of the teachers that he was a spy, and could say no more.

He was good at being a homemaker though. He was good at cooking and sewing and remembering what days I had to pack my gym clothes. He would draw on my paper lunch bags to show how much he loved me. He would draw a little gangster with a top hat on, holding a gun.

My job was just to keep him company and listen to his old stories about robbing stores and counterfeiting bus tickets and girls falling head over heels for him. I loved his hardscrabble tales set during the Depression. My father as a child became a sort of fictional character to me like Peter Pan, or Oliver Twist or Little Orphan Annie. He was from the time when terrible and wonderful things could still happen to children.

My dad turned eighty-seven years old last year. He was having trouble getting around. He was forced to give up his rambunctious dog because he couldn't walk it anymore. After this, he was overcome by sadness and stopped going outside at all. He said that there was really no place for him in the world. When I was done working, I would go over with some food and we would still sit on his bed talking and watching hours of CNN.

Then one day my dad turned off the television and said he was finished with it. He said he just wanted to tell me his own stories. It was the only thing that mattered to him anymore. And so I let him. There were no new stories. But in the same way that I had brought my favorite books along in my burgundy suitcase when I arrived in Montreal, my dad had favorite stories that he liked to tell too.

He often told me the story about the first movie he had ever seen. As a child, he had been given a nickel for his birthday and he wanted to use it to go to the cinema. There had been a huge fire in a movie theatre in Montreal and seventy-six children had died. After that the city had imposed a rule that children were not allowed in cinemas without their parents. My dad stood on the street corner with his nickel in his hand, asking men who were walking into the theatre if they would walk him in. A man agreed. My dad sat in the theatre and saw his first movie. It was *Snow White* and he said he could never describe how wonderful it was to behold. It was more real than real life. It made him feel that the world was filled with possibilities.

There was also the story about how his mother took him from Montreal to Prince Edward Island. She was from Prince Edward Island and thought they might fare better there, since they were starving in Montreal. She took my dad to see her cousin. While they were there, the cousin went and got a little plate with lemon cookies on it. My dad ate them all. They were delicious. He let the women talk while he enjoyed his good fortune.

As they were walking home, his mother asked him, "Why didn't you save a cookie for me?"

He was overcome with so much regret that he hadn't wrapped one up in a napkin and handed it to his mother. He was to feel awful about eating those cookies for the next seventy years. That was the thing about guilt. It's like amber, the way it traps an event in one's memory. You can look back at it decades later and there it is, exactly the same.

There was another story my dad told that involved his mother reading fortunes on playing cards. By this time they had gone back to Montreal. The war had begun and there was work to be found. She also read the fortunes of neighbors for pleasure and sometimes pennies. Her fortunes had a reputation for coming true.

One evening a neighbor in a dark blue coat and crushed hat came to the apartment. She asked my grandmother to look into the cards and see whether her son who was overseas was all right. My grandmother looked at the cards and saw the boy lying on the ground dead. Who knows what card could have told such a tragic event? Was it the three of spades? Was it the ace of hearts?

My grandmother told the neighbor that the cards weren't giving her an answer and handed back her coins. Afterwards she explained to my dad in the kitchen that she just wasn't brave enough to tell the woman the truth. My dad said he realized then that it was better not to know your future.

My dad also told me that I probably had psychic powers because if he wanted me to pick up Chinese food, he only had to think of it, and I would show up at the apartment with a container in my hands. There was also the story about a swan that followed him home from La Fontaine Park because it had fallen in love with him. And a story about a girl who had a crush on him and whose dad owned a chocolate factory, but whom he just couldn't love back. There was a story about a friend who insisted on wearing a combat helmet, even while playing at the beach in nothing else but his bathing suit, who ended up being killed in World War II.

There was one story he told me about someone named Mrs. Menard. Mrs. Menard was a woman who would come over to visit his mother and would always give him dirty looks and make snide comments about him. My dad always ended his tales of Mrs. Menard by saying, "I'll never know why she didn't like me."

Adults aren't supposed to let children know they don't like them. It violates a very basic social contract. It was his first hint that he would not fit into society as a whole.

The last story he told me was of when he had witnessed a crime when he was around eight years old. He was subpoenaed to appear in court. On the day of the trial, he climbed into the witness stand. The defense attorney looked at him and asked, "Do you know what happens to you if you lie?"

"You don't get to go to heaven," my dad answered.

The entire courtroom erupted in laughter. My dad had no idea why they were laughing, or what it was that he had gotten wrong about the universe this time.

My dad seemed so pale and weak the evening that he told the courtroom story. He was sad when I said I had to go. I tried to persuade him to come to stay with me at my apartment that night, but he wouldn't. "Not yet," he answered, as he always did when I asked him if he wanted to live with me. So I left, promising I would come back the next day. When I went by the following morning to check in on him, he had passed away during the night.

When my dad was middle aged and virile, getting into fights in the canned goods section of the supermarket, his stories all seemed like tough guy tales. My dad had lived through the Great Depression and now here he was, the stronger and tougher and funnier for it. But now I realized that the stories were incredibly sad. They were strange and beautiful and heartbreaking. They were essentially all tales of innocence.

—Heather O'Neill

I saw my big brother try to kill my father one September evening in 2001. It was a few days after the attacks on the World Trade Center and that's why I remember the exact date it happened. Or rather, why I can't forget it. With my father I'd watched the twin towers burst into flames, implode, collapse, my father draining a bottle of whisky in front of the television trying to get control of his grief and he was crying, crying, saying *Fuck now the sand niggers and ragheads they're gonna kill us, this here's the start of the war, I'm warning you my son get ready because this, I'm telling you now, I'm telling you we're bound to die, all of us* and he was moaning, warning *The next bomb they throw will be right in our faces, our French faces and then that'll be it for all of us for sure.* I was nine and I was crying too, like a kid who cries when he sees his parents cry, without really understanding, crying precisely because of this incomprehension, this void, crying because I was afraid of death and because I was too young to realize that

19

my father's words were only an expression of his violent and racist impulses, the words of a man I would learn to hate in two or three more years.

So then a week later, without any connection to the attacks except that the striking closeness of the events gives me a time frame for the attempted murder, right in the middle of dinner, in front of the rest of the family, my big brother grabs my father by the hair and starts bashing his head against the kitchen wall: he was killing him, and my father was howling, begging—I'd never seen my father beg anyone—with his face disappearing under the redness of the blood, under the accumulation of gaping, bleeding wounds, and my big brother was yelling *I'll fucking waste you, you son of a bitch I'll fucking waste you* while my mother tried to shield me. She was throwing glasses at my brother to stop him but missed every time and the glasses kept falling, exploding, shattering on the floor. She was shrieking, too, *Oh shit, don't, you'll kill each other, calm down,* hollering at the top of her lungs *He'll kill his father, he's gonna kill his own father,* then she'd whisper in my ear *Don't look sweetie, don't look, Mama's right here, don't look . . .*

But I wanted to look. Because I was the one who'd provoked this fight between my father and my brother, I'd wanted it. It was revenge.

The story of my revenge begins very early one morning. You have to imagine the scene: I'm drinking hot chocolate in the kitchen, sitting next to my mother and my big brother. They awakened a little while ago and are smoking while watching *The Fresh Prince of Bel-Air.* They've been up for only twenty minutes but have already smoked four or five cigarettes each and the room is stuffy with thick, cloudy smoke. I'm coughing, I had a lot of asthma in those days. My mother and brother are laughing in front of the television, throaty, booming laughs, and they're still smoking. My father and my sisters weren't there. I let my mother know that I have to go see a friend in the village to help him fix his bike. She nods without taking her eyes off the TV. I get dressed. I leave the house, I slam the door and head off into the cold, surrounded by the redbrick walls of northern France, by the smell of fog and manure and then, somehow or other, I realize that I've forgotten something in my room, so I turn around.

When I enter the house, without knocking on the door, I can see the huddled forms of my mother and brother in all the smoke, closer together than they were when I left.

And I see what's going on: my mother is taking advantage of the dim light and the fact that the others aren't there, she's giving money to my big brother and I know that my father has forbidden my mother to do this, he ordered her never to give him money again, not ever, because he knows that my brother will use it to buy alcohol and drugs and that once he's drunk he'll go tag supermarkets and bus stops or set fire to the stands in the village stadium, he's already done that several times. My father told my mother *Don't let me catch you again giving money to that troublemaker*, so when she sees that I've found her out, she gives a start. She comes over to me, furious: *You'd better not tattle to your father or else*, and then she hesitates. She hesitates over which strategy to adopt, she tries something else, she changes the tone, brings back that soft, imploring voice, *Your brother needs money to eat at the lycée but your father just refuses to understand that, so be nice to mama don't tell papa, you know how he can be such a jerk sometimes* . . . I give in. I don't say anything.

My mother makes the fatal mistake two weeks later. She doesn't know yet that she'll be paying for it before the day is over. On that morning I'm alone with her. We aren't talking to each other; we never talk to each other. I'm getting ready for school and when I open the door to leave she tells me something, without any particular reason, between two puffs on a cigarette (something she has often told me but rarely that harshly and bluntly), she tells me *You're really not the kid I'd have dreamed of having. Not even ten years old yet and you've already shamed the entire family. In the village everyone says you're a faggot. I don't know if it's true but us, we're stuck with that shame all on account of you.* I don't answer. I leave the house, I close the door without saying a thing and I don't know why I don't cry but the whole day after that tastes like my mother's words: the air tastes like her words, sounds taste like her words, food tastes like ashes. All day long I do not cry.

That same evening I went home after school. My mother was serving supper and my father turned on the television. He always said we shouldn't talk during meals, we should watch television, it was a question of good manners. He puts on *Walker, Texas Ranger* as usual and the entire family watches in silence.

Then suddenly in the middle of the meal I start shouting. I shout very fast and very loudly with my eyes closed *Mama's giving money to Vincent, she's still giving him money, I saw her, saw she was giving him some the other day and she told me not to tell you, she said Whatever you do don't tell your father, she asked me to lie to you and* but my father doesn't let me finish the sentence, he interrupts me, turns to my mother and asks *What the fuck is going on here?* He says to her *You're screwing around with me or what, what is all this bullshit* and he's raising his voice. He stands up, clenches his fists. I'd been sure that would be his reaction.

I can't help it, I look over at my mother, I want her to suffer for humiliating me that morning and I know provoking a fight between my brother and my father is the best way to hurt her; when our eyes meet she says to me *You you're a fucking little piece of shit,* she doesn't try to lie, she looks so disgusted she could throw up. My head droops, I start to feel ashamed of what I've just done but for the moment the pleasure of revenge is still on top (it's later that all I'll have left is the shame).

My father explodes, he can't stop himself anymore, he goes crazy like that when he's lied to, he throws his glass of red to shatter on the floor, he bellows *I'm the one in charge in this house, what's all this about hiding stuff from me goddamn it to hell*, and he yells so loudly that my mother is frightened, she takes me in her arms and she hides my sisters behind her, she tries to calm him, *It'll be OK honey I won't do it anymore* but he's not simmering down, I knew he wouldn't, he breaks another glass and my mother loses her temper too: *But you're completely out of control! I'm warning you—if you hurt a single one of my kids with any broken glass I'll cut your throat, I'll take you apart, just because I'm a woman doesn't mean you can scare me* and my father starts punching the wall saying *Fucking hell whatever did I do to piss off the good Lord and wind up with a family like this, what with a fruit* (that's me he's talking about) *and a drunk good for nothing but getting plastered, look at him, that one* (he points at my brother), *the loser*, and it's then, at that moment, that my big brother gets up and jumps on my father. He hits him, he hits him again to shut him up, my mother is shrieking in terror, shrill cries, pitifully shrill, my brother grabs my father by the hair, *I'll fucking waste you, you son of a bitch*, and he slams my father's head into the wall with his whole weight, his whole body, and then the cries of pain, the insults, the wails of sorrow, I could feel my mother's warm tears falling on my head, I was thinking *It serves her right, serves her right* and while she was trying to cover my eyes, I was watching the scene through her fingers, I saw the patches of purple blood on the yellow tiles. My brother left my father almost dead on the floor and fled.

A few years later I left my parents and the village of my childhood for good. And if I did so, it was because situations like that one made me understand that the problem with the family isn't just that it beats you down and buries you with its violence but also, and perhaps above all, it turns you into a cog in that violence, turns you into an active element, instills in you the desire to wound, instills longings for vengeance that you should not have had. The family is a curse, and like all curses it arouses passions in you that are not your own.

— Édouard Louis
Translated from the French by Linda Coverdale

It was at some point in the mid-eighties that Somalia became reminiscent of one of those ancient Amazonian species of flora that lie dormant for decades only to reanimate, flower and send their spores out into the wind. We went first, implanted into the claggy earth of England, followed by two grandmothers, three uncles, three aunts and just over twenty cousins, who were caught in the wire and tarpaulin refugee camps dotting the Somali-Ethiopian border.

One of those uncles, nicknamed Kettle in Somali due to his quick temper, had a strange journey. Deported from Saudi Arabia after many months in jail (a flogging every Friday) he was put, penniless, onto a ferry crossing the Red Sea to a country in the livid madness of civil war. His crime was to have been found with alcohol at a party (his own, celebrating his departure from the Kingdom) where a row between two of his guests had ended in murder. Kettle had had a difficult time even as a child: the youngest surviving child of a mother, Goldie, who had lost ten other children in infancy, and whom he tormented with his runtiness, fragility and inability to walk.

Goldie delivered him to as many traditional doctors as she could find—he was purged, burnt, cut, but to no avail. Eventually, he willed himself into health and finally left the sling on her back at the age of four to attend Qur'anic classes and then primary school. Kettle excelled at his studies and learned to speak English with the same measured, formal tones as his eldest brother, Osman, who worked for the BBC World Service. This knowledge of and perhaps even love for English and Arabic would carry him through life; he worked as a translator for numerous embassies in Saudi Arabia, including the Japanese, until he was selected to establish a Telex network across the country. From Bedouin settlements to oilfields to Texan-styled metropolises and the holy cities of Mecca and Medina, he established exchanges through which written messages could be sent internationally, long before fax, email and SMS came into use.

Despite his professional success, he was unable to sugarcoat his words or back down from a fight, two qualities that in Saudi Arabia can mean serious problems for a foreigner, especially an African. Kettle swaggered and wore big, billowing suits and shiny tiepins; he used corporate employment sponsors rather than endure the humiliation of a Saudi holding his passport and making unreasonable demands. He took the freedoms that Saudi men felt were their own, including drinking alcohol, and looked them in the eye. In a country where foreign maids are still executed for witchcraft and Africans are casually referred to as *abids* (slaves), he danced along that tightrope of maintaining both his dignity and his safety.

On that ferry, catching up on the news from Somalia from other passengers, he would have passed the "Gate of Tears" strait that squeezes the Red Sea into a swimming pool between Djibouti and Yemen. Government planes were eviscerating the two main towns in northern Somalia, Hargeisa and Burao, and the people were in flight: over the border to Ethiopia, or to the countryside or to Mogadishu, if they could afford it. Kettle's wife and five children were somewhere in that tempest. They had not communicated in nearly a year and suddenly the bachelor life he had been living in Saudi Arabia seemed a dereliction of duty, despite the impossibility of making a living in the Somali Democratic Republic. Would it have been possible to hear mortar fire or see circling bombers as the ferry docked in Berbera? I don't know, but that baking ancient port must have been both deserted and cacophonous, as fighters darted in and out of coral stone Ottoman mansions and looted depots.

The road from Berbera to Hargeisa stretches nearly a hundred miles and Google Maps tells me it is a thirty-two-hour walk. Kettle walked that distance on a rough, Chinese-built tarmac highway cut through the Guban desert. His grandfather, Farah of the Hundred Camels, wouldn't have broken a sweat but for small-boned, besuited Kettle it must have been hell. The Guban desert, just a few metres above sea level, shimmers with wet heat and multi-hued snakes. I imagine him holding his jacket over his head and sipping from a glass bottle of orange-flavoured Mirinda that he somehow purchased or inveigled in Berbera. No vehicles would have passed but as night came the temperature perhaps cooled by ten or so divine degrees and allowed him to make faster progress. It is a journey that could kill, that probably has killed many, but he survived and arrived at his family home in Hargeisa to find it abandoned.

Knowing how well Somalis keep tabs on each other, in normal society never mind during the dictatorship, a remaining neighbour or acquaintance must have told Kettle where his family had gone and the news was worse than he had expected. They had all been separated in the chaos of the first day of fighting and had fled in different directions. Wife. Five daughters. Son. Brother. Mother. Whom to pursue and where?

Following the weeping trail of lost shoes, burnt-out cars, and dead bodies out of the Hargeisa and towards the Haud desert that separates Somalia and Ethiopia, he searched for more news of his family. The deluge of refugees had slowed to a trickle, making the stragglers so much easier to pick off from the air and by roving groups of soldiers. I wonder how he prepared himself for what must have seemed an unavoidable meeting with death? He was courageous, always had been, but it is another thing when you are looking down the barrels of many Kalashnikovs. Who would bury him and rest his left cheek on the soil?

They were all in Ethiopia. In the scattering of makeshift camps cobbled together from what aid agencies working in other parts of Ethiopia could spare. Wife. Five daughters. Son. Brother. Mother. They were all alive. He survived the trek too and reunited them in increments, pulling the family together into one unit again, only to have his brother, Ahmed, succumb to an untreated heart condition. They were in that camp for many years before they could return and sleep in the ruins of their former home; Kettle rolling a blanket under the stars and listening to the World Service on a cherished radio.

Uncle Kettle told me all of this in the Star Hotel in Hargeisa, when we met for the first time in 2008. He was the last remaining member of my mother's family, and I expected someone like her—shy, private, watchful—but only the last description was true of him. He stirred his cappuccino and watched me set up my camcorder; I glanced back at him, reading his face for signs of my mother. I was doing research for a novel set during the Somali civil war and interviewing as many willing family members as possible. He was short and small-boned like my mother, but his face was darker and wolfish while she is soft-featured and golden. His small eyes were a rheumy blue and his teeth an astonishing melange of black, green and gold, but there was the same downturned, hooked nose that gave their faces a look of constant disapproval. He was impeccably dressed, working for the new government in Somaliland, a cushy job in an office with a chauffeur, but he was still rebellious, thinking about moving to Somalia to enter the shark's mouth of Mogadishu politics, to my mother's horror. He had a hodgepodge of health problems and his forearms were shockingly thin but life burnt out from him, nothing was forgotten, nothing forgiven. He was an Old

Testament prophet putting the world to rights, etching it into the hard drive of my camera, smiling sometimes at his own acerbity. There was something in him that I don't see often; a desire to see himself and the rest of world with brutal clarity, without evasion, fatalism, shame or care for propriety. I loved it and quickly grew to love him.

He carried my novels around with him in Hargeisa, where he finally decided to stay, to boast to friends and peers that his niece was a published author. He took wonderful care of his clothes and terrible care of himself and was hospitalized a few times, once clambering out of his bed, barely alive, so that he could go to his favourite restaurant, until he finally capitulated to the ruin of his heart, kidneys and liver.

Uncle Kettle is buried in what must be one of the world's most desolate cemeteries, in the hilly, scrubby, semi-desert outside of Hargeisa, his grave marked with a pile of rocks and his proper name, Mohamed Faarax Kaahin, painted onto a slab, two acacias standing sentinel nearby. My sense of belonging to Hargeisa, the city of my birth but not his, has dissipated in his absence. I still expect to see him there, to take him out for a large meal that he won't eat, to laugh at his sharp tongue. My heart still jumps when I see an older man in a billowing pinstripe suit, battling the wind, a thick wooden cane in his hand, walking in the particular straight-legged fashion of a certain Somali gentleman.

—Nadifa Mohamed

AMINATTA FORNA is a writer of fiction, memoir, and essays. She is currently the Lannan Visiting Chair of Poetics at Georgetown University.

Crossroads

AMINATTA FORNA

Two years ago I boarded a plane bound for Washington, DC. I passed through business class where the passengers were mainly white men, the world's officer class. In economy as I waited for the people in front of me to stow their baggage and ease into their seats, I looked around. It was a full flight. Dotted among the white faces were a good many black ones; DC is a city with a majority black population. I looked at the passengers and I thought: My God, the ancestors of the white people on this plane enslaved the ancestors of the black people and brought them to America.

A crime so large and yet there they were, the perpetrators and victims of that crime, reading in-flight magazines and sipping from plastic cups of water. I don't know what prompted the thought, or why it did not strike me every time I travelled to the United States. I would like to say I ruminated for a while, but I didn't. In the next few minutes I found my seat and like everyone else I embarked upon the routine of figuring out how best to organize my blanket, pillow, laptop, book and headset.

Two years later I moved to the DC area to live. This is not the first time I have lived in the United States. I spent a year in the 1990s in the Bay Area and more recently two semesters teaching in rural Western Massachusetts. It's not my first time in DC either; I've come here at least five or six times on book tours and visits. This, though, is my first time living here.

The summer of 2015 arrived by another name. It was the summer of Trayvon Martin, the summer of Eric Garner, of Freddie Gray in nearby Baltimore, of Sandra Bland. Of #blacklivesmatter. In Britain in the months before our departure we watched as in city after city across the United States, black people rose in protest against the police. Fury ignited neighbourhoods. By the time we arrived in late July my enthusiasm for the move had tempered. In my family we wear differently coloured skins. I am brown, my husband is white, our five-year-old son is brown. As I say, I had lived in America before, but perhaps it was the news events of the summer that made me feel differently this time, or the fact of having a child, someone to whom one must try to explain the workings of a world which frequently make no sense. I dread, as all parents of black children do, the day my son understands that the deal life handed him is not the same as the deal life has handed other of his friends. That hurting him is, for some people, a form of sport.

My apprehension was heightened by the surprisingly forceful opinions some American friends offered about where we should live. 'You want to live in the District,' 'Live in Maryland,' 'Whatever you do, don't live in Virginia' (Virginia being a Southern state and a Republican one). A white woman instructed me not to live in Georgetown. Georgetown is the area that grew up around the old port and, with its tree-lined roads and prettily painted row houses, is delightful. Why on earth would anyone *not* want a home there? 'You don't want to live next door to ageing white people, do you?' I said many members of my family and my husband's family were, in fact, ageing white people. What I was really thinking was: I'll live where I damn well please.

DC is one of the most segregated cities in America, split neatly down the middle, blacks to the east and whites to the west. Some areas are up to ninety-eight per cent black. Notably, nobody white suggested we live in a black area; whites recommended liberal white areas, because without it ever being said, 'black' means crime and 'black' means poverty. As it turned out Georgetown was unaffordable anyway, as was most of the District. Maryland meant a long commute and with Arlington just over the Key Bridge from Georgetown, I could walk to work. We went to live in Virginia.

One of the first things I realised about Virginia in the heat of summer was how much it reminds me of Sierra Leone. The Potomac, bounded by vegetation that rises from the shallows, looks like the wide, mangrove-frayed banks of the rivers back home. Nightfall brings with it the whirr of crickets, the call of night birds, the whine of the mosquito. Only the nightly recital of the Freetown dogs is missing. The sounds, which are the sounds of my childhood, are as comforting as they are familiar. Freetown is where I spent some of my earliest years. We lived in the city though my father had been born in the rural North. My mother is Scottish. My parents met, like Barack Obama's, when my father left Sierra Leone to study overseas on a scholarship programme. They returned to Sierra Leone part of the newly emerging professional classes.

The racially diverse family soon notices upon arriving in DC (well, America really) from London how comparatively rare they have suddenly become. In the first week a man photographs us as we walked three abreast down the Mall. The last time this happened to me was in London in the 1970s. I was skipping hand in hand with a white school friend. A man holding a camera with a telephoto lens leapt from nowhere and took our picture. We concocted wild stories: that the man was a spy, that he had been hired by prospective kidnappers. The man who takes our photograph on the Mall does so in much the same way as the man forty-odd years before, he doesn't ask, he walks directly towards us without varying his pace and only at the last minute he raises his camera, like a gun.

The other thing that happens a few times is this: we are waiting together at the head of a queue to fill in or submit some piece of paperwork that our new lives require. The person behind the desk, a white woman in each instance, looks up and says: 'Which one of you is first?' She doesn't simply wave both of us forward, which is what happens most everywhere I have ever been. She says: 'Which one of you is first?' She presumes we are not together, you see. It takes a while for us to figure this out. A couple of times when the queue is particularly long I take our son outside to play until my husband is called forward and then we join him at the desk. But when I do so I am challenged: 'Can I help you?' and 'Excuse me, ma'am, but I am serving this gentleman.' On this last occasion I am standing next to my husband, so close our shoulders touch, leaning with my elbows on the desk and reading our paperwork upside down. In the mind of the woman behind the desk I am apparently a stranger with no sense of personal space, butting in on the business of an Englishman altogether too polite to drive me away, because that's what absolute strangers do all the time, right? In her worldview it is more likely than that we might be together.

A friend describes how something similar happened to her when she unpacked her weekly shopping at the till in a supermarket, and the teller shouted at her: 'You may not touch that man's food, ma'am!' The man was her (white) husband. Really, you have to laugh. Only last week I went for the series of medical tests to which new clients must submit on behalf of their medical insurer. Waiting for a bone density test I was given a form upon which to declare my ethnicity. Black/White/Hispanic/Other. In Britain one is typically offered a buffet of choices under 'Mixed.' On the medical form I marked myself as 'Other,' because ethnicity has a bearing on bone density and medical science does not observe the 'one drop' rule. There followed an awkward conversation with the administrator whose computer would not accept an entry of 'Mixed,' but kept defaulting to 'White.'

Each country has its paradigm of race and America's size and culture might mean the American paradigm has been widely exported, plus the specific heinousness of the crime against black people in America lends it an extra authority. It can be hard to explain to people in America that there exist other and different experiences of being black. My cultural interpreters back when I first lived here twenty years ago tended to be people of colour from other lands who had lived longer in America than I had: West Indians, black Britons, Africans.

You are darker than me, therefore I will call you black. You are paler than me, therefore I will call you white.

In those days what I found curious was the way some people who were very fair skinned were nevertheless called 'black' by white people. They called themselves black too, but that was to me a matter of a different order, one rooted in knowledge, family and allegiance. The fact was that, to me, it seemed impossible simply by looking at many light-skinned people of colour to tell if they had any African blood at all. I said so to my African friends who quietly agreed. A British Jamaican friend warned me that I should not say so in the company of African Americans. The idea of 'passing' made no sense either. If you were light enough to look white, why didn't that make you white? Did I know about the 'one drop' rule back then? I think so, but the enduring nature of its legacy threw me. Did people really hold on to this way of thinking? Perhaps I should have been more thoughtful, because I did know that enslaved women were raped by their masters. So these then were their light-skinned descendants whose skin served as reminder of the plundering of their great-great-great grandmothers' bodies.

Behind the denials lies shame on both sides; this is the only answer I have. The result is silence. To me and my husband and child, the young white women, whether or not they knew it, were taking part in a nationwide pretense, saying, We're sorry but you are most unusual, this sort of thing really doesn't happen here (and let's not forget Virginia's anti-miscegenation laws were only overturned in 1967 in the delightfully named *Loving v. Virginia*). The light-skinned black people were saying, We do not wish to be reminded of what has happened to us in the past. Only on a recent trip to South Africa have I seen anything similar to the simultaneous separation and evident co-mingling of the races one sees in the United States, the energy expended on the self-deceiving lie that is the narrative of what is 'normal.'

In South Africa I would be considered 'coloured,' a designation and an entire community created by government decree to sweep into one place the untidy evidence of racial mixing, South Africa's version of the 'one drop' rule. In West Africa, in fact in pretty much every other African country I have ever travelled, those fair-skinned African Americans and I would be called 'white.' Filming a documentary in Mali where the brown-skinned Tuareg population is referred to as white, I tried to explain this to one of my English colleagues, who only continued to insist that this could not possibly be so. It was left to our Bambara fixer to tell him: 'You are in Africa now.'

Another thing that I have noticed in the US is the battle fatigue I saw first in black people when I was there in the 1990s, which we in Europe did not (yet) feel. Sometimes this showed itself as a kind of footslogging determination, or angry frustration, other times a withdrawal from the fray. I remember very well a couple I met at that time in San Francisco.

I had gone to interview the wife, about what I can't rightly remember; I was a journalist at the time. I do remember that I had been put in touch by a mutual acquaintance and that the house at which I arrived had an elegant interior and a garden with a flower-bordered lawn. During the interview we, the wife and I, found so much commonality that by the time the husband arrived home we had opened a bottle of wine in the garden. The husband was as handsome and warm as his wife was beautiful, funny and gracious. Within a short time he was insisting that I should bring my husband for dinner. A little later the conversation turned to race. 'I have nothing against them,' said the handsome husband smoothly. 'But I wouldn't have a white in my house. I work with them and I have no problems with it. But that's where it stops.' I looked over at his wife who, I imagined, would surely murmur some sort of admonishment, but she only smiled and offered me more wine. You're wondering if I protested? No. Do I feel guilty about that? Not really. I had never heard anyone talk that way, any person of colour I mean; I've heard plenty of whites say such things. Only there was no bitterness in the husband's voice, just a certain matter-of-factness. I sort of understood. The vigilance required of being black is too often exhausting; in relationships with white people the heavy lifting is inevitably borne by the black person: to circumvent conflict, to avoid all evidence of appearing chippy, to keep the white person at their ease. The couple from San Francisco had found their own solution. I did not challenge them, I was learning about race in America.

You can imagine, though, that we never did take them up on that dinner invitation.

In Sierra Leone before the war of 1991–2002 a certain kind of traveller disembarked regularly from flights from the United States, alongside the missionaries and Peace Corps volunteers. Around their necks they wore pendants in the shape of Africa, they dressed in shirts and skirts made of printed kente cloth and they had African names, which were not the names they had been given when they were born. They were African Americans come home.

My last visit to Sierra Leone before the war made it impossible was in 1991. In the company of a group of friends I celebrated my birthday at a restaurant called Old Wine, New Skins which had been set up by a family of African American 'returnees' (as we called them then; we would later retrieve the term to describe Sierra Leonians who came home from overseas at the end of the war). They were a man and his three wives—this made some among us roll our eyes, just as we were working to rid ourselves of polygamy. It was even said that one of the wives was white. They opened a restaurant and specialised in cooking our own food and then selling it to expats, which they did rather well, balancing the flavours to satisfy the requirements of local authenticity while serving Western tastes. Why hadn't one of us thought of it? The man wore dreadlocks and a *gara* shirt; when he came to take our order he called us 'sister' and 'brother.' The women wore long robes of Dutch wax print. All night we tried for a glimpse of the 'white wife,' but we achieved none.

If I am truthful I felt embarrassed for the returnees; to have come all the way here, to our little country dragging itself along the developmental floor, seemed like an act of desperation. I would later feel a similar discomfort in the United States faced with the same longing in African Americans, which found expression in Kwanzaa, books and posters about African kings and queens, tie-dye clothing. They seemed to know more about the history of my continent than I did. They yearned for what I possessed and took for granted, worse still failed to cherish, or perhaps could not cherish. Sierra Leone is a beautiful country: a coastline composed of curved beaches, pale and bright as cutlass blades, iridescent sunbirds that drink nectar from hibiscus cups, city streets lined with trees so heavily jewelled with fruit that in mango season you buy from the street sellers merely to save yourself the effort of reaching up with your own hand. But Sierra Leone is no Eden. People were always trying to fleece the returnees, and treated them with contempt. I knew because on the streets sometimes I was mistaken for one of them. There were other reasons, though, I could not share in the romance. My relationship with my paternal country was an abusive one. My father had been a political activist imprisoned by the regime more than once; during the years of my childhood we were followed and spied on even by those we trusted; our home was set upon by government thugs; in 1970 my stepmother, sister, brother and I were driven into exile in Britain for three years. By 1991 the rump of the same regime was in power and the country was heading into war.

I don't know what happened to the family; I'm guessing they left when the fighting came to Freetown in 1997, if they hadn't already gone by then. By all accounts America's evacuation of its citizens was nothing short of masterly. A warship was sent, helicopters landed in defiance of the rebel-proclaimed 'no fly zone,' marines went house to house collecting US citizens. A family friend opened the door to an armed unit come to remove his young son who happened to have dual citizenship. Only if you take me too, he said, and so they whisked him into a vehicle and a short time later he was out of the country. The whole evacuation lasted a mere matter of hours. The family at Old Wine, New Skins must have been grateful then for the eagle on the front of their passports. I wonder where they are now and whether they feel as ashamed for us, for our failure to spare ourselves the descent into hell, angry that we took their dream of Eden and desecrated it so thoroughly that it must have been impossible ever to dream the dream again.

Why did they choose us when others of their countrymen headed for Ghana, so much more developed, so much more distinguished? These were the days before you could acquire a DNA test for a handful of dollars, but the fact is whether or not they knew it, the family were more likely to share DNA with us than any other peoples on the West Coast of Africa. Sierra Leone's other name, the one it was known by to the outside world and for several hundred years, was the Slave Coast. Only a minority of all the slaves taken from West Africa went to North America, most ended up in South America and the West Indies, but of those who went north a good many came from Sierra Leone and a significant proportion from a single trading fort on a small island just off the coast of Sierra Leone called Bunce Island.

The ruins of a fort stand on Bunce still, surrounded by the rusted corpses of cannons. Great stone walls once enclosed the chief agent's residence, a Georgian-style mansion it is said, complete with a wrap-around verandah in the style of the great plantation houses of South Carolina, formal terraced gardens and even an orange walk. An arched doorway led through to rooms with high ceilings and at the back of the building a false fireplace (false because the temperature in Sierra Leone averages about thirty-five degrees centigrade year round). The slave yards where the captives were held were just behind the house; the chief agent could keep check on his goods from the upper windows of his house. In 1791 a British woman named Anna Maria Falconbridge dined at Bunce (or Bance as it was then called) Island Mansion and described the sight of the enslaved men and women: 'between two and three hundred wretched victims, chained and parcelled out in circles, just satisfying the cravings of nature from a trough of rice placed at the centre of each circle.' By the time of Anna Maria's visit the fort was operated by the company of John and Alexander Anderson, having been sold six years before by Grant, Oswald & Company. (Remember the name Oswald, because it will come up again, along with that of Richard Oswald's American trading partner Henry Laurens). Before that the fort was operated by the Royal African Company, which traded slaves on behalf of the British Crown.

Beneath the castle there is a cave, once an underground powder magazine, though local folklore says slaves were held there too. Step inside and you feel movement in the warm and stinking air, hear a sound like breathing and the rustle of a thousand wings: the cave roof is thick with bats. Beyond the old magazine a path skirts a series of dunes which, when I first realised that they were in fact eight-foot-high mounds of empty oyster shells, I imagined to have been tossed from the ramparts by gluttonous Englishmen. Later I learned they were used in the making of lime for the castle walls. If memory serves, the path continues around the perimeter of the tiny island, past a small cluster of graves which mark the last resting place of the white traders who died on Bunce.

Wade into the sea by the small landing beach and before the water has reached your knees you can find rum bottles, wood nails, pottery shards. Within minutes your hands are full of the jetsam and flotsam of slave ships and you throw the lot back into the waves. Standing on the remainder of a small stone jetty you call to the boatman on the shore who brought you to the island and now waits to bring you back. You watch him manoeuvre his dugout through the waves with a single paddle. You step off the island from the same place and in the same way as did thousands of departing Africans, only you will step off the boat again in a minute or two onto the shore, while they were transferred to the slave ships that lay anchored in deep water and, if they ever set foot on land again, did so thousands of miles away.

There are stories told in Sierra Leone, from centuries before I was born, of men who arrived on our shores, men who built their houses on the sea. These were not ordinary men, but the spirits of drowned corpses. Left long enough in water a black person's skin bleaches white. They had pale hair and green eyes because they ate fish and drank seawater. They captured men and women and carried them across the sea to feed to their god, a great devil who fed on human flesh.

At the thought of what awaited them some of the captives became catatonic. In the literature of the slaving ships it has a name: 'the lethargy.' In the days when the profits of Bunce went to the British Crown, the men and women and children were branded across their chests. R.A.C.E. (Royal African Company of England). R.A.C.E. The captives thought they were branded in order to be butchered and eaten like cattle. Catatonia causes the brain to shut down, rendering the sufferer mute and immobile. One theory suggests that catatonia may have once been an evolutionary fear response, originating in ancestral encounters with carnivores whose predatory instincts were triggered by movement. Captives struck by the lethargy often died of starvation, so the slavers stopped branding their prisoners and attached coloured strings to their wrists instead; they hired translators to explain to them what I suppose must have seemed a lesser fate.

For a long time afterwards people in Sierra Leone thought white people were cannibals. My stepmother remembers stories of cannibals, they were always waiting to catch children who misbehaved. One day she tells me about a colonial officer in her town who used to wait in his official car outside the railway station; she would see him when she and her friends came back from school and sometimes he would wind down the window, call one of them over and try to persuade her to come into the vehicle. My stepmother's grandmother warned her the man was a cannibal, she told her to run away if he ever tried to talk to her. My stepmother watches my expression carefully as she tells me this story.

You ran from cannibals, you avoided the crossroads, the meeting place of the spirits where men and women might be snatched and carried to the underworld. At night a grandmother urged her grand-daughter returning home to the next village to stay away from the path. Only strangers who did not know the countryside travelled the paths, slave-raiding strangers perhaps, and where the roads met was the place the unlucky traveller was most likely to encounter them.

The slavers were both black and white men, we know this. But it is the white men, men who could strike fear into the heart of a person such that they were turned into a creature of stone, who haunt the imagination.

My grandfather Pa Roke Forna kept five indentured men. My aunts and uncles tell me this, those of them who were alive when we had the conversation some years ago. They speak the names of the men for maybe the first time in decades. It takes a few moments to reel their minds back all those years, to the forties and fifties. Foday several of them remember, he seems to have been a favourite.

We always called my grandfather Pa Roke, but this was not his name, it was his title. My grandfather was an advisor to the Paramount Chief, like a chancellor I suppose; he presided over matters of law and heard many cases in the court in Magburaka. When a man who could not pay his debts came before the courts Pa Roke sometimes offered to square the debt out of his own pocket. Now indentured to my grandfather, the debtor would work on his farm until the debt was paid, which might take months or might take years. This was how Pa Roke acquired Foday and the other four men. They worked his lands which surrounded the village of Rogbonko where Pa Roke lived with his wives and children.

When I was a child my father would take us to visit Pa Roke often. I remember being ushered in to say hello and sent to sit outside again; sometimes during those long visits we ate together, gathered around a single dish of rice from which Pa Roke helped himself deftly using only the tips of his fingers while I used a spoon. Apart from saying hello and goodbye, though, we never spoke, for the reason that we did not share a common language. Pa Roke spoke Temne and I only spoke English. It was typical of my parents' generation, who came of age at the same time as their countries and who kept their gaze fixed firmly on the horizon, to neglect to teach their children the languages they grew up speaking. Pa Roke belonged to a world that was disappearing and I belonged in a future which had yet to arrive. Many years later I would try to remedy the omission and ask my stepmother to teach me Temne, constructing the grammar slowly together and on long walks because the language lacked a complete orthography. Linguists at Fourah Bay College had been in the process of compiling one when the war struck.

My aunts count Pa Roke's wives, aloud and on their fingers, until they reach sixteen. They start with the names of their own mothers and then of the mothers of their brothers and sisters who have already passed. Whenever there is an impasse they look to Adama who seems to have the best memory and is also the eldest. Pa Roke married sixteen women. The first wife was a praying wife, meaning she was the widow of an older brother or perhaps a cousin and had been given the choice, upon her husband's death, of taking one of his younger male relatives as a husband or returning to her own family. She had chosen Pa Roke. The second match was by all accounts a love marriage and there seems to have been some friction between this new wife and the praying wife (who seemed not to have stuck to praying), because the praying wife soon packed her bags and left. Among the other marriages several were dynastic. Pa Roke was not married to all his wives at once, he was well into his nineties when he died and had outlived all but the last. A good few would have died in childbirth as did my grandmother Ndora who was chosen personally by Pa Roke's second wife (she of the palace coup). Nobody remembers that much about her except that she came from the next village. She was only a sixth wife and she died bearing her third child.

It is said Pa Roke and Foday shared an enthusiasm for animal husbandry. Foday was in charge of the animals, though the farm mainly produced coffee and rice. Over the years and the birth and breeding of many sheep and goats the two men grew quite close. In the evenings Foday sometimes kept company with Pa Roke on the verandah of the big house overlooking the village square. The third person who joined them on occasion was Pa Yamba Mela, the diviner whom Pa Roke kept and housed in the village, even though Pa Roke was, by all accounts, a strict Muslim.

Whether the indentured men ever worked their way out of debt nobody can tell me. For the most part they stayed on in Rogbonko village. My uncles and aunts are keen for me to know that the men were well treated. They recall Foday's wedding; Pa Roke had paid the bride gift and covered the cost of all the celebrations. I do not ask whether he added the bill to Foday's debt, nor do I mention what seems evident to me—that Pa Roke now had two workers for the price of one.

What I also learn is that Pa Roke, who would later rule as Regent Chief on the death of the Paramount Chief, was once an indentured man himself. In his youth he had been sold into bondage by two of his uncles in order to raise campaign funds for a chieftaincy election in another chiefdom, one in which Pa Roke's mother was a member of the ruling family. In exchange for an unnamed sum Pa Roke spent two years working another man's land, just as Foday worked his. That was the way it was, a man could be born noble and owned by another and own men himself, all in the same lifetime and all in the same skin.

In 1997 I take my stepmother, who is then living with me in London after Freetown was overrun by rebel soldiers, to see the movie *Amistad*. We go to a cinema in Notting Hill Gate, a lovely old movie theatre with balconies and red velvet seats, one of the last cinemas where you could still smoke. The film is based on the true story of an uprising aboard the Portuguese slave ship *Amistad*. The rebels were Africans who had been abducted and enslaved from Sierra Leone in 1839. They killed the cook and the captain (in the film they kill loads more people) and ordered the crew to sail them back to Sierra Leone, but before they could make it the ship was sighted and seized by a US navy vessel, the Portuguese slavers were freed and the Sierra Leonians were imprisoned in New Haven, Connecticut.

In the making of the film the director Steven Spielberg took a decision not to subtitle a good deal of the dialogue spoken by the African actors. Apparently the purpose of this was to place the audience in the same position as the New Englanders faced with Africans babbling in incomprehensible tongues. The Mende-speaking extras were recruited from Sierra Leone and are clearly rising to the occasion. Also I suspect there must have been a good deal of repartee, perhaps even some ad-libbing because my stepmother who understands Mende keeps giggling.

The *Amistad* with its (by then) illegal cargo was bound for Cuba, as were many ships from Bunce. Once on holiday in Havana, I went to an art exhibition where I stood before a print of an African mask. The mask was one of those designed to be worn over the entire head with rings carved into the base, the features of the face were small and keen. It looked just like one I have at home, which has its origins in the women's secret society: the priestess wears it to lead the initiates in dance. I said: 'It's the Bundu devil.' A man standing nearby, a Cuban and the manager of the collective of artists, heard me and told me that it was more than likely exactly what I imagined it to be. I bought the print and carried it home to London.

The slave ships which crossed the Atlantic from Bunce and which were not headed for Cuba or the West Indies docked in South Carolina; from there the captives were bought and sold to plantations around the American South. Henry Laurens[1] owned and operated

1. In 1777 during the American Revolutionary War, Henry Laurens, by then America's envoy to Holland, was captured on the high seas by the British navy and imprisoned in the Tower of London, the highest-ranking American official ever so to be. His old friend Richard Oswald interceded on his behalf and even posted bail. After the American victory the British government appointed Richard Oswald to negotiate the Treaty of Paris. On the other side of the table, along with Benjamin Franklin and John Adams, was Henry Laurens. Together the old slaving partners struck a deal to return the slaves recruited into the British army back to their owners, a deal scuppered only by the British North American Commander Sir Guy Carleton who refused to hand over the slaves and sent them instead to Nova Scotia, from where the Black Loyalists (as they were called) petitioned to be sent to Sierra Leone. In 1792 fifteen ships carrying 1,196 people sailed from Halifax to Sierra Leone. The Nova Scotians and other

Austin and Laurens, the largest slave auction house in the whole of North America; he was Henry Oswald's main trading partner and bought the bulk of Oswald's Bunce Island captives.

Once, in Louisiana in search of a more detailed understanding of the lives of slaves, I visited a plantation house near Baton Rouge. The experience was bizarre. We wandered around the house (rather poky by the standards of a British manor house) and peered into glass-fronted cabinets containing, not the belongings of the family, but examples of the sort of items they would have owned, which were mainly European antiques. Nowhere, inside or out, was there any mention of the slaves who had worked the plantation. We were ushered out by a black woman in an antebellum crinoline dress. I asked her whether there were any displays about slavery we could see, slave quarters or suchlike. She shook her head, this way, this way. We'd seen a few French collectibles and now we were being hustled out. Finally in the gift shop I found one slim volume detailing the lives of slaves entitled: *We Lived in a Little Cabin in the Woods,* a collection of oral accounts of surviving slaves undertaken by the Federal Writers' Project.

In New Orleans I discovered the slaves of Louisiana had left behind more vivid evidence of their presence in other places, in the taste of jambalaya. In making jambalaya the rice is simmered with tomatoes, onion and water, the recipe calls for a mix of seafood, chicken and meat. In Sierra Leone we have an almost identical dish we call Jollof rice. You find people enjoying Jollof rice all over West Africa. Jollof, Djolof—derived from Wolof, a people of Senegal—Jollof rice is almost certainly the progenitor of jambalaya. At home

---

black former slaves from the US and also from Britain would settle there over the coming decades. The houses of the American settlers are there still, in the villages of Bathurst and Regent, slatted wooden houses, often brightly painted. Little pieces of Louisiana carried home.

in Sierra Leone we often serve Jollof rice with a condiment made of softly fried onions and Scotch bonnet peppers. The New Orleans recipe calls for andouille sausage, which is the French influence. Every cook has his or her own way of making jambalaya, it's more of a concept really, once you have grasped that you can make it anywhere with whatever is at hand.

In this way jambalaya is like gumbo, the other famous Louisiana dish, which shares the same trademark of mixed meats and fish and the recipe for which was almost certainly carried in the hearts of the enslaved. In Louisiana they like to make their gumbo with a roux base—the French again—but I won't have any truck with that. The West African way is to use okra. In fact, our 'gumbo' is really comprised mainly of stewed okra into which some pieces of chicken, smoked fish and meat are thrown. First each okra finger must be chopped into small pieces and then the whole thing simmered at length, probably the dish takes about four hours to prepare from start to finish. It's my homecoming dish. When my stepmother instructs the cooks she will tell them: 'Use a wooden spoon.' A wooden spoon rather than a metal spoon because wood makes the okra 'draw,' the way I like it best, but for a good many people the glutinous texture of okra is something of an acquired taste. Hence the roux sauce.

The Gullah people who are direct descendants of Sierra Leonian slaves make their gumbo with okra. By the time people from Sierra Leone were settled on Gullah Island the Slave Coast had been renamed the Rice Coast and slaves from Sierra Leone in particular were prized for their rice growing expertise. Henry Laurens himself owned several rice plantations. Captives were shipped from Bunce to Savannah to meet the demand, the rice trade grew and South Carolina became one of the wealthiest colonies in the Americas. But malaria and other diseases as well as rice flourished in the tropical climate of the Low Country and sea islands, driving away the white plantation owners who left the running of their estates to a small number of overseers and slaves acting as drivers. Free, relatively speaking, from the influence of white, Christian culture, the slaves held on to their cuisine, their stories and songs. Joseph Opala, an American anthropologist who did much to stitch together the history of Bunce Island, identified as Mende the language of an old recording of a song sung by an inhabitant of Gullah. The Sierra Leonians of Bunce brought their spirits with them too, the spirits swam, flew and walked on water in pursuit of the scurrying ships to live on in the religions of the Americas, in Candomblé, Santería, Voodoo. Mammy Wata, who offers great wealth to those who glimpse her in exchange for their unborn children; One Foot Jombie the bogeyman, who frightens children who won't go to sleep; and Baron Samedi, who holds the power of life and death, and is keeper of the crossroads.

I am kneeling on a compound floor of cracked, red earth, the sun is at its zenith. It must be well over forty degrees centigrade. It is the year 2000, close to the end of the civil war, Freetown is crowded with refugees and my aunt Adama is one, the last of the fighting is taking place near where my family live in the north which is also where the RUF have their headquarters. Today she is telling the story of the echoes of another war. The story will take several hours to hear during which time we, her listeners, will stand and shake limbs numb from squatting or sitting, will swipe at the flies that come to drink the sweat from our skin. Once I will ask my cousin, who is translating Adama's words for she tells her story in Temne, whether he wants to take a break and come back another day. No, he will shake his head, I have never heard this story. The story begins with these exact words: 'Your great-grandfather Pa Morlai was a warrior at the time of the Gbanka wars.' Adama tells us the tale of my great-grandparents, Pa Morlai and Ya Beyas and it goes like this:

Sometime in the 1880s the chiefs of Temneland were foolish enough to double-cross a young warrior by the name of Gbanka whom

49

they had hired to fight the Mende and force open the trade routes to the Bumpe and Ribi rivers and thereby gain access to the sea and the British and foreign vessels that bought gold and ivory along the West African coast. Gbanka was both Temne and Mende and when he lost faith in his father's Temne people he turned to those of his mother and fought for the Mende instead. The ensuing wars lasted many years, particularly once the northern Loko decided to ally with the Mende.

Pa Morlai was a Loko commander whose fighters overran the town of Mamunta deep in Temneland in an area ruled by the Obai Masamunta Akaik (King Great Beard). Mamunta was where Pa Morlai made his base until the wars were ended (by the British who, tired of the disruption to trade, captured and imprisoned Gbanka). With the end of hostilities Pa Morlai headed back north beyond the Katabai Hills to his village of Matoko accompanied by the retinue of slaves given to him by Masamunta Akaik as part of the peace settlement between the two men.

Among the slaves was one of Masamunta's own daughters, Beyas. Pa Morlai gifted her to his mother for her household and later, at his mother's behest, took Beyas as one of his wives and together and over time they had three sons and a daughter.

One day a basket-seller arrived in the town square of Matoko. Ya Beyas, as she was now known, recognised the weave and pattern of his shuku; they came from her hometown of Mamunta whose weavers are, even now, renowned for their basketry. Ya Beyas asked the shuku seller to carry a message to her family telling them where she was and begging that they free her. This the basket-seller promised to do, but when he returned the next year he had failed to pass on the message, for what reason we do not know. Ya Beyas gave her message to him a second time and waited another year and this time the basket-seller succeeded in his mission.

There were, in those days, strict rules by which a person could be redeemed from slavery. If the terms were met, then that person was free regardless of the wishes of their owner. When two of Ya Beyas's brothers arrived in Matoko they presented before a gathering of the chief and elders of Matoko and Pa Morlai this inventory of items:

Cow, 1
Barrel of palm oil, 1
Sack of rice, 1
Sack of salt, 1
Tie of tobacco leaves, 1
Country cloth, 1
Silver shillings, 4

Once the ceremony had been conducted Ya Beyas was a free woman, except that she wasn't, she was still Pa Morlai's wife. Thus when Ya Beyas declared she wanted to go home to Mamunta, Pa Morlai declined to allow her. She had a wound on her foot and this he used as an excuse to keep her in Matoko under the care of his healer. When her foot was better Ya Beyas once again told Pa Morlai she planned to travel to her hometown and to take their daughter Hawa to accompany her on the journey, but Pa Morlai refused his permission a second time. Hawa was betrothed to a young man in Matoko, he pointed out, Ya Beyas needed to stay for the marriage. In the end, though, he did relent and gave Ya Beyas his permission to go home; he appointed their second son Saidu to be her travelling companion and settled down to wait for her return. But Ya Beyas never came back.

Pa Morlai set out to follow his wife. The first time he entered Mamunta he had done so as a warrior at the head of an army. Now he entered as a suitor, preceded by a young girl bearing a heavy calabash upon her head. Pa Morlai went to Beyas's house and broke cola with her brothers, one of whom, heir to Masamunta Akaik, was now king, and he presented his calabash, the contents of which would certainly have looked very much like this:

Cola nuts (symbol of friendship)
Bitter cola nuts (symbol of hard times)
Alligator pepper, 1 (seeds to be kept in dried pod for union to hold)
Prayer mat, 1
Tie of tobacco, 1
Needle and thread
Gold
Silver
Precious stones

Pa Morlai had come to give Ya Beyas's family her bride gift, outstanding now for some twenty years or more. Ya Beyas accepted the calabash and in doing so she accepted Pa Morlai for her husband, this time as a free woman. Some days after the celebrations were over Pa Morlai decided it was time they returned home. When he told Ya Beyas to prepare for the journey Ya Beyas said, no.

She said no.

And so the story goes that Pa Morlai returned to Matoko alone where he died some years later while Ya Beyas and her son Saidu stayed in Mamunta. It is said Ya Beyas never laid eyes on Pa Morlai again.

I don't really know if Ya Beyas and Pa Morlai's story ended that way. It's true she never went back to Matoko. Her son, Saidu, my grandfather, grew up in Mamunta and would one day be indentured by the same brothers who had redeemed Ya Beyas. He would leave Mamunta and found a settlement of his own, which would become known as Rogbonko, the place in the forest. And on his estate indentured men would work. All of that is as Adama told it. What I am saying here is that I don't know whether the last act of defiance I like to give Ya Beyas in my retelling of the story is really true, that she looked Pa Morlai in the eye and spoke the word 'no.'

The last time I told Ya Beyas's story it was to a gathering of British people of West Indian heritage, descendants of people who had left Sierra Leone or some other African country and who when they left must have guessed that they did so without hope of return or redemption. When I came to the end of the story of my great-grandparents, to Ya Beyas's final declaration, people clapped and cheered and stamped their feet. And so I like to tell myself it really happened that way.

My aunt Adama died one year after we sat listening to her in that Freetown courtyard. She was the last member of our family who held the story of Ya Beyas and Pa Morlai. If I had not asked her to tell it to me, we would have lost it. So many things. We would have carried on thinking we were Temnes and never discovered our great-grandfather had been a Loko. The Sierra Leonians who landed in North Carolina and settled there and in Louisiana and around me here in Virginia and all over the United States brought with them only what they could carry in their memories and in their hearts. When I realised that I began to understand, in some small way, what it might feel like to lose the story of who you are.

To have it taken away from you.

HONORÉE FANONNE JEF-
FERS is a poet, a fiction writer,
a critic, and the author of four
books of poetry, most recently
The Glory Gets (2015). She
is the recipient of fellowships
from the National Endowment
for the Arts and the Witter
Bynner Foundation through the
Library of Congress, and she is
an elected member of the American Antiquarian Society. Honorée teaches at the University of
Oklahoma.

Lost Letter #1:
From Phillis Wheatley, of Boston, to Arbour Tanner, of Newport August 16, 1770[1]

HONORÉE FANONNE JEFFERS

Dear Sister:

I shiver at the other chance,
that had I not waited for my mistress
to take her midday rest, there would
be no wonder: my new friend.
Had I not disobeyed her word—
her concerns for the flames in my chest—
and stolen from the kitchen—
I would not have found you.
Even the coughing overtaking me
in the street was a benediction.
How God anoints us even in the midst of madness!
[dark coming over the water i was naked
but unaware of shame my mistress taught me

1. The poet Phillis Wheatley is the first African-American woman to publish a book. Kidnapped from Africa in early childhood and sold to a family in Boston, Massachusetts, Wheatley maintained a years-long friendship with another enslaved black woman who lived in Newport, Rhode Island, Obour (or Arbour) Tanner. No one knows how the two met.

that God hates a bare body now all men frighten me]
Your two names a comfort, though how shall I spell you?
"Arbour," an astounding, shady grove that protects.
"Obour," the name of "stone" in your homeland.
Until I decide, I have turned to Apostle Paul:
As slaves and women, we speak the same words.
Once, there was distance that kept
tongues hopeless. Now, we are blood,
no division between us.
[you have my mother's face i lie and say i cannot
remember but sister i do i do know her name]

I am your very humble servant,
and I pray, your long-time friend,

Phillis

Lost Letter #2:
From Obour Tanner, Newport, to Phillis Wheatley, Boston October 5, 1770

HONORÉE FANONNE JEFFERS

Dear Sister:

Before your letter, no one gave a care
for my name. Spell me how you wish,
for you have surely saved me.
That day we met, so much despair.
I walked to the pier on my errand—
on the right side of the city, the water,
and I was tired of brigs and schooners bringing
in the taken, our naked, shivering brethren.
Their eyes looking to me.
And I, a slave and woman. What can I do?
Even thoughts of canoes from long ago trouble me.
The thickened rivers of my homeland,
the danger, no matter the sun's love.
[taunting of the gulls that time on the water
i cannot seem to forget the sailors their touching
their grabbing the memories are ants crawling on me]
Your frantic chuffing on the cobblestones?
A gift.
I dropped my basket of dinner fish,

uncaring that my own mistress would scold.
My hand on your arm, keeping you from the fall.
So beloved in your frailty, my fellow traveler.
[i shall forget that time i must i pray my memories die
at least you understand the screaming the clenching of my chest
at night you understand oh sister thanks be to all our Gods]
Your breath calmed and we stood with
no explanation, until you reminded me—
my creatures lay dirty on the ground.
I knew I loved you when you did not
speak of ships.

A humble friend and fellow servant,

Obour

GARNETTE CADOGAN is editor-at-large of *Nonstop Metropolis: A New York City Atlas* (coedited by Rebecca Solnit and Joshua Jelly-Schapiro). He is currently a visiting fellow at the Institute for Advanced Studies in Culture at the University of Virginia, and a visiting scholar at the Institute for Public Knowledge at New York University.

A Family Name

GARNETTE CADOGAN

My earliest memory is of the world upside down, blurry, dark. My mother extracts me from the clutch of my fleeing father and hands me to my grandmother, who dashes back into the house as my mother face-pounds my father for stealing me from my crib in the dead of night.

My second-earliest memory is of my father standing on the sidewalk outside my house a few years later, waiting for me to come and talk to him. I walk to the front gate—"He can't steal you now, so you can go if you want," my mother or grandmother says to the five- or six-year-old me—and I stop at a distance at least twice his arm's length. "Do you know who I am?" he asks. I find him to be terrifying, although he's a skinny fellow not six feet tall, and although the front gate is now flanked by walls too high for him to scale. Perhaps my mother's regularly voiced scorn or my memory of being snatched out of sleep or his visible anger-coiled-in-humiliation—the physiognomy of burning resentment imbedded in the deep wrinkles that frame his glare—has made this man intimidating.

"You're Bryan."

"No, I'm your father!"

"No. Grandma is my father."

I run back inside. I leave Bryan Levy to fume from beyond the grill of the front gate, barred from talking to the son he wants to steal.

Years later, when I was fourteen or fifteen, my father pulls up to the gate in a compact sport-utility vehicle and sees me at play in the yard. He looks at me and through me and asks me for me. "Is Chris"—the name my family calls me—"there?" I recognize him. I always recognize him, although there is not a single photograph of him in the home. The only image of my father to be found has been the one painted by my mother's bitter words, creating a hologram that is mug shot one day, target practice the next. I have spotted him in supermarkets, record stores, pharmacies, and fast-food joints over the years. I have almost been hit by him as I was running across the street and he was speeding by. He stuck his head through the window and swore at me, the stranger who was playing a game of Frogger with his car. ("That's my father," I told the friend who saw it happen.) And here he is again, outside the gate a few feet from his son, the stranger. "Who wants to see him?" I ask. "His father," he snaps. "I'll go check to see if he's there," I promise.

"Bryan is outside," I tell my grandmother.

"What does he want?" she sneers.

"To see me."

"You're too big for him to steal, so you can go if you want."

I hesitantly head back outside, stand by the gate, and look past it at him. A mix of curiosity and fear glues my tongue to the base of my mouth. Annoyance and frustration seem to have taken over as his makeup artists, and he repeats, "Is Chris there?" "Yes," I answer. "I am Chris."

I never know how to answer this question often put to me: "Is it GARnette or garNETTE?" I usually say GARnette, rushing through the last syllable as if gobbling it up rather than laying it out, sometimes prompting people to mishear it as GARnit. Perhaps it is the way I garble my words—my sister Rene says my speech "sounds like you're talking with hot food in your mouth"—that leads people to call me Garet, Granet, Garfield, Garland, Garnash, and even Garnish. I answer to all of them, as long as I know it's me being referred to, and don't object unless the name is truly undesirable, like the one a Japanese ESL student bestowed on me, apparently having forgotten to swap a mnemonic with the real thing: Garbage.

But, my mushmouth tendencies aside, I hardly know how to properly pronounce my own name. After all, it was thrust upon nine-year-old me one Christmas holiday. My mother came home one day with Errol Cadogan, who had lived with us briefly when she dated him a year or so before, but who was so dreadful that my grandmother and I celebrated when he departed. But now he was back. And for good, apparently: they were now married. His scent hadn't even settled into the living room before he began to pump joy out of the house. He did this by force. I had to memorize "Garnette Neon Cadogan" and when I headed back to school after the break I was to instruct my teachers and classmates that I was no longer to be called Ethan Bryan Levy. New year, new name. My new middle name, Neon, suggested as much: with its origins in the Greek adjective *neos*, it meant "something new." I was so busy trying not to forget my new name and getting over the oddness of the middle name—"Wait, you mean like the loud lights?" my friends joked. "Wha kinda fluorescent name that, Ethan?"—that I never thought to ask which syllable of my first name I should lean down on.

I learned my new name, but a lot of my classmates weren't going to go to the trouble. They insisted on calling me Ethan Levy. And if it wasn't confusing enough for me to be calling myself one name while they were calling me another, at home the only name my brother, mother, stepfather, and grandmother would call me was Chris. My mother went to the trouble of legally changing my name to Garnette but somehow didn't think to assign me the name Chris, which I'd been called since I was a baby. As it was told to me, when I got home from the hospital my grandmother didn't think much of the name I'd been given, nor of the man I'd inherited it from, and so decided she would call me Christopher. My mother, who had fallen out with my father before I was born, settled for, perhaps even liked, the name Ethan, but my grandmother refused to call me that. My grandmother resorted to a stealthy obstinacy. She said Christopher often and persistently enough that my mother, out of exasperation, decided that Christopher would be my pet name, and over time its diminutive became the only tag family or close neighbors used for me.

To be precise, though, my mother had three other constant go-tos. When playful, she would call me "Bones" because of my skinny frame, or "Reds" because of my light-black complexion. When angry, she would call me Mr. Bloodcloth, creating the ultimate high-low mix by putting a personal title before that Jamaican curse word whose origins refer to a protective cloth used during menstruation. This backfired for both of us one afternoon when she repeatedly called me another curse word, Mr. Bombocloth, and I ignored her until she said, "Don't you hear me talking to you?" To which I responded, "I thought I was Mr. Bloodcloth." That rejoinder ensured she never again mixed up her curse words when addressing me, and the whaling I received guaranteed I would think hard before ever again being a wiseass to my mother.

When I looked closely at the names of my two younger brothers, I discovered that they shared the initials GNC. So, Garnette Neon Cadogan—for consistency's sake, I guess. But my younger brother whose name was changed from Damian Isaacs to G. N. Cadogan was—and, to this day, still is—called "Lippy" by the family, due to a lower lip that hung exaggeratedly, like an anchor anxious for the seabed, when he bawled. In Jamaica, it's not unusual to encounter people known to most of their family and friends and community by a nickname, their real names submerged except when they pop up on a check or in an obituary. I once taught in a school in which one parent was known to everyone in the community, including his children, as "Bagga." One day I mentioned "Bagga" to the school principal, only for her to flinch and rebuke me for saying his name. I objected that it was the man's name—his child at our school called him by it, after all!—and I knew no other. She would have none of it, nor would she explain why. I asked around, and found out that "Bagga" was short for "Bag a [bag of] shit."

When I bump into certain former classmates, I can't introduce them to people because I only remember them by a profanity, or some tamer but inappropriate moniker, like "Blacka," the only name I have for one very dark-complexioned guy I know. But even in a country where nicknames, or pet names, are ubiquitous, my family is unusual: none of us call the others by their real names.

My youngest brother, who has been between stout and fat since he was a baby, has from very early been called "Fatta" (as in "fatter"). I have two sisters whose real names I sometimes forget because, like everyone else in the family, I call them by their pet names "Tammy" and "Taz" (the latter nicknamed after my mother's favorite cartoon character, the Tasmanian Devil). My mother, whose first and middle birth names are Yvonne Maria, went by a long-standing pet name, Marlene, which my grandmother affectionately shortened to Mar, and which I began to use in my mid-teens. ("Don't call me Mom. Do I look like an old lady to you?" my mother, only eighteen years my senior, would warn.) And my grandmother, who was born Adria Maria Foote, was called "Titis," which non-discerning ears—not detecting the one-two uneven beat with an emphasis on the second syllable—thought was a reference to her chest, when in fact it was my mother's slight lisp as a baby, trying to say my grandmother's previous nickname, "Missis," that produced yet another name. (And my mother called her "Bigga," a reference to her size ["bigger"] that none of us children were allowed to use, not because it was considered offensive but because it was a term of affection reserved for my mother.)

Within the family, nicknames were generally a sign of affection; most of the nicknames originated with my mother, for whom humor seemed to be one of the few displays of affection she was capable of. Directed at people outside the family, however, the nicknames were synecdoche: following my mother's split from him, my stepfather, whose every other word was a lie, was called Remington Steele, after the con-artist title character from the 1980s television show. In a family with so many substitute names, it was easy for me, then, not to think of my name as anything but a temporary marker.

It's something of a mystery why my mother gave me my original name—could it really have origins as simple as her browsing through a name book for something interesting, as she once said?—but what is no mystery is why she changed it. She hated my father, a liar and a cheat, and wanted to be rid of the memory of him. The worst thing I could do as a child was to remind my mother of him. "Like your father" was her harshest indictment. "Don't behave like your father" made as much sense to me, though, as being told, "Stop speaking Mandarin." Every fault in me was scorned as bequeathed by him. And she was intent on purging any trace of him from within me. I wasn't sure of what I was to be; I just knew what I wasn't to be. It was identity by negation.

People change their names to give themselves a new identity. Some adopt a nom de plume to shape how others see them, to reveal how they see themselves. Samuel Clemens becomes Mark Twain, Mary Ann Evans becomes George Eliot, David Henry Thoreau becomes Henry David Thoreau. Some desire to throw off a name they don't like, or a name so offensive and alienating they consider it a "slave name," as some African Americans would poignantly term their birth names. In the popular 1970s television series *Roots*, one of the most gut-wrenching scenes is of the slave Kunta Kinte being violently whipped for refusing to accept his new name Toby. Some change their names after a religious conversion. Cassius Clay becomes Muhammad Ali, Ferdinand Lewis Alcindor Jr. becomes Kareem Abdul-Jabbar. Some take on a new name to project a more alluring persona. Robert Zimmerman becomes Bob Dylan, Declan Patrick MacManus becomes Elvis Costello. And some people are given names that are about their purpose, their fate. In Genesis, Abram ("exalted father") becomes Abraham ("father of multitudes"), Sarai ("princess") becomes Sarah ("mother of many"). Whether for reasons religious, political, or artistic, name changes are about assuming identity. But Ethan Levy became Garnette Cadogan not to give him a new identity, but because his mother wanted to give herself a new identity, one scrubbed of the memory of his father.

Wearing a new name is often an act of improvisation, a way of announcing yourself in the world. This is a difficult passage when you bear a new name you'd rather discard. I wore the name of an abusive man, the force of whose limbs I bore in my bruised limbs, and I had to wake up every day with that name, like a slave carrying his owner's surname. The name Cadogan, which sounded so distinguished, felt like a badge attached with safety pins that pierced through the flesh.

I learned, then, not to be precious about my name. I didn't care if people said it correctly; I had no attachment to it. And I learned to be playful about my name—put me on a couch and call it a defense mechanism, if you will—and embraced the fluidity of adopting different names and the different moods they evoked ("Ethan" felt down-home, "Garnette" felt sophisticated, "Chris" felt intimate and warm). To this day, I try on different names for the fun of it. At coffee shops I sometimes give my name as Kunta Kinte, which leads to situations like a barista (too young for *Roots*) chirping, "Hot chocolate for Kunta

Kinte!" On hospital intake forms for new patients, which I'm convinced doctors never read with care, I enter nonsense names when asked for my "preferred name." On one occasion a physical therapist stepped into the waiting room and announced, "Star Fleet Commander, we will see you now." Turns out someone reads the forms. And since I almost never correct people who get my name wrong I run into scenarios like the instance where an acquaintance wanted to introduce me to her boyfriend's friend Garfield, who turned out to be me, for I never thought to correct her boyfriend who had been calling me Garfield for a while.

The delight of having worn many names does become a nightmare, though, when it bumps against bureaucracy. A rather humorless bureaucrat who interviewed me for my application to become a permanent resident of the United States wanted to know why my father had a Jewish last name, my mother had an Indian last name (think Punjabi), and my surname was a Welsh name that neither my mother nor my father shared. Worse, he wondered aloud if Errol Cadogan was indeed my real father and if my mother was actually my stepmother. When I tried to renew my Jamaican passport a decade later in 2015, I ran into problems when the consular official looked at the forms. (They always look carefully at forms when it means giving permission to cross borders.) I got a headache trying to explain my situation to the supervisor. By the look on her face, she got a headache, too.

But no one is as annoyed by my name change as my father. I see the humiliation on his face whenever my legal name comes up. His eyes drop, then they dart up at me in accusation. When he has to introduce me to friends, he does a clumsy verbal dance: a pause, followed by a near-staccato, followed by a pause. "This is my son . . ." Sometimes he just lets it hang and leaves me to fill in the blank—"Garnette." I say the name he forgets, or refuses to remember.

One Saturday morning, near the end of the summer before my senior year in college, I received a phone call telling me that my father was on campus looking for me. I told the caller it wasn't my father—we'd had a falling-out some time ago, and had been on one of the years-long hiatuses that have characterized our dealings since he popped up outside the gate that last time. It had to be a mistake. The caller responded, as if in confirmation but with lingering sympathy for the imposter, "He was knocking on everyone's door and reading your name off a piece of paper. He didn't even know how to say it." Now that sounded like my father. "Is his name Bryan Levy?" I asked. Too-long pause. "Yes." "Oh, yeah, it's my father. Bring him over to my dorm."

It would have been easier to just change my name back to my birth name—and, for good measure, throw "Chris" in the middle— and I once considered doing so. But then I got to know my father, and I thought I'd stick with an undesirable name I had learned to live with instead of identifying with an unbearable man whose name I once had. After my stepfather was thrown out of the house—precipitated by me finally deciding I would no longer take his brutal beatings without a fight and picking up a machete to make it known—I had decided to get to know my father, to be able to say with certainty what it meant to be "like my father."

But getting to know him proved to be an exercise in understanding my mother's anger. I wanted to know him on his own terms, but couldn't extract myself from comprehending him through the terms my mother established. Her matrix of anger enveloped me, too. And he made it too easy. Shortly after he reappeared in my life, he took me to the airport and left me in the parking lot in his car saying, "Soon come." Now, under the best of circumstances, in Jamaica that statement is highly misleading; "soon come" could mean fifteen minutes, or it could mean five hours. It's more an existential promise than a temporal unit. Out of the mouth of my father it was a lesson in capriciousness. He showed up over a day later, and when he saw me fuming he got upset and complained, "Why didn't you drive and go get some food? I left the keys in the car, and there's money in the glove compartment." My protestations that I didn't have a license only elicited the defense, "A nuh license drive car. People drive car" (a statement that would return to haunt him a few years later when I drove his car unlicensed and got rear-ended, and the insurance company refused to pay for the damage). Tension and distrust quickly marked our relationship. So, in my early twenties, by which time all my close friends were calling me Garnette, I put aside the forms to change my name and my plans to reeducate everyone who knew me by it and decided that I would stick with it. It was the name that those I loved, those who loved me, were comfortable with. The name would be a marker of the distance between me and my father, and it would also be a declaration of the family-of-friends I chose to call my own.

Over time, the name Garnette took on rich meaning. It became the name I preferred because of who used it. My close friends who were family—my "auntie" Maxine, my "mom" and "dad" Arlene and Jim, my "brothers" and "sisters" Richard and Charmaine, and Shirley, and Kerry and Miguel—called me that name and imbued it with honor and affection. (The one thing on which my parents are agreed is that my friends mean too much to me, that they are more important than family. It's a partial truth. My close friends can't be more important than family—they *are* family.) My closest sibling-friend Christine, whom I only called "Sis," called me Chris, the one name I truly do get offended at being called by anyone outside my family or circle of very close friends. That name was like a shared secret between me and my grandmother, and in her mouth it was code for safety in a home where safety was scarce. So people who are new to me can call me whatever they think they hear, as long as they don't call me Chris.

The name Garnette has never felt exactly right, yet it is the name most attached to my sense of identity. It is the name that marks the years in which I began to walk out of love, and into love, rather than out of fear. It is, above all, the name I accept because it is the name that told me I was accepted.

Little Jewel

PATRICK MODIANO
TRANSLATED FROM THE FRENCH BY PENNY HUESTON

I had to go to Neuilly that afternoon to look after the little girl. I rang the doorbell of the Valadier home around three o'clock. Véra Valadier opened the door and seemed surprised to see me. It was as if I'd woken her up and she'd had to get dressed quickly.

'I didn't know you came on Thursdays as well.'

And when I asked if the little girl was there, Véra Valadier said no. Her daughter wasn't home from school yet. Even though it was Thursday and there was no school. But she explained that on Thursday afternoons the boarders played in the playground and the little girl was with them. I had noticed that neither Véra Valadier nor her husband ever called her by her name. They both referred to her as 'she.' And when they called out for their daughter, they merely said, 'Where are you? What are you doing?' They never uttered her first name. After all these years, I couldn't tell you now what that name was. I've forgotten it, and I wonder if I ever even knew it.

She took me into the ground-floor room where Monsieur Valadier usually made his phone calls, sitting on the corner of his desk. Why, I couldn't help asking, on her daughter's day off school, had she left her there with the boarders?

'But she really enjoys staying back there on Thursday afternoons . . .'

In the past, my mother used to say things like that, and always when I was so distraught that all I wanted to do was inhale the bottle of ether.

'You can go and collect her later . . . Otherwise she'll be perfectly happy to come home by herself. Will you excuse me for a moment?' Judging by her voice and her expression, she seemed to be somewhat upset. She disappeared in a hurry, leaving me in that room without a single chair. I was tempted to sit, like Monsieur Valadier, on the corner of the desk. It was gigantic, leather-topped, made out of light-coloured wood, with two drawers on either side, and not a single sheet of paper or even a pencil on top. Only a telephone. Perhaps Monsieur Valadier kept his files in the drawers. My curiosity got the better of me and I opened and shut the drawers in turn. They were empty, except that at the back of one I found a few business cards with the name Michel Valadier, but the address was not in Neuilly.

Sounds of an argument were coming from upstairs. I recognised Madame Valadier's voice, and I was surprised to hear her shouting and swearing, but, every now and again, her voice became plaintive. There was the sound of a man's voice answering her. They passed in front of the doorway. Madame Valadier's voice became softer. Now they were speaking very quietly in the lobby. Then the front door banged shut and, from the window, I watched as a dark-haired, quite short young man wearing a suede jacket and a scarf headed off.

Madame Valadier came back into the study. 'My apologies for deserting you . . .' She approached me and I could tell by her expression that she wanted to ask me something. 'Would you be able to help me do some tidying up?'

She led me to the stairs and I went up to the first floor behind her. We entered a big bedroom, at the end of which was a wide, low bed. It was the only item of furniture in the room. The bed was unmade, and there was a tray resting beside it, with two champagne glasses and an open bottle of champagne. A cork lay conspicuously in the middle of the grey carpet. The bedspread was hanging off the end of the bed. The sheets were tangled, the pillows scattered all over the bed, where a man's dressing gown in dark-blue silk had been tossed, along with a camisole and knickers and a pair of stockings. An ashtray filled with butts was on the floor.

Madame Valadier went to open the two windows. There was a sickly smell hanging in the air, a mixture of perfume and Virginia tobacco, the smell of people who have spent a long time in the same room and the same bed.

She picked up the blue dressing gown. 'I have to put this back in my husband's wardrobe,' she said.

When she came back, she asked if I wanted to help her make the bed. She pulled up the sheets and blanket. Her movements were abrupt and rapid, as if she was frightened of being caught out by someone, and I had trouble keeping up with her. She hid the lingerie and stockings under a pillow. As we finished straightening the bedspread, she caught sight of the tray.

'Oh, yes, I'd forgotten about that . . .'

She picked up the bottle of champagne and the two glasses and opened a wardrobe where lots of pairs of shoes were lined up on shelves. I had never seen so many shoes: different-coloured court shoes, ballerina flats, boots . . . She shoved the bottle and glasses to the back of the top shelf and shut the wardrobe. She looked like someone rushing to hide compromising evidence before the police arrived. All that was left now were the ashtray and the champagne cork. I picked them up. She took them out of my hands and went into the bathroom. The door was open and I heard the noise of the toilet flushing.

She looked at me strangely. She wanted to say something, but she didn't have time. Through the open windows, we could hear a diesel engine. She leaned out one of the windows. I was right behind her. Down below, Monsieur Valadier was getting out of a taxi. He was carrying an overnight bag and a black leather briefcase.

When we went down to join him, he was already on the phone, sitting on his desk, and he greeted us with a wave. Then he hung up. Madame Valadier asked him if his trip had gone well.

'Not great, Véra.'

She shook her head, absorbed. 'But you're not worried, are you?'

'Overall, things are fine, but there are still a few sticking points.'

He turned to me and smiled. 'Isn't she at school today?'

He was referring to his daughter, but I got the impression that he wasn't really interested and that he was merely asking out of politeness to me.

'I let her stay at school with the boarders,' said Madame Valadier.

Monsieur Valadier took off his navy-blue coat and placed it on his overnight bag, on the floor by the desk.

'You know, she can just as easily come home by herself . . .' He spoke softly, still smiling at me. He had the same attitude as his wife.

'There's something we want to discuss with you about our daughter,' said Madame Valadier. 'She'd like to have a dog.'

Monsieur Valadier was still sitting on the corner of his desk. He was swinging one leg in a steady rhythm. Where on earth could people sit if they came to meet him in this office? I wondered. Although I was pretty sure that no one ever came here.

'You'll have to explain to her that it's not possible,' Véra Valadier said. She seemed aghast at the idea that a dog might turn up in the house. 'Will you tell her later?'

She looked so anxious that I couldn't help myself from saying, 'Yes, madame.'

She smiled at me. That had clearly taken a load off her mind.

'I've already asked you to call me Véra, not madame.'

She was standing next to her husband, leaning against the desk.

'In fact, it would be much simpler if you just called us Véra and Michel.'

Her husband was smiling at me, too. There they were, across the room, with their smooth, unlined faces, still quite young.

For me, the evil curse and the bad memories all centred on one face, that of my mother. The little girl had to contend with these two individuals whose smiles and smooth skin were of the kind we're sometimes shocked to see on the faces of murderers who have long remained unpunished.

Monsieur Valadier removed a cigarillo from the top pocket of his jacket and lit it with his lighter. He took a puff and exhaled thoughtfully.

'I'm counting on you to sort out this dog business.'

I saw the little girl at once. She was sitting on the bench, reading a magazine. Around her, twenty or so older girls were scattered about the schoolyard. The boarders. She wasn't paying them the slightest attention, as if she had been waiting there all day without any idea why. She seemed surprised that I had come to collect her so early.

We went down Rue de la Ferme.

'We don't have to go home straightaway,' she said.

We had reached the end of the street and we set off into the section of the Bois de Boulogne where there are pine trees. It was odd to be walking on a late-November afternoon among trees that were reminiscent of summer and the sea. When I was her age, I didn't want to go home either. And could you even call it a home, that gigantic apartment where I had ended up with my mother, without it ever being clear to me why she was living there? The first time she took me there, I thought it belonged to some friends of hers, and I was surprised when the two of us stayed the night—'I'm going to show you your room,' she announced. And I was anxious when I had to go to bed. In that big empty room with the oversized bed, I expected someone to come and ask me what I was doing there. It was as if I had intuited that my mother and I were not really supposed to be on the premises.

'Have you been living in that house for long?' I asked the little girl. She had been there at the beginning of the year. But she couldn't remember exactly where she was living before that. What had struck me, the first time I went to the Valadier house, were all those empty rooms, which reminded me of the apartment where I'd lived with my mother when I was the same age as the little girl. I recalled that, in the kitchen, there was a board stuck on the wall, with white panels that lit up, the words in black lettering: DINING ROOM, STUDY and so on. I also recalled the words CHILDREN'S BEDROOM. Who could those children possibly be? They were probably going to come back at any moment and ask me why I was in their bedroom.

It was dusk and the little girl was still keen to delay our return. We had headed off in the other direction from her parents' home. But was it really their home? Twelve years on, who still knew, for example, that my mother had also lived in Avenue Malakoff, very near the Bois de Boulogne? That apartment didn't belong to us. I found out later that my mother was staying there while the owner was away. Frédérique and one of her women friends talked about it one evening at Fossombronne-la-Forêt, over dinner, when I was at the table. Certain words stick in children's minds and, even if they don't understand them at the time, they understand them twenty years later. It's a bit like the grenades we were told to watch out for at Fossombronne-la-Forêt. Apparently, ever since the war, there were one or two buried in Kraut's Field, and there was still a chance they could explode after all this time.

Yet another reason to be frightened. But we couldn't resist slipping out to that overgrown vacant block and playing hide-and-seek. Frédérique had gone to the apartment to try to find something my mother had forgotten when she left.

We had arrived at the edge of the little lake where people came to ice-skate in winter. The twilight was beautiful. The trees were outlined against a blue and pink sky.

'So, you'd like a dog.'

She was embarrassed, as if I had revealed her secret.

'Your parents told me.'

She frowned and pursed her lips, pouting. 'They don't want a dog,' she said.

'I'm going to try to speak to them about it. They'll come round sooner or later.'

She smiled at me. She seemed to trust me. She believed that I'd be able to persuade Véra and Michel Valadier. But I was under no illusion about those two: they were as tough as the Kraut. I had suspected as much from the beginning. With Véra, it was immediately obvious. She had a fake first name. And, in my opinion, his name wasn't Michel Valadier, either. He must have already gone by several other names. And, indeed, there was a different address on his business card. I wondered if he wasn't even more devious and more dangerous than his wife.

Now we had to head home, and I was regretting my empty promise to her. We were walking along the riding tracks to get back to the Jardin d'Acclimatation. I was certain that Véra and Michel Valadier wouldn't give in.

He opened the front door and went straight back to his study on the ground floor, without saying a word to us. I heard gales of raucous, vicious laughter. Madame Valadier—Véra—was yelling, but I couldn't make out what she was saying. Their voices were indistinguishable, each trying to shout over the top of the other. The little girl opened her eyes wide. She was frightened, but I sensed that she was used to this fear. In the lobby, she stood still, frozen; I should have taken her off somewhere else. But where? Madame Valadier came out of the study, looking calm and composed.

'Did you have a nice walk?' she asked.

Once again, she looked like those cold, mysterious blondes who glide through old American movies. Then Monsieur Valadier came out. He was also very calm. He was wearing an elegant black suit and there were big scratches down one of his cheeks, most likely from fingernails. Véra Valadier's fingernails? She kept hers rather long. The two of them were standing next to each other in the doorway, with their smooth faces of murderers who would remain unpunished, for lack of evidence. It looked as if they were posing for a photo, not for an official identity shot but for the cameras at the beginning of a soirée, as the guests arrive.

'Did mademoiselle explain about the dog?' asked Véra Valadier. Her tone was distant, not at all like the voices you hear around Rue de Douai, where she'd told me she was born. With another first name.

'Dogs are sweet,' she said. 'But they're very dirty.'

'Your maman is right,' Michel Valadier added, in the same tone as his wife. 'It would really not be a good idea to have a dog in the house.'

'When you're a big girl, you'll be able to have all the dogs you like . . . But not here and not now.'

Véra Valadier's voice had changed. She sounded bitter. Perhaps she was imagining a time in the future—time passes so quickly—when her daughter would be grown up and when she, Véra, would roam the corridors of the metro forever and ever, in a yellow coat.

The little girl didn't say a thing. She merely stared, wide-eyed.

'You see, with dogs you get diseases,' Monsieur Valadier said. 'And, well, they bite, too.'

Now he had a shifty look and an odd way of speaking, like an illegal street peddler keeping an eye out for the police.

I was finding it hard to remain quiet. I would gladly have stood up for the little girl, but I didn't want the conversation to get poisonous and for her then to get scared. Nevertheless, I couldn't stop myself from looking Michel Valadier straight in the eye. 'Did you hurt yourself, sir?'

I touched my finger to my cheek, the same spot where the long scratches ran down his cheek.

'No . . . Why?' he muttered.

'You really should put some disinfectant on that. It's like a dog bite. You can catch rabies.'

This time, I could tell he was out of his depth. And Véra Valadier was, too. They were looking at me warily. Under the glare of the chandelier, thrown off course, they were nothing but a suspicious couple who had just been rounded up in a raid.

'I think we're late,' she said, turning to her husband.

She had recovered her cold voice. Michel Valadier checked his bracelet watch.

'Yes, we must go,' he agreed, also feigning indifference.

'There's a slice of ham for you in the fridge,' she said to the little girl. 'I think we'll be home late tonight . . .'

The little girl drew nearer to me and took my hand, squeezing it like someone who wanted to be guided through the darkness.

'It would be better if you left,' Madame Valadier said. 'She has to get used to being by herself.' She took the little girl by the hand and pulled her away. 'Mademoiselle is going to leave now. You're to have dinner and put yourself to bed.'

The little girl looked at me once more, her eyes wide, as if she would never again be astonished by anything. Michel Valadier had moved in closer, and the little girl was now standing motionless between her parents.

'See you tomorrow,' I said to her.

'See you tomorrow.'

But she didn't seem very sure about it.

Outside, I sat down on a bench beside the path that runs along the Jardin d'Acclimatation. I had no idea what I was waiting for. After a while, I saw Madame and Monsieur Valadier leave the house. She was wearing a fur coat; he had on his navy-blue coat. They didn't walk close together. When they reached the black car, she got in the back seat and he took the wheel, as if he were her chauffeur. The car headed off towards Avenue de Madrid, and I realised that I would never know anything about these people, neither their real first names nor their real surnames, nor why a troubled look sometimes came over Madame Valadier, nor why there were no chairs in Monsieur Valadier's study, nor why the address on his business card was different from that of his office at home. And the little girl? She, at least, was not a mystery to me. I intuited what she might have been feeling. I had been, more or less, the same sort of child.

A light came on in her room on the second floor. I was tempted to go and keep her company. I thought I saw her shadow at the window. But I didn't ring the doorbell. I was feeling so miserable around that time that I scarcely felt up to helping someone else. What's more, the business with the dog had reminded me of an incident in my own childhood.

I walked to the Porte Maillot, relieved to get out of the Bois de Boulogne. During the day, when I was with the little girl at the edge of the skaters' lake, I could just about bear it. But now that it was night, I felt a sensation of emptiness which was far more horrific than the vertigo that overwhelmed me on the pavement in Rue Coustou, outside Zone Out.

On my right, the first trees marked the entrance to the Bois de Boulogne. One November evening, a dog went missing in that park; it was something I would be haunted by for the rest of my life, at times when I least expected it. During sleepless nights and lonely days, and even during summer. I should have explained to the little girl how dangerous it was, this business of having a dog.

When I entered the schoolyard earlier and saw her sitting on the bench, I thought back to another schoolyard. I was the same age as the little girl and there were older boarders in that schoolyard, too. They took care of us. Every morning, they helped us to get dressed and, in the evening, to get ready for bed. They mended our clothes. My 'big girl' was called Thérèse, like me. She had dark hair and blue eyes, and a tattoo on her arm. As I recall, she looked a bit like the pharmacist. The other boarders, and even the nuns, were wary of her, but she was always kind to me. She stole chocolate from the kitchen and sneaked it to me at night in the dormitory. During the day, she sometimes took me to a studio, not far from the chapel, where the big girls were learning how to iron.

One day, my mother came to collect me. She told me to get in the car and I sat on the front bench seat, next to her. I think she told me that I was never going back to that boarding school. There was a dog on the back seat. And the car was parked almost at the same spot where I'd been knocked down by the truck, not long before. The boarding school can't have been far from the Gare de Lyon. I remember, when Jean Borand used to wait for me outside the boarding school on Sundays, we would walk to his garage. And the day my mother took me away in the car with the dog, we went past the Gare de Lyon. In those days, the streets were deserted and I had the impression that the two of us in the car were the only people in Paris.

That was the day I went with her, for the first time, to the huge apartment near the Bois de Boulogne, the day she showed me MY ROOM. Before then, the few times Jean Borand took me to see her, we went by metro to the Place de l'Étoile, where she was still living in a hotel. Her room was smaller than my room in Rue Coustou. In the metal box, I found a telegram addressed to her at that hotel and in her real name: Suzanne Cardères, Hôtel San Remo, 8 Rue d'Armaillé. I was relieved every time I discovered the actual address of those places which I only vaguely remembered, but which appeared in my nightmares over and over again. If I knew their exact location and studied their facades, I was convinced they would become less threatening.

A dog. A black poodle. Right from the start, he slept in my room. My mother never looked after him and, moreover, would have been no more capable of looking after a dog than a child. No doubt someone had given her the dog as a present. For her, it was nothing more than a fashion accessory that she must have got bored with quickly. I still wonder by what twist of fate that dog and I ended up together in the car. Now that she was living in the huge apartment and her name was Sonia O'Dauyé, she probably needed a dog and a little girl.

I used to go for walks with the dog, beyond the apartment block and all the way along the avenue, down to the Porte Maillot. I can't recall the dog's name. It wasn't a name my mother had given him. It was around the beginning of the time I went to live with her in the apartment. She hadn't yet enrolled me in the Saint-André school and I wasn't yet known as Little Jewel. Jean Borand collected me on Thursdays and took me to his garage for the whole day. And I kept the dog with me. I knew already that my mother would forget to feed him. I was the one who got food ready for him. When Jean Borand came to collect me, we took the metro, and smuggled the dog onto the train, too. We walked from the Gare de Lyon to the garage. I wanted to remove his leash. There was no chance of him getting run over; there were no cars in the streets. But Jean Borand warned me not to take off his leash. After all, I had almost got run over by a truck in front of the school.

My mother enrolled me in Saint-André. I walked there alone every morning, and I came home every evening around six. Unfortunately, I couldn't take the dog to school, even though it was very close to the apartment, on Rue Pergolèse. I found the exact address on a scrap of paper in my mother's diary. Cours Saint-André, 58 Rue Pergolèse. On whose advice did she send me to that place? I stayed there all day long.

One evening, when I got home to the apartment, the dog wasn't there. I thought my mother had gone out with him. She had promised me that she'd walk him and feed him, tasks I'd already asked the cook to do, the Chinese man who prepared dinner and brought my mother a breakfast tray to her room every morning. My mother came home a bit later, without the dog. She said she'd lost it in the Bois de Boulogne. She had the leash in her bag and she handed it to me as if to prove that she wasn't lying. Her voice was very calm. She didn't look sad. She seemed to think it was all quite normal. 'You'll have to make up a lost-dog notice tomorrow, and perhaps someone will return him.' She took me to my room. But her tone was so calm, so blasé, that I had the feeling she was preoccupied with something else. I was the only one who thought about the dog. No one ever brought him back. I was too scared to turn out the light in my room. Since the dog had been sleeping with me, I wasn't used to being by myself at night, and now it was even worse than at boarding school. I pictured him in the darkness, lost in the middle of the Bois de Boulogne. That same evening, my mother went out, and I still remember the dress she was wearing. It was a blue dress with a veil. That dress has appeared in my nightmares for a long time, always worn by a skeleton.

I kept the light on all that night, and every other night. I never stopped being frightened. It would be my turn after the dog's, I was sure of it.

Strange thoughts came into my mind, so muddled that I waited ten or so years for them to take shape, before I could put them into words. One morning, sometime before seeing the woman in the yellow coat in the corridors of the metro, I woke up with a sentence running through my head, one of those sentences which seem incomprehensible, because they are the last shreds of a forgotten dream: You had to kill the Kraut to avenge the dog.

AMANDA REA is the recipient of a 2015 Rona Jaffe Foundation Writers' Award. Her fiction and nonfiction have appeared in *Electric Literature's Recommended Reading, Kenyon Review, Missouri Review,* the *Pushcart Prize* anthology, and elsewhere. She lives in Colorado.

Nola

AMANDA REA

I was thirteen when our father brought Nola home. She was the first woman he'd fallen for since he and our mother split, and I was de facto Queen of the Trailer House, commanding the master bedroom and no small amount of leeway when it came to bad moods, long showers, outbursts, hysteria, naps. My father and brother humored me in the weary way of men. Calm down, they said, patting my back with stiff hands, as though my personality might be catching. It's not the end of the world.

But it was. Everything was. Especially this: our father's girlfriend was coming down the driveway in a long white car. Somehow, I had failed to anticipate this, even dimly. Our parents' marriage had been so strained that I couldn't remember our father having loved a female who wasn't me. And now, he'd labored over a pot of spaghetti. He'd gone over the carpet with the vacuum, which had roared and clattered like a wood chipper. I looked around, nervous on his behalf. The three of us lived by the unspoken credo that life was too short for housekeeping. A made bed would soon be unmade; a working toilet would soon be broken again. Feral cats lounged on every outdoor surface. Every couple of years our father went on a shooting spree, but he never got them all, and the survivors wasted no time in inbreeding, becoming not so much cats as catlike wraiths. What kind of woman would make it through their yowling gauntlet, or down the driveway for that matter, culminating as it did in a disemboweled couch and a pile of old Christmas trees? Ever since we'd left our mother—our father first, us a few years later—our lives had felt provisional, like a slumber party with no clear end. We stayed up late. We guzzled milk from the jug. Trash piled up around us like a moat.

"Cozy," Nola said, as she got out of her car. "I like what you've done with the yard."

"We've kind of allowed it to go back to nature."

She kissed our father on the lips. She shook my brother's hand, then mine, with seeming sincerity. She had lively blue eyes with pleasing wrinkles at the outside edge, though of course they did not please me. Nor did I approve of her hair, which was blond and permed and scrunched too tightly around her head. There is no more exacting critic of female beauty than a homely teenage girl, and in a glance I registered that Nola was too doughy and chinless to be beautiful, but had instead a cultivated prettiness. She wore pink jeans and delicate earrings. Her lips shone with gloss. She smelled powerfully of strawberry. It was clear that she'd spent time in front of a mirror, turning from side to side, learning how to play up her assets. This was something I'd often wished our mother would do. She had many assets—in her youth she'd resembled Sophia Loren—but she didn't give a damn about any of them. She wore whatever people gave her. She went barefoot to "toughen her feet." She drank a twelve-pack of beer every night in lieu of dinner. When we asked her to stop, she said, "Mind your own business." When we threatened to go live with our father, she said, "Go ahead. You deserve each other."

Nola drank too, but her beer was an accessory she carried and occasionally sipped. She moved around the kitchen like she'd lived there for years, opening drawers, teasing us about the scarcity of forks. Her laughter was soft and tinkling. When darkness fell, our father made her a bed on the couch. But she wasn't there in the middle of the night when I crept out to check, and in the morning a satin bathrobe hung from our father's bedroom door like the flag of some foreign country. Sumptuous and turquoise, it was easily the fanciest thing that had ever been in our house, and I stared at it a long time before I worked up the nerve to lift the dangling belt and let it slide across my palm. Through the cracked door I could see them sleeping, two humped forms under my father's brown blanket.

Her things began to sprout all over: bracelets on the table, a toothbrush on the sink. Evenings found her on the couch, singing along while our father played his guitar. She had a good voice, rich and little bit throaty, possibly from cigarettes. Our father disapproved of smoking, and said this was all that kept him from getting down on one knee. Nola only smiled, and felt her pockets for a lighter. She liked to smoke out on the porch steps, where it was quiet and she could gaze at the faraway mountains. This was one of the only times I saw her still, and she looked unlike herself somehow, older maybe, or under the weight of some sadness. If she caught me looking, she'd force a bright smile. Stub out her cigarette. Jump to her feet.

She was always in a hurry to get somewhere. By day she was a receptionist in a dental office, and many nights she babysat for a friend. The friend had serious problems of an unnamed nature, so Nola occasionally had the children in tow. They were maybe five and six, a boy and a girl, with white-blond hair. From the living room we could see the tops of their heads in the back of her station wagon.

"Bring them in," our father said. "It's getting dark. They can play with the kids."

"Oh, I shouldn't. Their mother is really protective."

"Well, if she's that protective maybe she should watch them herself."

"You're telling me," Nola said, puffing her cheeks in exasperation. "But she's going through a hard time right now, and we've been friends forever. I'm the only one she trusts."

We only met the children once. We were at the mall with our father when we ran unexpectedly into Nola. She'd left our house only an hour before, on her way to work. It was the friend again, she explained. There had been a sobbing phone call, some drama involving an ex, and Nola had offered to take the kids until it all blew over. Anyway, here they are. This is Katie, this is Beau.

Meekly, the children smiled. We smiled too. The little girl tugged at Nola's sleeve.

"Mommy, can I have money for the gum-ball machine?"

Nola slapped the back of the child's head. "I told you not to call me that! Your mommy is not here. Do you understand?"

The child's eyes pooled with tears. Nola pressed a quarter in her hand. To us she said, "The poor thing. She gets so attached."

I don't remember what happened after this, except that we went our separate ways, vaguely bothered by the encounter. Wasn't it strange that Nola had struck her friend's child, and for such a sad and harmless error? And why had she been so animated, fluffing her hair and laughing too loud, even when no laughter was called for? Our father grimaced. "Maybe Nola isn't as cut out for babysitting as she thinks."

"That's because she's a moron," I said. My hatred for Nola came in surges, like the plunge of a carnival ride, only upward. In my diary, I referred to her as a "royal crown whore" and left it on the table for her to read. I walked around her like she was furniture. One evening over dinner I informed her that our father "jerked off with the eye of a needle"—a salvo I'd been crafting for days, expecting he would kill me, or at least overturn the table. Instead he gave me a pained look, as one might give a dog dragging its ass in the dirt, and said, "Go to bed."

Despite my behavior, Nola made an effort. She dropped by when our father wasn't home and asked questions about school, friends, boys. She offered to take me for manicures and ice cream. Always I declined, or gave an indifferent shrug. On pain of death I would not submit to Girls' Day. At moments like these, I felt an intense loyalty to my mother, and saw Nola as she might have: as a vapid, poodle-haired twat. And yet, I'd begun to soften toward Nola's chain-mail hair, and the way she had of rushing through the door late and sweetly frazzled, having lost her keys, lost track of time. I enjoyed her stories about barrel-racing and drinking with her girlfriends, and I never tired of looking at her tweezers and lip balms and pastel sweaters, and the heels she wore when our father took her out. She wasn't afraid to walk in them, nor was she afraid to buy tampons—I'd seen her drop a box right in the cart. She bought earrings and weight-loss shakes and little bottles of eye cream, and it was an endless wonder how she made these decisions, how she knew that an eye cream was needed and where to buy it. She embraced womanhood in a way I hoped to glean once she was my stepmother. Perhaps through close observation of Nola, I could become a normal woman, not so tough and stubborn as my mother, but happy. Yielding. A lover of chocolate and Christmas and jewelry.

Nola was babysitting one night when a man called our house. Our father answered in grave tones, his elbows on the table. It was a week before he told us the caller was Nola's husband. His name was Dean Bergstrom or something equally Nordic, and he was a hunting outfitter who lived a few miles west.

"All this time I thought my wife was working nights," he'd said, in a voice slowed by sadness or drink or both. "But come to find out she doesn't have a janitorial job at all."

Our father began to protest, but already the truth was sinking in. He could hear it in the hunter's voice. He could feel it in the back of his mind, where there lived a hundred niggling doubts. He'd never really believed Nola's stretch marks came from having once been very fat.

"Listen guy," he said. "Until this moment, I didn't know you existed."

"Well, I do. And I've got half a mind to drive over there and shoot you, but I probably won't."

We never saw Nola again. What pain our father felt he disguised with laughter. How crazy she was! What fools we'd been! We learned that she'd never worked at the dental office at all, but only hung around the desk visiting a friend. She was a housewife. And yet, hadn't we seen her with the phone to her ear, booking an appointment? Hadn't she gone on about tartar and the proper way to floss? We marveled at the volume of her lies, the stamina it must've taken to juggle two families in a way that's usually reserved for powerful men. But why acquire a second life no better than the first? Had she meant to leave her husband but couldn't bring herself to do it, or were we just a fleeting diversion?

Twenty years later, I still don't know. More than Nola, I find myself wondering about her daughter. Would she remember that day in the mall, and if so, would she forgive her mother's disavowal? Perhaps it would be a minor incident in a long, loving relationship. Or perhaps it would contribute to something larger, a pattern of disappointment that would cause her to reject her mother as I had done mine. Would she tell herself that no mother was better than a crazy one? Would she dwell on every harsh word and graceless act, forgetting all the rest? And would she, like me, grow up to have a daughter of her own? Would she be tugged and smeared and screamed at, and face the same pile of dishes night after night, and find in the mirror a person she barely remembers, from a life that had once seemed full of possibility? Would she ever feel an urge to say fuck it, and turn away from her life, as Nola had almost done, and my mother had done so decisively?

Of course, I didn't ask these questions when I was thirteen. I just shook my head. I twirled one finger around my ear. Nola became another story I told, a chimerical thing, half-imagined. I wore her turquoise robe for years, until I decided it was tacky and threw it in the trash.

The twelve collections published by poet SHARON OLDS include *Satan Says* (1980), *The Dead and The Living* (1984), *The Wellspring* (1996), and *Stag's Leap* (2012), which won both the Pulitzer and the T. S. Eliot prizes. Olds was New York State poet laureate from 1998 to 2000 and is currently a professor at New York University. Her newest book, *Odes*, will be out in fall 2016.

Ode to My Sister

SHARON OLDS

I know why they say the heart is in
the heart. When you think about people you love,
you get warm, there. I want to thank
my sister for loving me, which taught me
to love. I'm not sure what she loved in me,
besides my love for her—maybe
that I was a copy of her, half-size—
then three-quarters, then size. In the snapshots, you see her
keeping an eye on me, I was a little wild,
and I said silly things, and she would laugh her musical
serious laugh. She knew things,
sometimes she knew everything,
as if she'd been born knowing. And I
so did not know—my wonder went
along with me wherever we'd go,
as if I had it on a tool belt—
I understood almost nothing, and I
loved *pertinding*, and I loved to go into the
garden and dance with the flowers, which danced
with me without hardly moving their green
legs, I was like a music box
dropped on my head. And I was bad—
but I don't think my sister thought I was actually
bad, I was her somewhat smaller
littermate—nor did she need
my badness to establish her goodness. And she
was beautiful, with a moral beauty, she would

glide by, in the hall, like a queen
on a barge on the Nile, and she had straight black hair
which moved like a black waterfall, as
one thing, like a black silk skirt.
She was the human. I aspired to her.
And she stood between the god and me.
And her hair (*pertind*) was like a wing
of night, and in my dream she could hold it
over me, and hide me. Of course,
by day, if the god wanted you for something,
she took you. I think if the god had known how to
take my curly hair from my head,
she would have. And I think there was nothing
my sister wanted to take from me.
Why would she want to, she had everything—
in our room she had control of the door,
closed, or open, and the light switch,
dark, or bright. And if anything
had happened to me, I think my sister
would not have known who she was, I was
as essential to her, as she to me.
If anything had happened to her,
I think I would not be alive today,
and no one would remember me,
as if I had not lived.

Amaryllis Ode

SHARON OLDS

When the blossoms were wilting, I cut the stalk
and put it in a glass, before my trip—to have
waiting, for me, the damp withering
blooms to see, when I came back.
I thought of the female side of my gene-
alogy—the mothers, who have liked to have
waiting, upstairs, a daughter stripped
to be punished, and I realized I had been my mother's
conduit to the satisfaction
of being, in her own time,
the beater. I think she did not know what she was
doing. And it *is* nice, isn't it,
to have something waiting, the knowledge of which
will thrill you—how much drier will the blossoms
be, how everted each pistil-tip on its
coral stalk dusted with ochre
seed? My mother and I were a twosome, as her
mother and she had been, and her mother's
mother . . . Mine used to perform a song—
not while she was beating on me—
White coral bells, upon a silver stalk. It was
a pleasure, for me, to behead-head-head-head
the amaryllis, to slit its throat.
The ending to the song was *O don't you wish
that you could hear them ring?*

That will happen only when
the fairies sing—or in our case,
when the dead mothers weep—my mother would weep,
to read this.

Victuals Dream Ode

SHARON OLDS

Inside my father's testicle, tonight, it seems
bright and satiny, valentinaceous,
as if I had come from his heart and was
a part of him. And as soon as he gave me
up—fierce kiss goodbye—
I traveled into the mystery
of the half-human journeying toward the half
human, into the chamber, the vault
in the dark, and then his matter bumped
her matter and createred my spirit. He seemed
not to mind that I was partly my mother,
I think it was a kick, to him,
himself as a girl, sired off a lady.
That is why I like to believe
I was conceived in my father, carried in that rosy
hammock, because I felt he disliked me so much
less than she did, he did not uncare for
his eyes in me, or his oddball mind,
or his long legs—or her bones in me,
her cheeks and chin, her eyelids. All those dinners she cooked,
eaten in the silence he decreed. Peas
were interesting, the way they were rebels
in a group. Gravy could drown whole families.
And then there was chewing, big relief, and thank
god for meat, for what we regarded as the
lower creatures, and their vitals, liver
and lights, brains, eggs, balls and heart.

ALEKSANDAR HEMON is the author of *The Question of Bruno, Nowhere Man,* and *The Lazarus Project.* His latest short story collection, *Love and Obstacles,* was published in May 2009. His collection of autobiographical essays, *The Book of My Lives,* was published by Farrar Straus and Giroux in March 2013. He was awarded a Guggenheim Fellowship in 2003 and a "genius" grant from the MacArthur Foundation in 2004. His latest novel, *The Making of Zombie Wars,* was published by FSG in 2015. His book on the United Nations, *Behind the Glass Wall,* is forthcoming from FSG Originals. From 2010 to 2013 he served as editor of the *Best European Fiction* anthologies, published by Dalkey Archive Press. He is currently the Distinguished Writer-in-Residence at Columbia College Chicago. He lives in Chicago with his wife and daughters.

A Tomb for Uncle Julius

ALEKSANDAR HEMON

More than a century ago, my paternal ancestors emigrated to
Bosnia from Galicia and Bukovina (both now part of Ukraine),
the easternmost provinces in the Austro-Hungarian Empire. My
Ukrainian-speaking family believed there would be enough wood
in Bosnia to allow them to survive the winters. The Empire, having
occupied Bosnia since the 1878 Berlin Congress, gave land away,
encouraging colonization. The details of our migration are dim,
because none of our history was written down and everything—the
reasons, the dates, the difficulties, the fears, the family left behind—
was conveyed by way of stories whose exactness dwindled over
generations. What little is still remembered might be forgotten soon,
for a century later we are dispersed, after the most recent wars, all
over the world. Few in my family have died or will die in the country
of their birth.

Uncle Julius was my grandmother Mikhalyina's first cousin, born
in 1904, in Stara Dubrava, Bosnia. When they were about seven years
old, Mikhalyina and he sat under a blooming pear tree and swore
to each other that they would dedicate their lives to the freedom
of Ukraine. But before they could get around to doing any of their
freedom work, Uncle Julius left home. He was fourteen, and would

not see my grandmother for more than forty years, most of which he would spend in the prisons and gulags of the Soviet Union.

Twenty-five years ago, Uncle Julius shared the grand saga of his life and imprisonment with me. In 1990, I'd traveled from Sarajevo to Zagreb, where he lived, to spend a week interviewing him. On our bookshelf we'd had his memoir of his time in the Soviet labor camps, sitting next to Solzhenitsyn's *Gulag Archipelago* and Danilo Kiš's *Tomb for Boris Davidovich*. I'd skimmed his book, written in a testimonial style often turgid with ideological idioms (*working class, class struggle*, etc.), and had got the basic outline of his story. But I was a young and impatient journalist, and I wanted to hear the story of his terrible life directly from him. I wanted to write and edit his testimony. Besides, Fugazi, one of my favorite bands at the time, was playing a show in Zagreb that week.

This was the second (and the last) time I saw him. The first time I was about ten. My family had spent a summer vacation at his modest house in Mljet, a gorgeous island in the Adriatic. I remembered him as a kind but somewhat stern man who didn't talk much to my sister and me. I remembered his wife Olga as a warm, beautiful Russian woman with lilting laughter.

In the spring of 1990, I stayed with their daughter Nadezhda, whom I hadn't met before. In my family, cousins are liked a priori. The kinship bond guarantees a certain minimum amount of affection and the privileges that come with it: hospitality, for one. But I sensed that Nadezhda didn't like me, and I never felt welcomed around her. Once, she demanded that I flush the toilet more than once, her condescension suggesting that I appeared to her as an uncivilized, provincial Bosnian. Another time, I returned to find her in the dining room with the man who was her date that evening; they were listening to the tapes of gulag ballads, a genre unto itself, I learned, dealing with the horrors and joys of the labor camp experience. I was curious about it, but I could tell she didn't appreciate my curiosity, didn't want me around. She answered my questions curtly until I got the message and withdrew into my room.

Be that as it may, I walked every day for a week from Nadezhda's to her father's modest duplex in a quiet, woodsy part of Zagreb. At 11 AM sharp, we would have what for him and his Russian-born wife, Olga, was lunch, and for me breakfast. Then I'd follow Uncle Julius to his upstairs study for our interview, recording it on cassette tapes. He was eager to talk to me, he said, because younger generations needed to know the truth about the gulag.

During our lunch/breakfast, I noticed that Uncle Julius ate incredibly quickly. Once, as I was chitchatting with Olga, still serving food, I noted that Uncle Julius had already, before I'd even started, wiped his plate clean with a piece of bread. "A habit from the camp," he explained. "You had to eat fast before someone grabbed your food."

Uncle Julius's hunger likely preceded the gulag. With nine children, his parents had been horribly poor. His father had been a mason and tended some land, but that could never be enough to feed all the starving mouths. Uncle Julius's three-year-old sister had died from malnourishment, and things got even worse when World War I started. His father sold their house and all of their land for a few sacks of wheat and was soon sent to fight for the Empire, leaving his kids and wife homeless. The youngest child was six months old, the oldest eighteen years. Their mother then perished, followed by her youngest son. Back then, people had a lot of children in the hope that at least some of them might survive.

In 1918, Uncle Julius followed his older brother to wander from town to town, house to house, and beg for work, scraps of food and a night in the cow shed. His brother eventually found a way to make a living and they had to split. Uncle Julius wandered on to become a cobbler's apprentice; his duties included herding goats and receiving regular beatings. Eventually, he had enough, and got a job in a tannery. Alone and illiterate, he was not even fifteen.

In Uncle Julius's upstairs room, I envisioned the life of a teenager who'd suffered more than I ever could. I imagined him exhausted at the end of a fourteen-hour day, blisters peeling off the palms of his hands, his lungs sore with gore stench and lime. One day, he listens to some firebrand big-city student's tales about a land where people tore down the rotten edifice of exploitation and not only are getting paid decently, but actually own the fruits of their labor. I knew then, as I know now, that I would've just as readily dreamed of escaping from the pit of low-wage suffering into the actualized utopia of the Soviet land. I've had no doubt that if I had found myself in Uncle Julius's self-cobbled shoes I would've been just as quick to sign on for the grand project of social justice people used to call Communism.

And sign on Uncle Julius did. He joined the newly founded Yugoslav Communist Youth in 1924, and became a full Party member in 1926. After he got out of the army, the Party decided to send him to the USSR for education. His papers were not in order, he had only fifty dollars, but he was eager to plunge into the better future. He lingered in Poland for a while, waiting for his papers to be sorted out, but then got too anxious and decided to cross illegally into the USSR. As the Polish border patrol shot at him, he ran across a frozen river; the ice cracked, but the river was shallow; the tails of his coat were riddled with bullet holes.

Before he could practice the utopian freedom of the USSR, he was first detained for a few months. The GPU (the state security, soon to bloom into full notoriety as Stalin's NKVD) interrogated him, and he managed to convince them he was not a spy but a fellow Yugoslav Communist. Once out of detention, he was dispatched to Voronezh to work in a tanning factory. He attended night school; met a woman, Antonina; married her; and they had a son, Volodya. The GPU was still watching him closely, but his new life was panning out nicely: once his Yugoslav Communist papers checked out, he joined the Soviet Party. One summer, as a Communist of Ukrainian background, he was deployed to take part in the collectivization process in Ukraine. He saw the kulaks arrested and beaten; he saw piles of collected wheat rotting in village squares as the villagers were starving; he saw carts of corpses trundling by to be emptied into mass graves. As a loyal soldier of the revolution, he had believed that the purges of the kulaks were necessary for the advancement of socialism, part of the revolutionary process. But to me he confessed that he, like many a Communist at the time, had been willingly blind.

He enrolled in a Moscow university to study forestry; Antonina, Volodya and Valya, his brand-new daughter, soon joined him. He mingled in the epicenter of the revolutionary state; he had a cordial relationship with Nikita Khrushchev; he met Nadezhda Alliluyeva, Stalin's wife, who would disappear from public life in 1932; he spent time with Tito and other Yugoslav Communists who were there at the time, and after whom many a factory or street in the future socialist Yugoslavia would be named.

Soon he realized something was off; the times were, to put it mildly, perilous. In the thirties, Stalin was at the height of his power and paranoia; arbitrary purges were an ongoing operation. People got arrested and vanished for exhibiting symptoms of bourgeois weakness, for wearing a tie or carrying an umbrella. To Uncle Julius the stories of disappearances were malicious rumors, or, at worst, honestly mistaken arrests. He was convinced he had nothing to fear, as he did nothing wrong; he worked hard and was a committed Communist, believing that all the sacrifices, personal and collective, would be justified by the arrival of the glorious future.

But there, in Uncle Julius's miscarried future, was I, listening as he talked to me and my cassette tape recorder in his voice of a sage teacher, in his Russian-accented Serbo-Croatian. Now and then he seemed impatient with my questions. It's possible I was projecting, but in his narration I smelled a whiff of contempt for the likes of me, for those who, devoid of idealism and willingness to suffer and/ or inflict suffering for a better, just world, were symptomatic of the future having gone wrong. Maybe he felt I didn't care. The Berlin Wall had gone down the year before; Eastern Europe was waking up from a nightmare, while the relatively liberal Yugoslavia was looking up at a future of free-market democracy, whatever that meant. Perhaps he could sense that I thought the project he'd dedicated his life to failed terribly; that it'd never been viable, if for no other reason than the magnitude of criminality involved; that the demise had been long in coming and then, when it happened, practically overnight, I was perfectly cool with it. Or he could sense that I interviewed him not to spread the truth about Stalinist crimes, but to get some good writing material: I was more interested in his story than in his history. I cared and empathized, sure, but strictly theoretically: the great suffering was an indication of a great crime; the great crime should be opposed on principle; and people have suffered terribly. But he also provided access to fertile narrative soil, and I fancied myself a writer, eager to plunge into new-era narration.

In 1937, Uncle Julius, working and living in Kalinin (Tver today), was arrested. He endured what in American free-market democracy passes as "enhanced interrogation"—sleep and food deprivation, painfully uncomfortable poses, beatings, threats of execution—but back in the days of candid Stalinism was unabashed, honest torture. He repeatedly refused to sign the interrogation record that would've amounted to a false confession. He would not incriminate anyone, insisting he himself was innocent. One of his interrogators explained to him that if he was guiltless he wouldn't have been arrested—the Soviet state never made the mistake of arresting innocent people.

Uncle Julius shared his crammed cell with informers, provocateurs, fools and those who were certain they'd be shot. There were Russians, Romanians, Poles and those who never said a word. He became close with a Jew named Lieberman, who was also adamant in refusing to sign the record or implicate anyone. Lieberman made chess figures of bread, and Uncle Julius and he played to pass the time. At night, they'd hear desperate screams from other cells of people on their way to execution.

Uncle Julius was charged with espionage, organizing a spy ring, and connection with the foreign bourgeoisie, all under the infamous Article 58 of the Soviet Penal Code. His Yugoslav and Comintern connections played an important role in the narrative established by the prosecutors. He was sentenced to ten years of hard labor. He refused to sign the paper acknowledging the verdict. Before his departure, he managed to see Antonina. He implored her to save herself and the children by signing a statement renouncing his counterrevolutionary activities, but she just kept weeping. On the same long-traveling transport heading north toward the gulag Arctic, he and Lieberman comforted and helped each other.

I asked him if he'd ever found out who it was that informed on him and implicated him in the international conspiracy. He had, but would not say his name on record. So I turned off the recorder, and he told me the name of a Yugoslav Communist, which I recognized as one that had graced the schools, streets and factories of my childhood. He'd been his comrade, Uncle Julius said, tears streaming down his cheeks. I sat in silence, waiting for him to resume. Before he did, he insisted again that no one was to know. I couldn't have told him that even if I wanted to divulge to the public that one of the great Yugoslav Communists had in fact been a snitch and/or a weak, terrified prisoner, it no longer mattered. Many schools and streets had already acquired different names, and the renamed factories were well on their way to free-market collapse. Twenty-five year later the great Yugoslav Communists are all forgotten, their heroism and moral feebleness fully merged in historical and human oblivion. As for me, I forgot within weeks the name he told me.

In 1938, Uncle Julius commenced his tour of the Arkhangelsk Gulag: Nyandoma, Sukhaya Bay, Ostrovnoy, Anufriyevka, Yertsov, Alekseyevka, etc. Those names meant nothing to me; they were just arbitrary markers for the locations whose sole purpose was continuous production of death and degradation. The multitude of names was fitting for that Babylon of torment, where Russians, Ukrainians, Belarusians, the Kyrgyz, Ossetians, Georgians, Tatars, Uzbeks, the Chinese, Koreans, Romanians, Yugoslavs, Jews, Hungarians, Bulgarians, and Austrians, and those who never said a word, were imprisoned and dropped off like multilingual flies.

The prisoners' allotment of food depended on their meeting the work quota, which presumably helped the camp achieve the plan imposed by Stalin's government. Those who didn't meet the quota ate less, becoming less likely to earn more food, thus destined to perish in the spiral of exhaustion and starvation. The labor camps were chaotic, many of them controlled by criminals with the tacit approval of the authorities and the NKVD, which had its own quota of arrests to fulfill. The guards killed people at will, or threw them into isolators—wooden cages hanging ten feet aboveground, where the prisoner could not even stand up and would often freeze in the cold.

Uncle Julius particularly remembered the children in the gulag. Once a transport of two hundred high-school-age boys and girls, sentenced for truancy, arrived. Weak and starving, they couldn't possibly meet their quota; they lingered in rags by the fires, waiting for a chance to snatch a piece of bread, some of them mutilating themselves to get to the camp hospital. Girls were passed around among the criminals, who treated them as property. Uncle Julius remembered Valya, a teenage girl, whose beauty was particularly appreciated by those with power. She was feisty, assaulted other prisoners, gambled with the criminals. They shared her with the guards, one of whom dared to presume she could belong to him alone. To teach him a lesson, the criminals set her up to lose in a card game, where the bet was the young guard's head. Valya lost, walked up, ax in hand, to the guard warming by the fire, and split his head like a watermelon.

There was also a fourteen-year-old boy, Vanya, so intransigent he could not be tamed. He resisted the guards, fought with the NKVD goons and would often end up in the isolator. As they dragged him away, he would shout under a rain of blows: "Thank you, Stalin, for my happy childhood!" Soon, he disappeared from the camp and the word was that he, like many other disorderly ones, was sent to the infamously harsh islands off Kamchatka.

Even in the gulag, one was perpetually suspect: at the height of the war, Uncle Julius was charged once again under Article 58, this time for being part of a conspiracy of Ukrainians, who, according to the NKVD, devised a plan to have the Germans parachute weapons and tanks into the Arkhangelsk area so the Red Army could be attacked from the rear. He was resentenced and sent to a harsher camp, where one of his tasks was filling mass graves with dead bodies. The job sometimes demanded stomping on top of the dead to meet the quota of cadavers per hole. Once, he went to pick up a corpse from the isolator. As he put it on the cart, the corpse moaned: "Let me die! Let me die!" It turned out it was Vanya, who managed to recover enough to tell Uncle Julius how he had tried to escape from the island with two other inmates. They killed a guard, then wandered through the frozen wasteland until two of them conspired to kill the third one and eat him. Soon, Vanya killed the other man, and ate him too. "Did you let him die?" I asked Uncle Julius. I don't remember his answer, but I am sure he was crying again.

Back in 1990, I was a devout smoker. As Uncle Julius spoke about life and death in the gulag, sometimes barely aware of my presence, I kept craving a cigarette, longing for a break in his discourse to step out and light up. My attention sometimes flagged to the point of drowsiness as he outlined the infernal geography of the Arkhangelsk Gulag, or expounded on forest-cutting methodologies. I was going to have it all on tape anyway, and I could listen and edit at my convenience. But when he told me the story of Vanya, I was all ears—perhaps because I'd been an intransigent teenager myself not so long before. Or because the story best contained the distilled evil of Stalinism or any totalitarian system: the reproduction of absolute power by arbitrarily purging the weak ones while converting the strong ones into monsters.

Never agreeing to accept the charges inflicted upon him, Uncle Julius kept writing official complaints, insisting on his innocence, and sending them to Moscow. He didn't know what had happened to his wife and kids. After World War II ended, there was a limited amnesty, mainly for criminals, but the camps refilled with new prisoners, many of them Red Army soldiers who suffered the indignity of having been POWs. Uncle Julius's forestry expertise and camp experience made him needed and allowed for a more bearable life. One day, upon returning from work, he saw two teenagers, emaciated and in rags, loitering at the camp gate. It took him a while to realize they were his children, Volodya and Valya. He hadn't seen them since his arrest.

Volodya told him that Antonina had been fired from her job and expelled from the Party soon after her husband's arrest. She'd signed a statement renouncing him, but they'd still been thrown out of their apartment and forced to relocate to a smaller one. A complete stranger had then moved in with them. They'd suffered from hunger, and were beaten by the stranger all the time. Antonina had another child, the war started and the man left, and they became even more impoverished. At the age of eleven Volodya had to go to work, while Valya begged in the streets. Then Kalinin had to be evacuated before the advancing Germans. Antonina and her children tagged along with a Red Army unit, which took care of them through the end of the war. Upon return to Kalinin, they found their place in ruins and lived in the train station, panhandling to survive. Volodya eventually found a job, but they were desperate. Then they heard their father was in the Arkhangelsk region and went to ask for help.

Uncle Julius found a way to get more food, replaced their rags, even borrowed scarce money for his destitute children. They accepted it all, but still remained far too hardened to indulge their father with a warmth that could sustain him upon their departure. Valya was particularly withdrawn and quiet; only as they were parting did she throw herself into his arms, weeping, convinced that she would never see him again. (And she never would: a few years later, she married a man who demanded she cut off all contact with her politically contaminated father.)

Uncle Julius never lost his belief in Communism. He remained convinced that Stalin's terror was but an aberration, a criminal betrayal of the revolution's original, Leninist principles. Even in the worst of circumstances, he hadn't abandoned his devotion to his ideals. As he outlined with pride the ways in which he, a forestry engineer, improved tree-cutting processes in the gulag, exceeded the plan, and thus helped the advance of Soviet socialism, I recalled reading about a Christian saint who had been grilled alive by the Romans. When they asked him if he was ready to renounce his faith, he said: "This side is done. Flip me over!"

One day, Uncle Julius showed me the letter he'd written to Gorbachev personally, on the occasion of the 1986 USSR Communist Party Congress, which would announce perestroika as the official policy. In the letter, he begged Gorbachev not to abandon the path of Leninist socialism, for if he did, all of the suffering and sacrifices would've been in vain. Listening to Uncle Julius, I realized that even if I felt nothing but disdain for grand social projects built on human bones, I still admired him, his unflagging devotion and his willingness to endure for a noble idea. And I realized that if he, the last true Communist in a dying Yugoslavia, were in power, I'd be imprisoned, what with my blatantly bourgeois sensibilities (love of rock 'n' roll, ironic capacity, disrespect for authority and rule of law, etc.) And it was clear to me that I would not have lasted in a labor camp for a fucking day, not only because I was a happily pampered city boy who'd never known what it was like to be hungry, but also because there was no idea I could believe in strongly enough to sustain me in extremely difficult circumstances, nothing worth enduring for, except, maybe, love.

Sometime in 1945, in one of the camps, Uncle Julius met Olga. She was young, struggling to stay out of the criminals' paws, and Uncle Julius tried to help her by assigning survivable work to her. There was no dating in the gulag, but when he was transferred to another camp, he couldn't stop thinking about her. He wrote to her and proposed a marriage. By way of a released friend, she sent a message accepting. Uncle Julius was still a prisoner, not sure he'd ever be able to escape the NKVD grip. He pulled what frayed strings he had to have her transferred to his camp. But before they could enter the gulag version of marital bliss, he was once again accused of being a foreign agent. In 1948, Tito and the Yugoslav Communist Party changed their theretofore obedient tack and decided to slip out of Stalin's grip. All relations between the countries were broken off; Soviet tanks loomed on the Yugoslav border, rearing for invasion. Uncle Julius, a Yugoslav Communist who had written letters to Tito from the camp, was suspect again. He underwent interrogations and feared another Article 58 charge and sentence. Instead, and somewhat miraculously, he was released and deported to Krasnoyarsk, in the heart of Siberia. He thought he would never see Olga again. But in November 1949 she showed up in Krasnoyarsk, and they took up their cohabitation. Life became easier but nowhere near easy. As a forestry engineer, Uncle Julius worked on taiga exploitation, and they hopped all over the region, dealing with corruption and petty conspiracies to expose him as a serial anti-Soviet plotter. Soon Nadezhda was born; they acquired some property: a little house, a cow, a pig. And then the rumors reached them that Stalin had died. For a while, no one dared believe or even talk about what it meant.

The story goes that in 1955, after Stalin's death, Khrushchev came to Yugoslavia to apologize to Tito and repair the relations broken in 1948. At the meeting, Tito gave Khrushchev a list of about a hundred Yugoslav Communists who'd disappeared into the gulag. He wanted to know what happened to them. Krushchev promised to look into it and soon informed Tito that only thirteen of those hundred could be tracked down. One of them was Uncle Julius.

In 1956, he and the five-year-old Nadezhda disembarked from the train in Belgrade. Being Russian, Olga was not allowed to come with them. As soon as his foot touched his native soil, Uncle Julius was arrested by Yugoslav security. Nadezhda was left to wander around the train station, not knowing the language or anyone there, until some strangers took her home. A week or so later, Uncle Julius was released and reunited with his daughter. Soon the Soviets let Olga go too, quite possibly after Tito's intervention.

A few years after his return from the USSR, Uncle Julius saw my grandmother again. Nearly fifty years later, she'd had ten children and had lived through World War II, typically terrible in Bosnia. They both recalled their oath under the pear tree. Uncle Julius also criticized Mikhalyina's religious faith and the related lack of enthusiasm for salvation by way of socialism.

After a week with Uncle Julius, I had about fifteen hours of conversation recorded on cassette tapes, plus a notebook of cursory notes. I'd planned to transcribe the interview for publication, but I only wrote a short magazine piece. Laziness interfered: the prospect of transcribing fifteen hours of the twentieth century's prime horrors was too daunting. Thus the long story was ever forthcoming—one day I'd do it, or maybe the day before, as my father liked to joke. And then I, like everyone else, ran out of days. The war started in Croatia in 1991, and in Bosnia in 1992, and then I was in Chicago, exhausted by low-wage work. The first time I returned to Sarajevo after the war, in 1997, the tapes and the notes were nowhere to be found, much like the rest of my previous life.

But I always retained what Uncle Julius told me. I used some of those memories for "Islands," the second story I ever wrote in English, which became part of *The Question of Bruno*, my first book, and which, my sister told me, Nadezhda found objectionable for its misrepresentation of Uncle Julius. In random conversations, I'd serve up tidbits of his life to make a point about trauma and suffering—recalling, for instance, how, decades after his imprisonment he still ate as though someone might rip the food out of his hands. Only rarely—say, after a few exceptionally strong drinks—I'd inflict the full range of Uncle Julius's gulag experience upon some innocent American who may have asked me if I was Russian. "No, I am not, but my father had an uncle . . . ," I'd begin, and soon they'd be sorry for misjudging the situation as conducive to the casual appreciation of *other cultures*.

In 2003, I traveled to Eastern Europe to do research for my novel *The Lazarus Project*. The novel was about a young Jewish man who had survived the Kishinev pogrom of 1905, orchestrated by Russian nationalists, only to be shot in 1908 by the chief of the Chicago police, for no discernible reason. I roamed around western Ukraine—Galicia and Bukovina, my ancestral lands—and bowed my head at the Jewish cemetery in Chisinau (formerly Kishinev). After the trip, I went with my then wife for a vacation to Mljet, where I hadn't been since my family's visit to Uncle Julius. I'd lost touch with him in the war years, and then I heard that he'd died, but didn't know when or how.

In Mljet, we rented a very small house right on one of the saltwater "lakes"—the sea came inland through a narrow strait—so devoid of waves that they resembled pools of green olive oil. The area was a national park, and therefore quaintly underdeveloped, so that silence and cicadas reigned all day, while at night the only light often came from the moon and the stars. I'd wake up early to read *Moby Dick* and gaze at the stillness of the water instead. One morning, I saw a gray-haired woman swimming. She parted the water as though pushing through a wheat field, while a German shepherd ardently paddled in her wake. When they were done, she helped the dog out of the water, and then wrapped a towel under its hind legs to lift them. The dog hopped uphill on its front legs as the woman carried its behind. They went up the stairs, out of my sight.

Later I stopped by the only tavern in that part of the island. Talking to the owner, I mentioned that I'd once come here and stayed with Uncle Julius and his wife. "Well, Olga's here," the tavern owner said. "She swims every morning with her dog." Eagerly, I went to look for her, finding the little house with some difficulty. When I walked in the gate, the German shepherd moved toward me dragging its hind end on the dirt in a mockery of running. The dog's name was Dasha.

For the next few days, I'd watch Olga swim with Dasha in the morning; in the afternoon, I'd go talk to her. This was the first time she'd visited Mljet since before the war, and she wouldn't have done it if Nadezhda hadn't pretty much forced her. She told me Uncle Julius had died in 2000, at the age of ninety-six. When I asked what he died from, she just shrugged. There didn't seem to be a particular illness; his body was so old and tired it simply stopped working—his life just ended by itself.

One afternoon, she abruptly asked: "So, what are you doing in America to spread the truth about the Stalinist crimes?" I was startled by the question. The honest answer, of course, was: "Absolutely nothing." But, in desperate confusion, I mentioned that I'd often taught the works of Danilo Kiš, who had exposed the malignant depths of Stalinism in *A Tomb for Boris Davidovich*, and that, moreover, I'd written a preface for one of his books. She glared at me, not quite appreciative of my efforts.

"You do know he was a Jew," she said.

"His father was Jewish and perished in Auschwitz," I said. "So?"

"Well, it was the Jews," she said, and I still couldn't comprehend what she was saying.

It was the Jews that controlled the camps and manipulated Stalin, she told me. *It was the Jews* who were the main source of all that suffering.

I managed to offer that I didn't think that was actually the case, but it was not up for discussion—my gulag experience, or the total absence thereof, disqualified me entirely. Never did "the Jews" as a sinister force come up in my conversations with Uncle Julius, even if he had some strange historical ideas. (He insisted that Serbs and Croats were actually Ukrainians.) In his memoir, he speaks warmly of Lieberman, as someone who managed to retain his decency and dignity in hellish conditions.

But it wasn't so much the anti-Semitism that took me aback. My heart sank at the fact that nothing seemed to have been learned from the horrific experience; the agony did not lead to wisdom, nor knowledge, nor grasp of history. That lovely summer afternoon in Edenic Mljet it appeared clear to me that we lived and died in anonymous struggle, until whatever edifice that might have borne our name was reduced to nothing and we were fully forgotten.

Which is why I'd wanted to write Uncle Julius's story for years but never could imagine doing it without including Olga's terrible punch line, which entombed in oblivion Uncle Julius's personal history.

Then, last year, I finally wrote the piece, partly prompted by a news story about Putin's appreciation of Stalin's alleged managerial capabilities, partly because I needed money. But I did not want to finish it before I talked to Olga and asked her if she still stuck by her claim. Because Olga, now in her early nineties, still lived in Croatia, I accepted an invitation to give a reading in Zagreb. I wanted her to have the final word. Perhaps her absurd proposition was due to some temporary blackout, to a kind of moral stress resulting from the most recent wars. I hoped she'd recant her claim and Uncle Julius would rise from oblivion, his life restored to its full value.

As soon as I was in Zagreb, I called, and Nadezhda picked up. I greeted her and told her I'd love to see Olga that weekend.

"We will not be here," she said.

"Are you going to Mljet?" I asked.

"No," she said.

And even though I offered a feeble, cowardly suggestion that we could, perhaps, meet next time I'm in Zagreb, I knew well enough I'd never speak again to that side of my family. The last word in my narrative of Uncle Julius's life would be that *No*, the final slamming of the tomb's door.

Tunnel

MO YAN

TRANSLATED FROM THE CHINESE BY HOWARD GOLDBLATT

A note: The wife in this story is not named. She is merely called Laopo (wife) by the narrator and by the husband. The 1965 film Tunnel War was a must-see throughout the country on the eve of the Cultural Revolution, when anti-Japanese sentiments were fostered by the authorities, and was still being shown more than a decade later, when the now abandoned one-child policy was carried out often with inhumane diligence.

A predawn chorus of dog barks alerted Fang Shan, who jumped down off the *kang* and cautiously opened the door, then stood quietly in the yard, listening intently to what was happening out on the street. Hearing the shouts of men and the wails of women off to the west, he rushed back inside and roused his pregnant wife out of a deep sleep.

"Are they coming?" Laopo asked.

"Pretty sure they are," he said anxiously. "We can't take any chances. We'll have to hide."

"It's coming any day now, I can tell," she said, "so what can they do?"

"Don't be a fool. It'll be much worse this time. It's not a human being as long as it's still in there. They'll induce labor at 7:59 for an 8:00 birth."

"So let them."

"What are you saying? That baby would be dead in three days."

Laopo picked up the prepared bundle and dragged herself off the *kang*, grumbling as she headed to the door, "I really don't want to go down in that rat hole of yours."

"My dear Laopo, wait till you see how nice it is down there," Fang Shan said.

A seven- or eight-year-old girl rolled over and sat up on the *kang*. "Where are you going?" she asked, sleepy-eyed.

"Hush, Pandi," Fang Shan whispered. "Stay home and watch your sisters. I'm taking your mother to a hiding place. We'll be back when it's safe."

She nodded knowingly. She was a spindly girl with a nest of unruly hair.

"There's dry food on the stove and water in the vat if you're hungry or need a drink. If anybody asks where your mother and I are, tell them we went to your grandparents' house."

The girl nodded.

Fang Shan took a worried look back at the *kang*, where two more little girls were fast asleep. The dogs were barking louder now, intensifying his sense of anxiety and his fervor. After dragging his wife outside and up to the wall, he bent down and removed a battered, overturned pot lid to reveal a hole in the ground that showed traces of frequent activity.

"Down you go," he said.

Laopo: "In my condition? I'll suffocate down there."

Fang Shan: "Don't worry about that. I'll make sure you and my son are safe."

Taking Laopo's arm, Fang Shan helped her down into the hole and followed her in. From the top step, he replaced the lid.

When she reached the bottom, she filled her lungs with tunnel air. Fang Shan heard her moan. "What's wrong?" he asked.

"I hurt myself on my way down."

"You're about to have a baby," he said dismissively, "so shrug it off."

He took a pocket flashlight out of the bundle and lit the way ahead with a narrow beam of light.

"That's really far!" his startled wife blurted out.

"What do you think I've been doing down here for six months?" he said proudly. "I tell you, this thing goes all the way down to the riverbank. Come on, let's get going."

Lighting the way through the twists and turns of the tunnel with his flashlight, he crawled ahead, pressing her to keep up. "Do you think it's easy carrying all this weight?" Laopo wheezed.

Fang Shan laughed. He was in a buoyant mood. "OK, slow down." Once they were thirty meters in, the tunnel spread out and upward. Slowly they straightened up until they could both stand upright. He took down a box of matches and lit a lantern in a wall niche, creating a burst of warmth and light all around, including a bed of golden straw in one corner, warm and inviting, a full earthen jug of water, and a basket of dry provisions. It was a cozy nest.

"Do you plan to live down here?" she asked.

Fang Shan rolled a cigarette and lit it from the lantern. He took a deep drag as a sly smile creased his face, which resembled a dried walnut. A stumpy, short-limbed man, he had hands like the searching paws of a blind rat. His wife treasured his tiny eyes and the thin, nearly transparent ears that poked out from a tangle of hair. "No wonder people call you a rat!" she said with a little laugh.

Fang Shan: "That's the name my dad was stuck with, and it was passed down to me after he died."

"If a man's a rat, won't his son be one too?" Laopo teased. "I'm afraid this thing I'm carrying is another rat."

Fang Shan: "A rat or a cat, I don't care, as long as it's a male."

Laopo: "No promises. We'll know when it's out."

Fang Shan: "I'll strangle you if it's another female."

Laopo: "You horrid man! Who wants a female anyway? If the first one had been a boy, I wouldn't have suffered through all these pregnancies, afraid of my shadow, always hiding, a life more like a ghost than a human being. If this one's a girl, I'm going to tie off my tubes. Enough is enough!"

Fang Shan: "Don't even think about it! Do you want to end my family line?"

Laopo: "Why not? It's not a line to gloat about."

Fang Shan: "Says who? Eight generations of tenant farmers. We're red to our core."

Laopo: "Stop talking about the past. These days being rich is a glorious thing. Being poor is out."

Fang Shan: "I miss old Chairman Mao." He heaved an emotional sigh.

Fang Shan shone his flashlight on a Mao poster hanging on the wall.

Laopo: "I didn't see that."

Fang Shan: "It's to ward off evil and keep us safe."

Laopo: "Are we really going to live down here?"

Fang Shan: "With this place we have nothing to fear. If you have another girl, we'll just try again."

Laopo: "Isn't all this just like the movie *Tunnel War*?"

Fang Shan: "That's what gave me the idea."

Laopo: "But if they find the entrance they could fill the tunnel with water, and we'd drown like rats."

Fang Shan: "They won't waste the water. It comes out of wells and flows into rivers."

Laopo: "What if they use poison gas?"

Fang Shan: "Can't happen. They're not like the Japs, and, besides, where would they get poison gas in the first place?"

Laopo: "Who knows, but if you can dig a tunnel, they can lay their hands on poison gas. After more than eight hundred showings, everybody's seen *Tunnel War*."

Fang Shan: "Sure, everybody's seen it, but no one else has thought of digging a tunnel, have they? It's a case of, 'If you pay attention you're in the know; if you don't you just watch the show.'"

"Rats are born knowing how to dig a hole," Laopo remarked.

Fang Shan: "I'm a male rat, and you're a female rat."

That got a laugh out of them, but they clammed up as a ray of light entered the tunnel. They could hear the croaking of frogs on the riverbank.

"Is the river right outside?" Laopo asked.

Fang Shan: "No, it's beyond some bushes and willow trees."

Laopo: "The sun's up."

Fang Shan: "Now that it's light out, I'll go up and look around. Wait here and keep still."

He got down on all fours and crawled to the opening in a grove of willow trees halfway up the embankment. The river flowed below. Looking through a green latticework of willow branches, he saw the bright orange sun clinging to the water, its shadow stretched out across the surface. Willow branches bowed low to merge with exposed brown roots. He noted that dirt packed around the opening had formed a shoal fronting the clear water. He took pride in knowing that in six short months of nightly hard work, he had secretly carried out a huge undertaking, especially for such a little man. There were no sounds of human presence on the embankment, but the village on the other side of the river was alive with activity. By parting willow branches and making an opening in the bushes he was able to crawl out of the opening and climb up the embankment by holding on to a willow branch; he hid himself in a thicket of indigo bushes to watch the goings-on in the village.

What he saw was a throng of people and a red caterpillar tractor rumbling in high gear down the street, sunlight glinting off the wheels spinning beneath tracks that dug deeply into the thick layer of roadway dust. Streaks of light from the headlights were stronger than the sun's rays. People trotting behind it were led by a man barely five feet tall in a green uniform with brass buttons and a wide-brimmed hat. He carried a red battery-powered bullhorn. The others were trotting; he had to run to keep up on stumpy legs, pounding the ground rapidly like drumsticks. Fang Shan knew who the little man was: the infamous Chairman Guo of the village family planning office. They called him Master Death. When women of childbearing age caught sight of Master Death they hated their parents for only giving them two legs. Fang Shan silently congratulated himself. The young men in Chairman Guo's wake, all in khaki uniforms, moved at a crouch, like infantrymen following a tank.

The tractor stopped in front of a new house with a tiled roof belonging to Yuan Datou, a notorious offender against the one-child policy. Yuan was a butcher who made a good living selling pork. Heavy fines for having more children than were allowed barely made a dent in the family's wealth.

Chairman Guo had the men fasten one end of a steel cable to Yuan's house and the other to the tractor's rear bumper. He switched on his bullhorn.

"Listen up, villagers," he announced, "especially you serial offenders against the one-child policy. New instructions have come down from our superiors: 'Better a ruined home than a lost nation' is one. 'No cut ropes for those who hang themselves and no antidotes for those who take poison' is another. As chairman I am going to teach you all a lesson. Yuan Datou, send out your wife to have her pregnancy terminated."

No sound emerged from Yuan's house.

"You have five minutes," Chairman Guo trumpeted. "If you don't come out and your house comes down around you and your family, you're to blame, not Chairman Guo and certainly not the country."

Still no sound from Yuan's house.

Chairman Guo gave the signal. "Go!" he shouted.

A shrill noise preceded bursts of white smoke from the tractor's vertical exhaust pipe. The driver's dark glasses and a black bandanna covering his mouth obscured Fang Shan's view of him.

The tractor moved slowly, drawing the cable taut. At first Yuan's house seemed immobile, but as the driver revved the engine higher and higher, the building began to shake, and heartrending howls emerged from inside. The door flew open, and the family—a pregnant woman; three little girls, neatly stepped in order of age; and an old woman with a cane—came out, led by Yuan Datou, butcher knife in hand.

"I'm coming for you, Master Death!" Yuan Datou roared.

Chairman Guo: "Come on, then, come on. Kill me and you'll pay with your life." He stood his ground.

Yuan Datou: "I don't give a damn!" Yuan swung his glinting knife at Guo, who crouched down and lost his hat.

"Grab him!" Guo shouted, protecting his head with his hands. "Grab him!"

A dozen young men rushed up, knocked Yuan to the ground, and hog-tied him. "Now grab his wife and take her to the clinic," Chairman Guo ordered, having regained his composure. "Get that damned tractor moving and show those sons-of-bitches who they're dealing with!"

The tractor roared to life and moved ahead at full power. Yuan's house came down, as if in slow motion, sending a cloud of dust into the sky.

"All you people who removed your IUDs," he announced, "and all you illegally pregnant women come out right now." He waved a sheet of paper. "Don't try to put something over on me. I've got a list of names right here!"

A clutch of grimy, ragged women formed around Chairman Guo. He began calling out names.

"Yang Dacheng's wife."

A weeping woman raised her hand.

"Li Jingang's wife."

A pasty-faced woman stepped up.

"Fang Shan's wife."

No one came forward.

"Fang Shan's wife . . ."

Chairman Guo: "The monk can run away, but not the temple."

Fang Shan slid down the embankment and scurried into the hole.

"They're out for blood today," he said to his wife.

Laopo: "What was that noise a moment ago?"

Fang Shan: "A tractor pulled down Yuan Datou's house."

Laopo: "What about our house?"

Fang Shan: "I'm afraid we're going to lose it."

Laopo: "Where will we live?"

Fang Shan: "It's three run-down rooms. They can have it."

Laopo: "A worthless house is still a house."

Fang Shan: "This tunnel is warm in the winter and cool in the summer."

She sighed. "We'd really be rats then."

Fang Shan: "Stop complaining. I'll go up and bring the children down."

Laopo: "I . . . I'm worried the baby's coming . . ."

Fang Shan finally noticed that his wife's face was wet with sweat and that she was already bleeding. "Good, that's great!" he said excitedly. "Be a good wife and give me a son. That will hit them where it hurts."

"I don't feel right," she said. "I never bled this much when I had the girls."

Fang Shan: "Then it must be a boy."

Laopo: "Don't go up yet. You have to help me."

Babies come when it's time; melons drop to the ground when they're ripe. What "help" could he manage? Fang Shan turned down her request, but helped her over to the straw bed and took off her pants once she was lying down. He gazed at the taut mound of her belly, on which the word "son" had been drawn. He could not help laughing.

She was panting from the strain. "Damn you!" she cursed. "I'm like this and you're in a laughing mood . . ."

Fang Shan pointed to the word on her belly. "What do you expect me to do when I see my 'son'?"

She struggled to sit up, grabbed his hand, and sank her teeth into it.

Fang Shan yelped in pain. "Ouch, you bit me!" He rubbed the bloody wound.

Laopo: "I'm usually the one who bleeds. Now it's your turn."

Fang Shan: "Be a good wife and have your baby while I go up and rescue the girls. I can't let those guys bring the house down around our daughters."

Laopo (pleading): "Won't you be a good husband and stay with me? Something doesn't feel right. You probably poked a hole in my womb when you removed the IUD."

Fang Shan: "Don't be silly." He ignored her plea. "I knew what I was doing." He began crawling toward the opening in their yard.

The pungent smell of earth was intoxicating. It was that earthy smell that had driven him to get up night after night to dig like a madman. At first, of course, he was digging for his wife, but before long he was doing it solely for himself. During that time he daily

127

dragged his weary body back from the field, looking like a dead fish and feeling that if he lay down he might never get up. But his spirits rose as soon as he was under the ground and strength returned to his body. His digging tools were a pair of short-handled hoes, which he dug into the fresh yellow dirt that he let fall on his head, into his mouth, and all over his naked body. His eyes shone in the darkness, through which he had no trouble seeing the dirt fall and the scars his hoes cut into the soil. The lantern was solely for his wife's benefit, and he would not have wasted money on a flashlight except to make it easier for her to be down there. The unspoiled roots he encountered were like delicacies. Finding them was part of what kept him digging. He crawled nimbly, experiencing a sensation like flowing water.

As he stood in the opening, peering through a hole in the upturned lid, he was treated to the sight of a rosy sunrise.

All the time he was underground, his senses were especially keen, and the thought occurred to him that he really might be a reincarnated rat.

He heard Chairman Guo interrogating his daughters in the house.

The girls answered the chairman's questions just the way he had told them to.

He heard Chairman Guo tell his men to carry the girls outside.

He heard the girls bite their captors' hands.

He smiled proudly.

He heard Chairman Guo curse: "They really are a family of rats! You in the tractor, take the house down. I won't stop till this rat's nest has been cleared out."

He heard his daughters weep as they were dragged outside. He heard the tractor come to life. He heard the steel cable being attached. He heard Chairman Guo give the order. He heard a rumble.

A collapsed wall crushed the upturned lid and sent down a cascade of dirt. He scurried back into the tunnel.

He felt free and relaxed.

When Fang Shan entered the roomy part of the tunnel he saw a squirming mound of flesh between his wife's legs. He rushed up and spotted a peanut-sized growth between the meaty object's legs.

"Son! A son!" he shouted. His gums itched; he bit off a clod of hard dirt. To him, it was like butter, not gritty.

Taking a pair of scissors from his wife's bundle, he cut the umbilical cord. "What a wonderful wife," he said as he patted her cheeks. She looked up at him through the grayness of her eyes. Using toilet paper, he cleaned the baby's face, which was just like his: tiny mouth and big ears. He wrapped him in the bundle cover and picked him up.

"Laopo," he exclaimed, "we won!"

MARLON JAMES was born in Jamaica in 1970 and is the author of three novels. His most recent, *A Brief History of Seven Killings*, was the winner of the 2015 Man Booker Prize, the American Book Award, the Anisfield-Wolf Book Prize for Fiction, the Green Carnation Prize, and the Minnesota Book Award. His first novel, *John Crow's Devil*, was published in 2005 and his second, *The Book of Night Women*, was published in 2008. His short fiction and nonfiction have appeared in *Esquire*, *New York Times Magazine*, *Granta*, and *Harper's*. He lives in Minnesota and teaches at Macalester College.

One Day I Will Write About My Mother

MARLON JAMES

My father's doctors discovered too late in 2011 that they had missed his colon cancer spreading, despite operations and chemo. By the time they shifted blame for metastasis slipping right past them, he was dead. But it wasn't the cancer that killed him. A blood clot, launched from his left leg or right, took easy passage through his veins, struck the lung, and shut his heart down before my mother could park her car to see him for the second time that weekend. I heard of his death from my sister, a quick phone call where the only way she could keep herself together was to resort to doctor jargon, *Daddy didn't make it.* The language threw me off despite her repeating it twice and it wasn't until I heard my mother scream, off in his room, that I knew.

The thing is, this is not a story about my father. I always write about him, but never about my mother. Even before my friends and I found ourselves in the burying years, my father took up a curious space in my life; there but not always present when I was growing up. Present, but not always there when he got sick. Always ready to talk Shakespeare, Coleridge, or Kahlil Gibran, but only once asking if I had a girlfriend. Between us was always distance and static—the only kid who could talk to him about poetry was the kid he could never figure out. All of which makes for two paragraphs of prose where the act of trying to map a man becomes the point of the prose itself. It is as if that man-sized void that fathers leave is perfect for waxing poetic, but for the ever-present mother, I've got nothing.

She was the one always there, and yet the one harder to write about. It's easy to spin a clever fiction about my father. Not so easy to string words about my mom, the person who applied bandages and bought schoolbooks, but also the adult often around during long stretches of holiday boredom. Even on a purely linguistic level, 'the man who wasn't there' sounds sexier than 'the woman who was always present.' That might be because writers and readers place longing at a high value.

But there goes my daddy again, hijacking a story about my mother.

Things I remember. The first time I saw my mother cry was in 1978, when news came from England that my sister-in-law had died. I was eight years old and adults didn't cry. Adults were never weak. Adults knew the answer to everything. Adults whipped the living shit out of me while simultaneously convincing me that this was hurting them far more than it was hurting me. Or this: if big people did cry, it was because of being in physical pain. But this was different. She was crying over something that I couldn't see, hear or touch. Actually sobbing. But then she stopped and within an hour it was as if it never happened. She did the same when my father died, my sister told me. The sound I heard over the phone, long, loud and out of breath, like a gasp, a shout and a cry all at once. On the way back home, with my sister driving, she sat there silent. Done.

My mother has lost her temper more than once. Early eighties when she found out my older brother was smoking weed. She slapped him, not like a mother disciplining her son, but like a woman enraged that a man had disappointed her again. The time she snapped at me in the car despite being angry with someone else. Neither of us apologized or brought it up again.

Also this: my mother is a liar. A grand, elaborate liar with a stunning ability to convince, possibly the most hilarious thing about her. Somehow she managed to convince each of us at six that she was a hundred years old, enough that we would relay the same information in class with such a straight face that even the teacher started to wonder. That time when she told us we were moving to a big house uptown, and sat there on the couch while we started to decide what to take and what to leave, and which friends to stop talking to, now that we were going to be posh.

My mother thinks the hospital killed my father. She never had much use for bullshitting or pussyfooting, sometimes crossing the line from honest to tactless. Hard to say if it's true, of course, but all bets are off in a Jamaican hospital, and the most they did to prevent deep vein thrombosis was to tell the patient to get up and walk. A sick man, killed by the hospital that expected him to be Lazarus; she has called them murderers more than once to my sister and me. And while I say, *Mummy, you can't walk around with such things in your head*, I know it's true.

She was born in Linstead, St. Catherine, in 1936. Her sisters still say she was the most beautiful of the Dillon girls, which is saying something since everybody in Linstead knew the beauty of the Dillon girls, but the old pictures back them up. There is one of her, hair curled and pressed close like Billie Holiday's, and all dolled up like in a 50s film. There is another of her and three other women, dressed mod in miniskirts and beehive hair and leaning up against a sports car. They look as if they're at the beach. They look like soul sisters more than real sisters, but I have no idea who these women were.

The photo makes me think about who she was before marriage and motherhood. My mother having fun. My mother rolling deep with her chick posse, and maybe even getting into a little trouble. My mother, a woman hanging with woman friends. It haunts me because the mother I know had friends mostly from work, and by the late 80s they were all gone. She said to me back when I was eighteen, *Well you know I don't have anybody to talk to*. And that statement, tossed off like an afterthought, may be the reason why marriage always seemed like purgatory to me.

This is a bargain that I still see women make, including friends who are not friends anymore. *Now that I am a married woman, my life is husband and family*. Friends fade. This was something that women of her time were told to buy into, that friendship was something to bide the time until you found your true purpose as wife and mother. Happiness was something you provided for your children, not yourself. My mother was the first person to make a contradiction real to me. Something I saw in two of my friends who had fucked around on their wives, and one who probably would. Men and women, in the midst of ever-expanding family, who were still the loneliest people on the planet.

Also this: she is an epic farter. I tell her all the time that one day she'll blast herself into orbit.

My cousins are amazed by her infinite capacity for sweetness. To them she is *that* aunt. Somebody who can hug you soft and sweet with just words, even words as simple as *Happy Holidays*. Around her sisters and brothers, she becomes big sis, the one who stayed in Jamaica, the last of her sisters to marry and the last to think she should marry my father. At her mother's funeral in 1976, she held two of her sisters tight as they lost it. Tired herself, her arms wrapped around my aunts, her eyes hidden in the shadow of her black, wide-brimmed hat. A single tear rolling down her right cheek. She's the one they lean on, even now.

And this: she still calls me baby in public. And she does it like this, *Bye bayyybeeeee*. It used to annoy the crap out of me when I was twenty-one and a man, but now, whenever we part, at home, or the airport, I hang there suspended, waiting for her to say it.

There was this time, a slow Sunday afternoon back when I was either fifteen or sixteen, when my daddy was in the kitchen teaching me how to cook lobster and I caught him stealing glances out the window, which looked out to the garden. He beckoned me over with his left hand, his right jabbing lobsters with a giant fork, dunking them deep in popping fat. Out in the garden knelt my mother and inside were the two of us, looking at her planting flowers as if she were a stranger about to walk out of the frame. *You see her? The smartest woman I ever know. But she too proud. She fail just one of her general exams and never took it again. We have any more garlic?* Years later, at Christmas dinner when everybody was raving about my father's lobster, roast pork and curried goat, she said to no one, again in that tossed-off way she communicated disappointment, *Nobody ever say anything when I cook.*

She has never said a swear word. Ever. Not even shit.

Flannery O'Connor once said great stories resist paraphrase. I have a feeling that my mother's story resists story. Or that maybe I can only recall, not reconfigure or rearrange into anything like narrative. That at best, I might hit something like Michael Ondaatje's "7 or 8 Things I Know About Her." I have a feeling it's something simpler, the fact that I might not even know my mother. I know she loves cream soda and still calls it aerated water. She still calls umbrellas parasols. But put a boxing match on TV and she shrieks frenetic, like Norman Mailer watching black men beat each other.

One late morning years ago we were alone in the house. I still lived there, so I was probably twenty-four or twenty-five. I can't remember why we were alone, but I do remember her knocking on my room door, walking in jittery and anxious.

"Get up," she said, "quick."

I did what twentysomethings did and asked why. I lay on the bed, trying to decide between Jane's Addiction and Mother Love Bone CDs.

"Just get up," she said. "Dance with me."

I didn't know what to do. Worse, this looked like a serious request, not a joke. She stood there waiting, in the same sundress she always wore, her hair rolled up.

"I don't dance," I said.

She didn't hear me but started singing, and it was only when she got to the chorus that I realized it was "Tennessee Waltz," by Patti Page. She said it was her favorite song but had never heard it on the radio. She had probably not heard it in forty years. She was still by the door waiting. I was still on the bed waiting for her to leave and the awkwardness between us grew thick. As she walked away I wondered if that was her last shot at being who she was forty years ago, and my last shot at seeing her when she was younger than me.

The morning of my exorcism I came with a list of grievances against my father. I had gone to a church in uptown Kingston, because I didn't want anyone from my own church to know. And because that demon in me, the one who wanted to see Jake Gyllenhaal and Hugh Jackman naked, was taking over my life, meaning taking over my computer. And the church pamphlet that I kept for years to remind me that men I thought I wanted to fuck were really men I wanted to be, was wearing out. Sin—guilt—confession—forgiveness—rinse—repeat.

I just wanted to be normal. That's not true. I didn't want to be normal at all. I wanted to want it. I didn't want a wife and children,

I wanted to want them. I didn't want a house and two cars in the suburbs and a normal job with a normal Tuesday morning breakfast scene watching TV and sending children off to school. I wanted to want it. I didn't say any of that when the deliverers, a man and a woman, walked into the twelve-by-twelve beige room with three chairs and two vomit bags on the floor. They asked me why I was there. I shot off all the reasons why my father pissed me off, disappointed me, offended me and earned my disfavor, because all faggots are looking for their fathers.

"Tell me about your mother," the man said.

I opened my mouth and a scream came out.

Since my father died, my mother has been wearing pants again. She hasn't since the 70s. Now she wears jeans, a brand-new thing for her. My youngest sister, who now lives with her, has been introducing her to the practice of glamming up, so now she has foundation on her face. But my father's death also stripped her of man-pleasing bullshit, so her hair is now cut super-short with tight, shiny curls. She tells her daughter things she would never tell her sons, including her terrible fear of being alone. Her sons live abroad and she travels every year. But not to my house—I'm terrified of how much work it would take to de-gay it.

The week her last child left her house, Aunt Elise took up pottery. My mother, who spent most of her life building work and family, never built a room of her own. And other than for church, she doesn't know how to make room for anything else, despite a surplus of space. She is never going to take up pottery, or anything new for that matter, that old fear of failure stopping her from trying. But this woman still walks a mile to church, cooks all her own meals, drives like a total boss and holds her brothers and sisters together. My best friend's mother took to retirement by sitting in the armchair beside the TV, and waiting for the death that came seven years later.

137

I don't think my mother has given up, no woman who just dis-covered jeans has given up, but I wonder about the limbo she seems to be in. A limbo where she does find-a-word puzzles and e-mails her nephews, nieces and grandchildren. We are all shuddering over that moment when she discovers Facebook. I don't have the nerve to ask if she's happy, though I think she is. Well, she is whenever she thinks of her children, grandchildren and church.

And even when she thinks of my father. They were best friends who should never have gotten married. But they did, produced four children and near the end of his life, when there was nothing left to be bitter about, went back to being best friends. It was something to see, the rhythm of late-term man-woman friendship and com-panionship, with none of the complicated bullshit that comes from marriage. She doesn't miss a husband—that man was never really there, but she misses her friend, and she still grieves for him.

There was once a man who invited me to Paris for Christmas. It was 2005, and I didn't find him attractive but that wasn't why I didn't go. All I could think of was what my mother would think if she found out I was gay. That she would just throw herself more into church with a mission to pray my gay away, or worse, atone for her failure as a mother. I think the reason I screamed in the exorcism room was that I realized right then that I had built my terrible life around not disappointing my mother, though she had never asked for that. And even after realizing that I was gay anyway, that meant coming to terms with being cool with her no longer being in my life. There again was me reading my mother not as a person, but as a concept that I could project my fear and desire onto and then react. *How could she not know? I've never had a girlfriend. How could she know, we never speak about such things*, in fact we're a family that doesn't talk, something that nearly devastated my sister.

March 15, 2015, I came out in the *New York Times Magazine*. It didn't feel like a coming out to me but was treated as such and the article went viral. I had finally gotten to the point where I didn't care what people thought, and reaction, positive or negative, didn't interest me. The weekend before, I had lunch with my older brother. I honestly thought this would be the last time we were in the same room together, while he thought he was just getting lunch with his little bro. It was a strange week of kiss-offs, my acting as if I was going through the funeral rites of my relationships. So it was funny that I got the anticlimax I spent thirty years hoping for, in which friends and family would be in my corner post–coming out, and instantly over it.

But even my brothers wondered if I had heard from my mother. They said I should call her and explain, since she would be hearing it the same time as a few million other people, and who knows how she would react to not being told. And I agreed with this until it hit me that I was done explaining myself. And then I won the Booker Prize, and every news story led with "openly gay Jamaican author." My mother followed my Google alerts—surely she would know now. I wasn't going to tell her. Maurice Sendak never came out to his mother either.

All this openly gay business made me wonder if I would ever hear from my mother again. That's too dramatic, of course I knew I would hear from her, but I wondered if she would say anything other than family business. How the hedge needs cutting and who no longer comes to church. Also this: my mother has sung me "Happy Birthday" every November 24 since I was one year old. She even called me in Nigeria two years earlier. I had resigned myself to never getting that call again. Not out of malice or bitterness, but because our family disease of non-talk would spread even to her singing.

But at 9 AM on my birthday, when I was hungover and waking up in London, my cell phone rang. It was her number. She did not say hello or anything, just took a small breath and sang.

Tell Me How It Ends
(An Essay in Forty Questions)

VALERIA LUISELLI

I. TOWARD THE BORDER

"Why did you come to the United States?" That's question number
one in the intake questionnaire for unaccompanied child migrants.
I started working as an interpreter in the court of immigration in
New York City almost a year ago. My task there is a simple one: I
translate children's stories from Spanish into English. I ask questions,
following a questionnaire, and the child answers them. A lawyer then
decides whether the child has any avenues of immigration relief, and
eventually, whether to take on the child's case or not.

But nothing is ever that simple. I hear words, spoken in the mouths
of children, threaded in complex narratives. They are delivered with
hesitance, sometimes distrust, always with fear. I transform them into
written words, succinct sentences, and barren terms. The children's
stories are always shuffled, stuttered, and shattered beyond the repair
of a narrative order. The problem with telling their story is that it has
no beginning, no middle, and no end.

"Why did you come to the United States?" The children's answers
vary, but they often point to reunification with a parent or some

other relative who migrated to the US years earlier. Other times, the answers have to do with the circumstances they are fleeing from: extreme violence, persecution and coercion by gangs, mental and physical abuse, forced labor, neglect. It is perhaps not the American dream that they pursue, but the more modest aspiration to wake up from the nightmare in which they were born.

I watch our own children sleep pleasantly in the backseat of the car as we cross the George Washington Bridge into New Jersey. Their mouths are open wide. Boy and girl, foreheads pearled with sweat, cheeks red and streaked white with dry drool. They occupy the entire space, spread out and heavy, breathing so calmly. I glance back at them now and then from the copilot's seat, and turn around again to study the map of the country—a map too big to be unfolded entirely. At the wheel, my husband adjusts his glasses and dries his forehead with the back of his hand.

It is July 2014. We are driving from Manhattan to Cochise, Arizona, near the US-Mexico border, to spend the rest of the summer there. We are waiting for our green cards to be either granted or denied, and in the meantime we are not allowed to leave the country without losing status. We joke, somewhat frivolously, about the possible definitions of our new migratory situation: "pending aliens," "aliens seeking status," "alien writers," "pending Mexicans." But we knew what applying for green cards implied. And when we applied, we also decided that if we were going to stay in this country as residents, we had to at least get to know where we were going to live a little better. So when summer arrived, we bought maps, got driver's licenses, rented a car, packed a few basics, made playlists, bought provisions in the supermarket, and left New York.

The green card questionnaire is nothing like the intake questionnaire for undocumented minors. When you apply for a green card you have to answer things like: "Do you intend to practice polygamy?" and "Are you a member of the Communist Party?" and "Have you ever knowingly committed a crime of moral turpitude?" And although nothing can or should be taken lightly when you are in the fragile situation of asking for permission to live in a country that is not your own, there is almost something innocent and endearing in the green card questionnaire's preoccupations and visions of the future and its possible threats—like a sci-fi film that you remember watching long ago on VHS or Beta. The current undocumented children's questionnaire, on the other hand, is colder, more cynical, and conspicuous. It's impossible not to read and answer it with a growing feeling that the world has indeed become a more fucked-up place than what we all imagined it could be.

B efore the undocumented children are asked why they came to the United States, the person conducting the intake interview has to fill in basic biographic details, such as the child's name, age, country of birth, the name of his or her sponsor in the US, and the people with whom he or she lives.

A few lines down, another two questions float across the page like an uncomfortable silence, separated by an empty space:

Where is the child's mother?_____father?_____

A s we make our way across the map of the country, the summer heat becomes drier, the light thinner and whiter, the roads more solitary. For a couple of days, in our long westbound drives, we've been following a news story on the radio. It's a sad story, which hits close to home, and yet seems unimaginable, almost unreal: tens of thousands of migrant children from Mexico and Central America have been detained at the border, and are awaiting either deportation or political asylum. They have come without their fathers, without their mothers, without suitcases, without passports. Why did they come to the United States? And why did we? I don't know if anyone knows the reasons. Perhaps, when the story is over, we will all understand. But before anything can be understood it has to be narrated many times, told in many different words and angles, by many different minds.

Then comes question number two in the intake questionnaire: "When did you enter the US?" Most children don't know the exact date. They smile and say "last year" or "a few months ago" or simply "I don't know." They've fled their towns and cities, they've walked and swum and hidden and run and mounted freight trains and trucks. They've turned themselves in to Border Patrol officers. They've come all this way looking for—for what, for whom?

As we get closer to the Southwest, we start collecting local newspapers. They pile on the floor of our car, in front of my copilot seat. We do constant, quick online searches, and tune in to the radio every time we can catch a signal. Questions, speculations, and opinions flash-flood the news for the days that follow. What will happen to these children? Where are the parents? Where will they go next? Nothing is clear in the initial coverage of the situation—which will soon be known more widely as the 2014 American Immigration Crisis, though others will advocate for the more accurate term "refugee crisis."

Naturally, newspapers and other publications react differently: some denounce the maltreatment of child migrants at the border, some elaborate lucid and complex conjectures on the origin and cause of the sudden surge in their influx, some endorse the protests against them. A caption in a web publication explains an unsettling photograph of men and women waving flags, banners, and rifles in the air: "Protesters, some exercising their open-carry rights, assemble outside of the Wolverine Center in Vassar [Michigan] that would house illegal juveniles to show their dismay for the situation." A caption in a Reuters image explains another photograph, where elderly men and women sit in beach chairs holding banners saying "Illegal Is a Crime": "Thelma and Don Christie (C) of Tucson demonstrate against the arrival of undocumented immigrants in Oracle, Arizona."

In varying degrees, some papers and webpages announce the arrival of the undocumented children like a biblical plague. Beware: the locusts! They will cover the face of the ground so that it cannot be seen—these menacing coffee-colored boys and girls, with their obsidian hair and slant eyes. They will fall from the skies, on our cars, on our green lawns, on our heads, on our schools, on our Sundays. They will make a racket, they will bring their chaos, their sickness, their dirt, their brownness. They will cloud the pretty views, they will fill the future with bad omens, they will fill our tongues with barbarisms. And if they are allowed to stay here they will—eventually—reproduce!

We read the papers, and listen to the radio, and wonder. We wonder if the reactions would be different if all these children were of a lighter color; of better, purer breeds and nationalities. Would they be treated more like people, more like children? In a diner in Roswell, New Mexico, we hear that hundreds of kids, some traveling with their mothers, some traveling alone, are being put on airplanes and will be deported that same day back to Honduras. These planes, full of "alien" children, will depart from an airport not far from the famous UFO museum. The term "alien," which only a few weeks ago made us laugh and speculate, which we still passed around the car as an inside family joke when we decided to visit the UFO sites in New Mexico, is suddenly shown to us under a bleaker light. It's strange how concepts can erode so easily into dust, how words we once used lightly can alchemize abruptly into something toxic.

The next day, driving out of Roswell, we look for news on what happened with those first summer deportees who were sent back to San Pedro Sula, Honduras. We come across these two lines in a Reuters report that read like the beginning of a cruel, absurdist story by Mikhail Bulgakov or Daniil Kharms: "Looking happy, the deported children exited the airport on an overcast and sweltering afternoon. One by one, they filed into a bus, playing with balloons they had been given." We dwell for a while on the adjective "happy," and the strangely meticulous description of the local weather in San Pedro: "an overcast and sweltering afternoon." But what we really cannot stop reproducing, somewhere in the dark back of our minds, is the image of the children holding those sinister balloons.

In our long daily drives, when our children are awake in the backseat of the car, they ask for attention, they ask for bathroom stops, they ask for snacks. But above all they ask:

When will we get there?

How many more hours?

To appease them, to fill in the empty hours, we sometimes tell them stories about the old American Southwest, back when it used to be part of Mexico. We also tell them stories about Apaches, and Bluecoats, and Pancho Villa. Other times we fall silent, and listen to our children's delirious backseat games. And when we drive through towns, we turn on the radio and listen to the news about what's happening just outside the small and protected world of our rented car. We hear bits and pieces about the crisis, we talk it over and consider its many angles. We answer our kids' questions, and discuss their ideas—yet the wider picture always remains blurry. All of it resists a rational explanation.

The third and fourth questions in the intake questionnaire are ones that our children, too, ask many times, though in their own words: "With whom did you travel to this country? Did you travel with anyone you knew?" Sometimes, when our children fall asleep again, I look back at them, or hear them breathe, and wonder if they would survive in the hands of coyotes, and what would happen to them if they were then deposited at the US border, left either on their own or in the custody of officials. Were they to find themselves alone, crossing borders and countries, would my own children survive?

The fifth and sixth questions are: "What countries did you pass through?" and "How did you travel here?" To the first one, almost everyone immediately answers "Mexico," and some also list "Guatemala," "El Salvador," and "Honduras." To the second question, with a blend of pride and horror, most say: "I came on *La Bestia*," which literally means "the beast," and refers to the freight trains that cross Mexico, on top of which as many as half a million Central American migrants ride annually. There are no passenger services along the routes, so migrants have to ride atop the railcars. Thousands have died or been gravely injured aboard La Bestia, either because of its constant derailments, or by falling off during the night, or by falling into the hands of smugglers, policemen, and thieves. But people continue to take the risk, because there is no other route to take if you cannot pay. La Bestia's routes start either in the town of Tapachula, in the state of Chiapas, or in Tenosique, Tabasco—both towns near the Mexico-Guatemala border. They slowly make their way up to the US-Mexico border following either the eastern Gulf route to Reynosa, the border town near the southeasternmost tip of Texas, or the western routes that lead either to Ciudad Juárez, Chihuahua; or to Nogales, Sonora, which share borders with Texas and Arizona, respectively.

In driving from southwestern New Mexico toward southeastern Arizona, it becomes difficult to ignore the uncomfortable irony of it: we are traveling in the direction opposite to the children whose

147

stories we are now following so closely. As we get closer to the border, and begin taking back roads, we do not see a single migrant—child or adult. We see other things, though, that indicate their ghostly presence, past or future. Along the narrow dirt road that goes from a ghost town called Shakespeare, in New Mexico, to another town called Animas, and from there to Apache, in Arizona, we see a discreet trail of flags that volunteer groups tie to trees or fences, in order to indicate that there are tanks filled with water there for people to drink as they cross the desert. As we approach Animas, we begin to see fleeting herds of border patrol cars like ominous white stallions racing toward the horizon. Occasionally, we are overtaken by big pickup trucks with big men, and imagine they carry big guns. In the Dantean city of Douglas, right at the Arizona-Sonora border, we get lost in a layout of concentric streets with ominous Old Testament-sounding names, like "Limbo of the Patriarchs" and "Limbo of the Fathers." We decide not to tell anyone in diners and gas stations that we are Mexican, just in case. But we are stopped a few times by immigration officials, and have to show our passports, and display big smiles when we explain we are just writers and just on vacation. Why are we there and what are we writing—they always want to know. We are writing a Western, we say. We are writing a Western, and we are there for the open skies and the silence and the emptiness—this second part is more true than the part about writing the Western, which is mostly untrue. Handing back our passports, one official says sardonically:

So you come all the way down here for *the inspiration*.

We will not contradict anyone who carries a badge, a gun, and a repertoire of sarcastic sneers, so we just say:

Yes sir.

How do you explain that it is never inspiration that drives you to tell a story, but rather, a combination of anger and clarity? How do you say: we do not find inspiration here, but we find a country that is as beautiful as it is broken, and we are somehow now part of it, so we are also broken with it and think we have to do something about that.

As we drive back to New York in mid-August, my husband tells the children about the life of Geronimo, the Chiricahua Apache. His words perhaps bring time closer to us, containing it inside the car instead of letting it stretch out beyond us like an unattainable goal. I listen to portions of the story: Geronimo was the last man in the Americas to surrender to the Europeans. He became a medicine man. Mexican soldiers had killed his three children, his mother, and his wife. He never learned English. He acted as an interpreter between Apache and Spanish for Chief Cochise. When my husband falls silent again, distracted from the story by a sudden bifurcation in the route, I look for a music playlist and press shuffle. One song that often comes up is "Straight to Hell," by the Clash. In a way, it has become the leitmotif of our trip. There's a line that drills its way into my brain: "There ain't no asylum here. King Solomon he never lived 'round here."

Questions seven and eight on the intake questionnaire for children are: "Did anything happen on your trip to the US that scared you or hurt you?" and "Has anyone hurt you, threatened or frightened you since you came to the US?" The children seldom give details of such experiences upon a first screening. But the numbers tell horror stories: eighty percent of the women and girls who cross Mexico to get to the US border are raped on the way. The situation is so common that most of them take contraceptive precautions as they begin the journey north. But rape is a minor risk compared with other horrors. In 2010, the bodies of seventy-two Central American migrants were found piled up inside

149

a ranch in Tamaulipas. Some had been tortured and all had been shot in the back of the head. What did number seventy-two think when the seventy-first gunshot was heard? Three people had faked their death and, though wounded, survived. Later, they explained that members of the drug cartel Los Zetas perpetrated the mass murder, after the migrants had refused to work for them and did not have money to pay to be released. That same year, a sixteen-year-old boy on the Mexican side of the border was shot to death by an American officer on the US side, who claimed the boy and other people had thrown rocks at him. Bullets for rocks. In 2013, the US Border Patrol found the remains of 463 migrants—most of whose deaths were unaccounted for, and most of whom were found near Tucson, on the US side of the border. Mexican newspapers pointed fingers at civilian vigilantes and ranch owners.

The numbers tell horror stories, but perhaps the stories of deepest horror are those for which there are no numbers, no possible accountability, no words ever written or spoken by anyone. And perhaps the only way to make some justice, if that were at all possible, is by beginning to peel off the surface of their scab. By beginning to want to hear and to record those stories, over and over again—so that they are not forgotten, so that they remain in the annals of our little histories and then come back, always, to haunt and shame us. Because we can all be made accountable if something happens under our noses and we don't dare even look.

II. IN COURT

We returned to Manhattan at the end of the summer of 2014. The family's green cards were waiting for us in a stack of mail piled high by the door—all of them except mine. The children went back to school, we went back to work, and life was back to almost normal. I still had to figure out what to do with my lost green card—and so began to talk to my lawyer regularly on the phone. We had to come up with plans B and C. We applied for a temporary work permit, and that came in the mail a few months later. But there was still no sign of my green card. We continued to look for possible solutions, until one day my lawyer told me she had to hand over my case to someone else, because she had just been offered another job in a nonprofit organization, working on cases defending child migrants, and she had to abandon her private practice.

Ever since I was left somewhat alone, without gods, I became a ferocious believer in the power of small coincidences. That is how chance works, at least for those of us who do not have the certitude of grander schemes. It was thanks to my lost green card, and thanks to my lawyer abandoning my green card case, that I became involved with a much larger problem. My more trivial pursuits as an "alien writer" or "pending Mexican" suddenly took me into the heart of something larger and more important. Listening to my lawyer over the phone as I walked down Broadway one morning, I decided to inquire further into what she was really telling me. She explained that the Obama administration had decided to create a priority juvenile docket in immigration courts to speed up the deportation proceedings of thousands of undocumented children. That is why she was taking on this new job. I asked if I could be of any help in court. She said I could, and gave me an appointment with a lawyer from AILA (American Immigration Lawyers Association). I still had questions before we hung up, but not the right words to articulate them at that moment: What was the priority docket? Which court? Who was defending these children? Who was accusing them? Of what crime exactly?

The next questions in the intake questionnaire—nine, ten, and eleven—are: "How do you like where you're living now? Are you happy there? Do you feel safe?" I think about these questions often, and wonder what images flash through a child's mind the second before he or she gives me an answer.

By January 2015, the picture was a little clearer for everyone who had been following news related to the immigration crisis. Or, if it was not clearer in its deeper causes and consequences, there was at least a better sense of its magnitude now. Although the flow of youth migrating to the United States from Mexico and Central America had been observed for years, there had been a considerable and sudden increase in the numbers: from October 2013 to the moment in which the crisis was declared in June 2014, the total number of child migrants detained at the border approached the figure of 80,000. Later, in the summer of 2015, it was known that between April 2014 and August 2015, more than 102,000 unaccompanied children had been detained at the border.

The majority of the children come from Guatemala, El Salvador, and Honduras—the so-called Northern Triangle. Almost all the children are fleeing the violence and coercion of the *gangas*, or criminal groups associated with drug trafficking, such as the Mara Salvatrucha 13 (MS 13) and Barrio 18 in Honduras and El Salvador. Some children flee domestic violence, abandonment, and forced labor. Many arrive looking for their parents, who migrated to the United States years before they did. Others look for relatives who have been sending money for years, or who have kept close enough contact to still be reachable.

Questions number twelve and thirteen in the intake questionnaire are for children whose parents or siblings are already in the US: "Have your parents or siblings been the victim of a crime since they came to the US?" and "Was it reported to the police?" The reason for these two questions is that victims of crimes in the US may be eligible for a type of relief, which, if granted, is a path to lawful permanent residency for the crime victims and their families. Questions fourteen, fifteen, and sixteen open a window into understanding, among other things, how this mass migration of children is shifting the basic structure of the family unit: "Do you still have any family members that live in your home country? Are you in touch with anyone in your home country? Who/how often?" Most children have someone both in their home country and in the US. The family tree of migrant families is always split in two trunks: those who leave and those who stay.

Those who usually stay behind are the youngest and the eldest. The ones who travel are mostly the teenagers. But in this recent surge, children as young as age three have made the journey north without a parent. The children usually leave their home country under the care of coyotes, who charge anywhere from $3,000 to $7,000 to deliver one child to the US-Mexico border. The coyotes rarely go beyond the dividing line between the two countries, and they cannot be made accountable if anything goes wrong during the journey.

Once they cross the border, the children know their best bet is to be caught by Border Patrol officers. Crossing the desert beyond the border, alone, is too dangerous. They also know that if they are not caught at this point, or if they do not surrender themselves to the law, their fate will be to remain undocumented, like most of their parents or adult relatives already in the US. Remaining undocumented is perhaps not worse than what they are fleeing, but it is certainly not the life that anyone wants.

If the children are Mexican, and the Border Patrol officer interviewing them determines that they are not victims of human trafficking and do not have fear of returning to Mexico, they are immediately deported back to Mexico under a process called "voluntary return." This is per a 2008 amendment to the Trafficking Victims Protection Reauthorization Act, signed by President G.W.

Bush, which states that the US can return children from contiguous countries Mexico and Canada under negotiated repatriation agreements, and without formal immigration proceedings in the court. If the children are Central American, however, US law protects them with the right to a formal immigration hearing in federal court, where they have a right to hire their own attorney at no expense to the US government and can contest their deportation and seek any available avenues of relief that could allow them to lawfully remain in the US.

Once the Border Patrol catches them they are placed in a detention center commonly known as the *hielera* or the "icebox." The icebox derives its name from its frigid temperature, but also because in it the children are under ICE custody (Immigration and Customs Enforcement). They remain there for up to seventy-two hours, though many complaints have been made because children are kept for longer, subject not only to the inhumane temperatures, but also to verbal and physical mistreatment. They are underfed, have nowhere to lie down to sleep, and are not allowed to use the bathrooms as often as they should be. In July 2015, for example, AILA filed a complaint after learning that in a detention center in Dilley, Texas, 250 children were mistakenly given adult-strength hepatitis A vaccinations, and became gravely ill.

If the children make it out of the icebox, they are placed in custody with the Office of Refugee Resettlement and sent to shelters in a border town. There, they are given a window in which they must manage to contact a family member or acquaintance who will declare him- or herself as their official sponsor. If they manage to make that contact, they are put on a plane, usually paid for by their sponsor, and sent to the city where the sponsor lives.

After a few months in their new home, they receive an order to present themselves in court, where they're told it is their responsibility to find a lawyer to defend them. Questions seventeen and eighteen refer to the sponsors: "Do you have any other close family members who live in the US? Immigration status?" The immigration status of the children's family members is almost always "undocumented." This, of course, means that presenting themselves in court in the company of a sponsor is also a way of exposing other members of their family to a system that they have been dodging and hiding from, sometimes for decades, naturally fearing deportation. The new situation creates tensions and complications within families. Sponsors have to give all their details when the children are screened, from their names to their exact addresses. Many feel that they are putting themselves in a position of utter vulnerability. And yet thousands of children and their sponsors have presented themselves in court since the surge began and the crisis was declared. The states with the highest number of children released to sponsors since the crisis was declared are Texas (above 10,000 children), California (almost 9,000 children), and New York (above 8,000 children).

In March 2015, my nineteen-year-old niece and I started working as interpreters in the court of immigration in New York City. On our first visit to court, we were given basic training by members of The Door—a Manhattan-based nonprofit organization that provides comprehensive youth development services, from legal assistance to English classes to counseling and creative activities—and were handed the intake questionnaire to begin working that same day: it was a busy day and they needed all the help they could get, even if the volunteers were newcomers.

The process by which a child is asked questions during the first court appearance is called screening, a term that is as cynical as it is appropriate: the child like a reel of footage, the translator-interpreter like an obsolete apparatus used to channel that footage, the legal system a screen, itself too worn out, too filthy and tattered to allow any clarity, any attention to detail. All the stories become generalized, distorted, appear out of focus.

In court, screeners ask children questions, one after the other. First one, two, then three, and then, eventually, questions nineteen and twenty:

Who did you live with in your home country?

How did you get along with the people with whom you lived?

"The people with whom you lived" is an elastic category. It refers to immediate family. But it could also refer to neighbors, and schoolmates, and everyone within the radius of a person's everyday circuit. And what happens when an entire community has been broken down by violence? To this question, the children's answers vary, but the tableaux they sum up to is a single depiction of an entire continent that is being crushed to pieces by political negligence, by corruption on all levels, and by fear of "the people with whom you live." The maps of political violence and the routes of new migrations have to be superimposed, at least in the Americas, with those of drug production, trafficking, and consumption. The American continent is united, no doubt, finally, by the trail of bloodshed that drug trafficking leaves behind it. Yet, there is little talk of this, from Patagonia to Alaska. There is little talk of drug legalization, of arms being trafficked from the US to Mexico and Central America, of the role that absolutely everyone, from producers to consumers, plays in the great theater of devastation, thinking that they are merely part of an audience in perhaps one of the bloodiest and cruelest spectacles that the twenty-first century has given.

Children run and flee. They have an instinct for survival, perhaps, that allows them to endure almost anything just to make it to the other side of horror, whatever may be waiting there for them. They flee, looking for protection against other family members, neighbors, teachers, kingpins, policemen, gang members, paramilitary soldiers. Undocumented, they leave their countries and cross Mexico in the hands of a coyote, riding La Bestia. They have to try not to fall into the hands of rapists, corrupt policemen, murderous soldiers, and other drug gangs, who might enslave them in poppy or marijuana fields, if they don't shoot them in the head and mass-bury them. Then, at the US border, they have to face officers who will say things like: "Speak English! You are now in America!" Then, if they are not deported, and make it to a shelter, they have to start looking for their parents, if they have parents. Question number twenty-one: "Did you stay in touch with your parents?" Some say yes and some say no. Reunited with their parents, or with a sponsor when they do not have parents, they may or may not find the security and support they've been migrating toward.

After a few weeks, or sometimes months, in their new home, unaccompanied children receive a Notice to Appear, ordering them to present themselves in immigration court. If they don't show up (because they fear going to court, or perhaps only because they have since changed address, or didn't get the notice) they risk an order to be removed *in absentia*—in their absence. In court, an immigration judge, assisted by a translator, informs them they have the right to an attorney, but at no expense to the US government. In other words, it is the children's responsibility to find and pay for a lawyer, or find a free lawyer, who can help them defend their case against the US government attorney seeking to deport them. A typical first immigration hearing begins with the judge stating the basic facts:

This is September 15, 2014, New York, state of New York.

This is immigration judge (name of judge).

This is in the matter of (name of the child respondent).

Then come a few questions directed at the accused, such as if he or she responds to Spanish, and whether he or she lives at a given address. Then the judge states that he will be speaking to the attorney, and asks:

How do you plead?

We admit the charges.

But what are the charges, exactly? Fundamentally, that the child came to the United States without lawful permission. Admitting these charges alone would lead to deportation unless the child's attorney can find those potential avenues of relief that form a defense against deportation.

Questions twenty-two, twenty-three, and twenty-four are:

Did you go to school in your home country?

When did you stop going to school?

Why?

In the end, the question will always be—Why? The questions in the intake questionnaire are meant to lead up to a "potential relief" section in which the screener determines whether the minor is potentially eligible for either asylum, SIJS (Special Immigrant Juvenile Status), a U visa, or a T visa, any of which, if successful, would provide a defense against deportation, allow the child to remain in the US lawfully, and pave the way toward an eventual path to lawful permanent residency. Most commonly, the kind of harm the children are fleeing makes them eligible for asylum or SIJS. Asylum is granted to people who are fleeing persecution (or who have a fear of future persecution) based on their race, religion, nationality, and/or association with a particular social or political group. It is very difficult to be granted asylum because it is not enough that these children have suffered unspeakable harm. The harm or persecution has to be proved to be *because of* at least one of those four classifications. If asylum is granted, this means the children can never return to their home country where they fear being perse-cuted without jeopardizing their immigration status in the US. The SIJS visa is for children who, according to a family court, are impeded from reunification with their parents because of abuse, abandonment, neglect, or a similar basis under state law, and for whom reunification in their home country is not in their best interests. Less common is the U visa, which may be granted to victims of certain crimes that occurred in the United States, who have suffered mental or physical abuse, and who—and this is the crux of the matter—have also cooperated with the government in the persecution of criminal activity. Finally, the T visa is for victims of human trafficking, which is less common and rare for victims to self-disclose within a brief interview.

Before the crisis was declared in the summer of 2014, minors seeking asylum had approximately twelve months to find a lawyer to represent their case before their first court hearing. When the crisis was declared and the priority docket created, this window was reduced to twenty-one days. The problem is that priority dockets push cases ahead and proceed more quickly than institutions and organizations can usually respond, so many children are deported even before they have time to find a lawyer. It is almost nonsensical: What child can find a lawyer in twenty-one days? What family, without legal counsel or resources, can respond to the urgency of a priority docket?

I remember leaving court with my niece after our first morning doing screenings for The Door. We left with a feeling of frustration, a sense of defeat. All we could do in court, it was clear, was to serve as a fragile and slippery bridge between children and the court system. We stopped to buy a coffee in the nearest deli, and as we walked out she said:

You know, I think I'm going to major in law instead of social work.

Why law? I asked.

Though of course, in the context, my question was trivial. According to a comprehensive report issued in October 2015 by

159

the Migration Policy Institute, the majority of children who do find a lawyer do appear in court and are granted some form of relief. All the others are deported, either *in absentia* or in person.

Child migrants in court proceedings are not entitled to free legal counsel, so volunteer organizations have stepped in to do the job themselves, either pro bono or at very low costs. This has always made me marvel at the US. It is a country full of holes, which individuals, out of a deep sense of duty toward other people perhaps, fill in. In New York, organizations such as AILA, The Door, KIND (Kids in Need of Defense), Catholic Charities, CARECEN (Central American Resource Center), and Safe Passage Project are a few of the groups that are always present in the NY Immigration Court. The problem is that nonprofit organizations can only provide a kind of patchwork and not even the sum of all of them can ever manage to fill in all the need-gaps.

Questions twenty-five, twenty-six, and twenty-seven: "Did you work in your home country? What sort of work did you do? How many hours did you work each day?"

I note down key points, in English. I write them in as much detail as possible. I also try to look for general categories that may tip the legal scale in favor of the future client in a future trial—categories like "abandonment," "prostitution," "sex trafficking," "gang violence," and "death threats." But I cannot make up the answers in their favor, nor can I lead the children to tell me what is best for their case, as much as I would like that. It's sometimes confusing and bewildering, and I find myself not knowing where translation begins, and where interpretation starts. I sometimes note their answers in the first person and sometimes in the third:

I crossed the border by foot.

She swam across the river.

He comes from San Pedro Sula.

She comes from Tegucigalpa.

She comes from Guatemala City.

He has not ever met his father.

Yes I have met my mother.

But she doesn't remember the last time she saw her.

He doesn't know if she abandoned him.

She sent money every month.

No, my father didn't send money at all.

I worked in the fields, ten or maybe fifteen hours a day.

The MS-13 shot my sister. She died.

Yes, my uncle hit me often.

No, my grandmother never hit us.

If the child answers the questionnaire "correctly" he or she is more likely to have a strong enough case, which will increase the child's chances of being placed with a pro bono attorney. An answer is "correct" if it strengthens the child's case and provides a potential avenue of relief. So in the warped world of immigration, for example, a correct answer is when a girl reveals that her father is an alcoholic who physically or sexually abused her, or when a boy reports that he received death threats, or that he was beaten repeatedly by several gang members after refusing to acquiesce to recruitment at school. These are the kinds of answers that may open doors to potential immigration relief. When children don't have enough battle wounds to show, they may not have any way to successfully defend their case, and are most likely to be "removed" back to their home country.

According to the same report issued in October 2015 by the Migration Policy Institute, despite the creation of the priority docket, many cases filed between October 2013 and August 2015 (55,513) remain unresolved: that's more than forty percent of them.

There have been 14,024 removals *in absentia*, and 3,360 removal orders and "voluntary departures" in person. On the other hand, 11,610 children have been given "informal" relief, such as prosecutorial discretion; but only 313 cases have received formal relief. Understanding the difference between the two forms of relief is fundamental: formal relief means the child can lawfully remain in the US and has a path to a green card and eventually US citizenship, such as through SIJS, asylum, or the less common T and U visas. Informal relief simply means that the government exercised what is called Prosecutorial Discretion, a decision not to prosecute the case against the child, with the result that the child no longer has an active removal case—i.e., will not be immediately deported—but has also not been granted any immigration status, and has no path to a green card.

The problem for children granted informal relief is, of course, that even though they don't have a formal removal case pending, they remain in the US without legal status. And without legal status, they are likely to live and work in the shadows, without access to social safety nets like health insurance and without legal representation to determine if they have any other routes to pursue lawful immigration status. So they are a particularly vulnerable part of a new population. They will stay. But under what conditions? They will remain in a kind of migratory limbo—and remain there indeterminately, unless they are able to seek help or representation outside the immigration court system, through the USCIS (United States Citizenship and Immigration Services) agency.

Since my niece and I started working in court, my five-year-old daughter asks a lot about "those kids who in-migrated." We tell her some of the stories. We tell them during dinner to the rest of the family, we tell them in the morning to ourselves, we tell them to each other right after we leave the court. Perhaps retelling is a way of understanding the unthinkable, but also, a way of forgetting the initial stab that inches its way through the stomach when a child tells his or her story for the first time. As predictable as some of the children's answers start to become after months of screening, nobody is ever fully prepared to hear them.

I write their answers in my notebook before I copy them down neatly on the intake questionnaire. He says: "The gang followed me after school, and I ran, with my eyes closed I ran fast." And so I write all that down and then note: (persecution?). He says more: "And they followed me to school and later they followed me home with a gun." And I write that down, and then note: (death threats?). And then he says: "They kicked the door open and shot my brother." So I write that and note: (home country poses life-threatening danger?). And then I find myself not wanting to write anymore, so I just sit there, quietly listening, wishing that the bullet had missed. But it hadn't. And later the screening is filed, and sent away to a possible lawyer: a snapshot of a life that would wait in the dark until maybe someone found it.

But tell me how it ends, Mamma, my daughter often insists.
Part of the problem is also that all stories lack an ending when one first hears them, because the children involved have to wait months, sometimes years, before their case is fully resolved. My daughter often comes back to them, days or weeks later, demanding a proper conclusion.

What happened later? she wants to know.

There is one story that obsesses her, a story for which I have not yet been able to offer a real ending. It begins with two girls in a courtroom. They are five and seven years old. They sit at one end of a long mahogany table. The younger one is working on a coloring book with a set of crayons, while the older one answers

163

my questions. She is a little shy but tries to be clear and precise in her answers, delivering all of them with a big smile, toothless here and there.

Why did you come to the United States?

I don't know.

How did you travel here?

A man brought us.

A coyote?

No, a man.

Was he nice to you?

Yes, he was nice.

Where did you cross the border?

I don't know.

Texas? Arizona?

Yes! Texas Arizona.

The two girls are from a small village in Guatemala. When the younger one turned two, their mother left them there under their grandmother's care. She crossed two national borders, with no documents, and settled in Long Island, where she had a cousin. Four years went by. The girls grew up, talking to their mother on the telephone, hearing stories about snow falling, and big avenues, and traffic jams, and, later, about their mother's new husband and their new baby brother. Questions twenty-eight, twenty-nine, and thirty: "Did you ever get in trouble at home when you lived in your home country? How did your parent/relative punish you if you did something wrong? How often did this happen?"

No.

No.

Never—the older one answers, while the little one undresses a crayon and scratches its trunk with her fingernail.

One day their grandmother told them that a man was going to help them get back to their mother. She said it would be a long trip, but that they would be safe in his hands. He had already taken another person from their village safely across the two borders, and was charging less than others for the service. He would take them across Guatemala, across Mexico, and deliver them to the US-Mexico border. Once there, there would be other people to help them travel the rest of the way to New York.

The day before they left, their grandmother sewed a ten-digit telephone number on the collars of the dresses they would each wear throughout the entire trip. Over and over she repeated a single instruction: they should never take this dress off, and, as soon as they reached America, as soon as they met the first American policeman, they had to show the inside of the dress's collar to him. He would then dial the number sewed onto it and let them speak to their mother. The rest would follow.

The rest did follow: the two girls made it to the border, made it to a shelter, and after a few weeks were put on a plane and flown to JFK, where their mother, baby brother, and stepfather were waiting for them. But family reunification is not really where it all ends. Their case, for example, is one that was not immediately channeled to a lawyer after their first screening, as it did not seem "strong enough." I do not know if the two girls will be given relief.

Tell me how it ends, Mamma.

I don't know how it ends.

I sit outside on a bench in Battery Park one day with a friend. It's September and I've just got out of a court screening. We watch those noisy New York bateaux-mouches endlessly depart for and arrive from New Jersey. I tell him a little about what happened in court that day. He remembers some lines from a prayer, "La oración del migrante," that he learnt while working on a documentary about La Bestia: "Partir es morir un poco / Llegar nunca es llegar"—To leave is to die a little / To arrive is never to arrive.

III. HOME

Toward the end of the intake interview, some of the most difficult questions have to be asked. Thirty-one, for example: "Did you ever have trouble with gangs or crime in your home country?" Smaller children look back at you in bewilderment after hearing that question; some laugh at it, even though many of them have perhaps already heard the words *ganga* or *pandillero* before. Older children and teenagers have had, in most cases, direct trouble with gangas and pandillas. The degree of their contact and involvement with pandilleros varies, but they've all been touched in one way or the other by the reaching tentacles of groups like the MS-13 and Barrio 18. The teenage girls, for example, are not usually coerced into gangs, but are often sexually harassed by them or recruited to be girlfriends of gang members. Boys who are being coerced are told that their little sister, or cousin, or girlfriend will be raped if they don't man up and join.

The first person I ever screened in court was a boy from Honduras, age sixteen. Let's call him Manu. I met him in March 2015. His aunt, Alina, was sponsoring him. She sat in the general waiting area keeping her two-year-old daughter entertained with a coloring book and crayons provided by the court workers, while Manu and I spoke, seated at one end of the long mahogany table where interviews are conducted.

Why did you come to the United States?

He says nothing and looks at me, and shrugs a little. I reassure him:

I'm no policewoman, I'm no official anyone, I'm not even a lawyer. I'm also not a gringa, you know? In fact, I can't help you at all.

So why are *you* here then?

I'm just here to translate for you.

And what are you?

I'm a *chilanga*.

I'm a *catracho*—he says—so we're enemies. And in a way he's right: I'm from Mexico City and he's from Honduras.

Yeah—I say—but only in football, and I suck at football anyway so you've already scored five goals against me.

He smiles, perhaps almost laughs. I know he's going to let me go on with the questions now. I haven't won his trust, of course, but at least I have his attention. Both newcomers to this situation, we proceed, slowly and hesitantly. He delivers his answers like a whisper or a murmur, and looks down at his clasped hands or turns around to find his aunt and baby cousin.

Although I try to convey my words neutrally, every question seems to either embarrass or annoy him. He answers in short sentences, sometimes only silent shrugs. No, he had never met his father. No, he did not live with his mother in his home country. He had met her, yes, but she came and went as she pleased. She liked the streets, perhaps. He doesn't like talking about her. He grew up with his grandmother, but she died a few months ago. Everyone always disappears. Six months now, exactly, since she died. She used to take care of them, in Honduras, but it was his aunt, the same aunt now sitting in the back of the courtroom, who had always sent money.

How do you like living with your aunt?

He likes her. But even though she is family, he's never really known her. She had always been just a voice inside the telephone. She called in regularly, from New York, to see how they were all doing. I ask who "they" were, to get a clearer picture. Or, in other words, question nineteen, with its respective branches, which in turn branch out, into always more and more complex stories:

Who else did you live with in your home country?

I lived with my grandmother and my two cousins, Patricia and Marta.

How old are they?

Nineteen and thirteen. No, wait, nineteen and fourteen.

Are they still there now? Do you talk to them?

No.

So where are they?

They are on their way here.

To the US?

Yes.

With whom?

A coyote of course.

Paid by whom?

My aunt, sitting over there.

Is she their aunt too?

No, she's their mother.

The reason for the trip that the two girls are also now making, following Manu's trip, doesn't become clear to me until we finally come to questions thirty-one, -two, and -three:

Did you ever have trouble with gangs or crime in your home country?

Yes, I did, he says.

He later pulls out a folded piece of paper from his pocket. It's a copy of a police report he filed against gang members, who waited for him outside his high school every day. He's held on to the report for a couple of years now, guarded it during his journey north like a sort of passport or talisman.

Can you tell me more about that incident?

He tells a confusing, fragmented story about the MS-13 and their ongoing fight against the Barrio 18. One was trying to recruit him. The other was going after him. One day some boys from Barrio 18 waited for him and his best friend outside their school. When they saw them there, Manu and his friend knew they couldn't fight them. There were too many of them. He and his friend walked away. They were followed.

They tried running. They ran, ran for a block or two, until there was a gunshot. Manu turned around—still running—and saw that his friend had fallen. More gunshots followed, but he carried on running.

Questions thirty-four and thirty-five:

Any problems with the government in your home country? If you did, what happened?

My government? They don't do anything, that's the only problem.

That night, after the incident with the gang, he called his aunt in New York. They decided he would leave the country as soon as possible. He didn't attend his friend's funeral. He didn't leave the house during the weeks that followed. Until the day came when the coyote arrived at his door. His aunt paid the coyote $4,000. He and Manu left at dawn one day. Manu explains that boys cost $4,000 and girls $3,000.

Why?

Because boys are the worst, he says, smiling wide.

We go over the rest of the story: from Tegucigalpa to Guatemala by bus, to the Mexican border, to Arriaga and then aboard La Bestia, to the US-Mexico border, the icebox, the shelter, the airplane, and finally Long Island, New York. But he suddenly narrates an unexpected turn: Just weeks after he left, his two cousins, Patricia and Marta, began to be harassed by the same gang that had killed his best friend. That's when his aunt, Alina, decided that she'd rather pay the $3,000 for each of her daughters, and put them through the dangers of the journey north, than let them stay. That's why the two girls are now on their way to the US.

The next time I see Manu, six months later, we're in a large room on the twenty-somethingth floor of a corporate building next to South Ferry. We can see Staten Island from the window, and if we stretch our necks to the right, we can see the Statue of Liberty. The setting is almost unreal, as if we've been thrust into a high-budget production of a bad Hollywood movie. I sense his disbelief and perhaps he senses mine, too.

An organization in court has found him pro bono lawyers in this large firm, and they've called me to continue translating for his case. We sit around a large black table: Manu, his aunt, three lawyers who speak only English, and me. We are offered coffee and snacks. Alina and I say yes to the coffee. Manu says he'll have some of everything if it's free. I translate:

He says, yes please, that's very kind of you.

The meeting serves the sole purpose of preparing Manu's SIJS application, though he's probably more likely eligible for asylum. An asylum application, however, is more complex, and its granting also entails harsher consequences, like not being able to return to his home country. So we go through the lawyers' contract, and then through his application. Everything runs smoothly, until the lawyers ask if Manu is still enrolled in school. He is, he says. He's at Hempstead High School. But he wants to leave as soon as possible.

Why? they want to know. They remind him that if he wants to be considered for any type of formal relief, he has to be enrolled in school.

He hesitates. But he suddenly opens his mouth wide, showing his teeth and gums. He's missing two teeth on the top row. He closes his mouth again and says:

I used to laugh at my grandma 'cause she had no front teeth, and now I look in the mirror and I laugh at me.

He talks slowly and in a low voice, but perhaps more confidently than when I first met him in court, months ago. He looks down at his clasped hands now and again as he talks. Hempstead High School, he then tells us, is a hub for MS-13 and Barrio 18. I turn cold at hearing this statement, which he delivers in the tone one might use to talk about items in a supermarket. He's afraid of Barrio 18. They beat his teeth out of his mouth. MS-13 boys saved him from losing the rest of his teeth.

Suddenly, we all want to ask questions thirty-six and thirty-seven: "Have you ever been a member of a gang? Any tattoos?" No, he has no tattoos. And no, he's never been part of a gang. The MS-13 in Hempstead wants him, but he's not going to fall for it. Not now, more than ever. He'd rather disappear than join them, now more than ever.

What do you mean by now more than ever, Manu? I ask, forgetting for a moment my role as translator.

I mean now that my two cousins are here with us and I have to look out for them better 'cause New York is a shithole just as full of pandilleros.

When I asked Manu after the meeting what he thought of Hempstead, he said it was almost as ugly as Tegucigalpa, but that at least it was home to Method Man, from the Wu-Tang Clan. I told him Hempstead was also, coincidentally, the town in which I had just started teaching. He promised to show me around one day. He hasn't. In a later web search, to corroborate the strange fact about Method Man, I find that Hempstead is also where Walt Whitman lived for a while, and where the fourth most obese man in the world was born. I start reading about the town: it is a broken community, which has served as a kind of stage for the Bloods and the Crips for more than forty years. There is a 1999 album by the rapper A+, called *Hempstead High*. The hit single from the album is called "Enjoy Yourself," and in the final stanza A+ says: "Actin' all wild, unprofession-al / Who got beef, I knock teeth out ya smile / But my lyrical lubricant keeps the crowd movin'." I hear the song over and over as I ride the Long Island Railroad one day on my way to Hempstead—the irony of those words pounding in my head.

There is a saying in Spanish: *De Guatemala a Guatepeor*—from Guatebad to Guateworse. Almost 5,000 kilometers separate Tapachula, the Guatemala-Mexico border town from which La Bestia departs, from New York. Hundreds of thousands of kids have made the journey, tens of thousands have made it to the border, thousands to New York. Why did you come to the United States? To find, at school, in their new neighborhoods, the very things they were running from?

Thirty-eight: "What do you think will happen if you go back home?" Some months later, in a phone interview with Alina in which I am still trying to put some pieces of the story together, she tells me that she had brought Manu over from Honduras when she realized it was no longer a joke, "no longer children's games," she says.

They killed his friend in front of him you know, and I knew he'd be next, she said.

Thirty-nine: "Are you scared to return?" Alina also tells me that she brought the girls over after some pandilleros started waiting outside her eldest daughter's college every day, following her slowly back home on motorbikes as she walked along the side of the road, trying not to look back. The same coyote that brought Manu to the US brought them. The one that is now nineteen was put in jail after she crossed the border, because she was not a minor, and Alina had to pay $7,500 to get her out. I don't ask where she's getting all the money. I suppose that her life savings, and her husband's, have all gone into bringing their three teenagers over. It was unimaginable to put them through the danger of the journey north, until it became unimaginable to let them stay over there. Forty: "Who would take care of you if you were to return to your home country?"

US law guarantees education for all children, no matter their nationality or immigration status. Every child is entitled to free public education. But not all children know this, nor do their parents necessarily know it. With the large influx of new migrant children, many schools in the country are overwhelmed, and negligent administrators simply push parents back when they call to ask about enrolling their children. Many school districts have reacted by creating more obstacles for newcomers. One of these is New York's Nassau County, which has the fifth-largest population of migrant children in the country. It is also the district where I work. Public schools in Nassau County have denied entrance to many children, based on their not having appropriate immigration papers—something that is by all means an illegal practice. In the summer of 2015, the New York State Education Department held a compliance review and in the end determined that no public school was allowed to ask students for immigration documents of any type.

But not all schools are complying. For months now, Alina has been trying to find a different school for Manu. The two girls are not as vulnerable to gang coercion, she thinks, but she would also like to move them. In fact, the older one is supposed to be in college, not in high school, but they've told her that her English is not good enough for college yet. They've told her that Manu's English is not good enough for another high school either, and his documents are not complete and in order, and there is no space anywhere anyway. I ask her who "they" are. She's silent for a moment and then says:

Whoever answers the telephone when I call a school.

So what happens next? I ask her.

Tell me how it ends, Mamma, she asks me.

What happened later? she wants to know.

Sometimes I make up an ending, a happy one. But most of the time I just say:

I don't know yet.

IV. A COMMUNITY (CODA)

As I begin to write this piece, it is late in November of 2015. My niece is majoring in law, and working for a research initiative at City College on the Politics of Sexual Violence, with one of the most lucid activists in the area. My green card has still not arrived, and my provisional work permit expired a few days ago. I am not illegal but it is now illegal for me to work in the US. I am not allowed to volunteer, either, according to immigration law. I have wondered if I am "allowed" to write—writing is work, after all. But of course I do write and I will write, because it's the only thing I can do to not go crazy.

I have had to resign temporarily from my teaching job, leaving fifty college students without a teacher right before their finals. Ten of those fifty students had been hearing me ramble on about the 2014 American Immigration Crisis in a class we all decided to call a "migration think tank" rather than the "Spanish conversation" course I was supposed to be teaching. During our first encounters these ten students looked at me very silently and with a sort of congealed bewilderment, which I usually prefer to attribute to their excess of hormones and lack of sleep rather than to their apathy or my want of better teaching skills. And I think I may have been right this time not to judge them or myself too harshly, too quickly. Midway into the semester, they started to speak up. They began asking difficult questions, and started articulating sophisticated opinions. Conscious of my own limitations in the subject matter, I brought in experts to talk to us: immigration lawyers, social workers, activists, and political scientists. The semester rolled on, and it seemed to me that for once, a class I was giving was not just following a syllabus but was growing quite naturally out of our group's shared concerns and questions.

One October morning, my students came to class particularly anxious. All the while they shuffled in their seats, whispered to each other, looked around the classroom and out the window. I stopped class and asked what was wrong with them—expecting to hear nothing back. But someone at last said:

Nothing, Prof.

Nothing?

Nothing. We just want to tell you something, another said.

What is it? I asked, sure that they would boycott, or that they would ask to leave early that day.

Well you know how you brought in that professor to talk to us?

Professor Gowrinathan?

Yes, that one.

Yes, I remember.

And remember, Prof, how she said that we had to try to turn emotional capital into political capital?

Yes, I remember.

Well we want to suggest a political student organization that does that.

What do you mean? I asked.

An organization for teenage migrants so we can do something instead of just talking about things, another one said.

You know, Prof—we don't want to be voluntourists in our own town, so we have to do something more concrete.

So these ten college students drafted a constitution, appointed duties, and got the university's approval. Their organization is called LA TIIA—which plays on the Spanish *tía*, or "aunt," and stands for Teenage Immigrant Integration Association. Their idea was simple and brilliant: if the immigration crisis started at the US-Mexico border, in southern Arizona or Texas, and then moved up all the way to the NY immigration court, and now there are children and teenage migrants living in the most remote towns of Long Island, it's not going to end there. The crisis will deepen and spread, and things will fall apart, unless all those kids find a way

175

to become quickly and fully integrated. These kids have just been through the worst. They arrive to find an unfamiliar country, a new language, but also a group of strangers that they must now call their family. They have to deal with family reunifications, interrupted education, acculturation, and trauma.

Because Long Island, and Nassau County in particular, is so terribly deficient when it comes to public education and services, the private universities in the area have to offer some kind of sustained relief, my students say. We have the space here, the resources, the classrooms, the football fields, and the radio station. The solutions have to be simple and concrete, they say. No "let's empower the migrants" kind of empty jargon. There have to be intensive English classes, college prep sessions, team sports, a radio program, and a civil rights and duties discussion group. They want to partner with organizations such as The Door, in Manhattan, and S.T.R.O.N.G., a nonprofit that focuses on teenagers in Long Island who are particularly vulnerable to falling into gangs.

It only takes a group of ten motivated students to begin making a small difference. LA TIIA will begin formal activities in the early months of 2016.

The question comes back to me often now that it is not clear if my green card is going to arrive: "Why did you come to the United States?" I don't have an answer. No one does, really. But you will end up trying to stay in America, the country, as if it were a denser space than all the others—its gravitational pull so irresistible. You begin to imagine the place where you originally came from as a backyard might look from a high window in the deep of winter: a space impossible to resuscitate, a past filled with objects obsolete and out of place. You will end up wanting to play a part in the great theater of belonging. You will unlearn the universal metric system so you can buy a pound and a half of cooked ham, accept that thirty-two degrees, and not zero, is where the line falls that divides cold and freezing. You might even begin to celebrate the pilgrims who removed the alien Indians, and the veterans who maybe killed other aliens, and the day of a president who will eventually declare a war on all the other so-called aliens. No matter the cost. No matter the cost of the rent, and milk, and cigarettes. You will give everything. You will convince yourself that it is only a matter of time before you can be yourself again, in America, despite the added layers of its otherness, already so well adhered to your skin. But perhaps you will never want to be your former self again. There are things that ground you to this life as if it were an inevitable, necessary place. Why did you come to the United States? Because there is more to America, and the cruelty of its borders is only a thin crust. There is a sense of community that, though so often so crippled, is what brought you here.

A NOTE ON INTERVIEWS AND ACKNOWLEDGMENTS

The stories told in this essay are true. All names of the children I have interviewed in court, as well as specific facts about their biographical information and that of their sponsors, have been changed in order to protect them. The dates of specific events and the order in which they may have occurred have also been modified for the same reason.

I want to thank the following organizations and think tanks: The Door, Safe Passage, S.T.R.O.N.G., the Migration Policy Institute, the Politics of Sexual Violence Initiative, the American Immigration Lawyers Association, and the Teenage Immigrant Integration Association. For their insights, support, and enthusiasm I want to give special thanks to Rebecca Sosa, Michael Vargas, Angela Hernández, Nimmi Gowrinathan, and Ana Puente; and to my students at

Hofstra University: Gardenia Benros, Jacqueline Berkovsky, Nicole Caico, Lourdes Carballo, Maria Carbone, Benjamin Cope, Pauleen Samantha Jean-Louis, Brandon Jurewicz, Amanda Moncada, and Jessica Simonelli.

BIBLIOGRAPHIC AND OTHER SOURCES

Beyond the interviews with children and their family members, for my research I have also used policy reports, fact sheets, documentaries, newspaper articles, and email exchanges. These are mentioned below in the order in which they appear and in relation to the sentence/s in the text that they support.

1. *Nothing is clear in the initial coverage of the situation—which will soon be known more widely as the 2014 American Immigration Crisis, though others will advocate for the more accurate term "refugee crisis."* Source: Sonia Nazario, "The Children of the Drug Wars: A Refugee Crisis, Not an Immigration Crisis," *New York Times*, July 11, 2014. [See page 144]

2. *"Protesters, some exercising their open-carry rights, assemble outside of the Wolverine Center in Vassar [Michigan] that would house illegal juveniles to show their dismay for the situation."* Source: Lindsay Knake, "Protesters Carry AR Rifles, Flags in March Against Central American Teens Coming to Vassar," Michigan Live (MLive.com), July 15, 2014. [Page 144]

3. *A caption in a Reuters image explains another photograph, where elderly men and women sit in beach chairs holding banners saying "Illegal Is a Crime"; "Thelma and Don Christie (C) of Tucson demonstrate against the arrival of undocumented immigrants in Oracle, Arizona."* Source: Paul Ingram, "Arizona Town Protests Arrival of Undocumented Migrant Kids," Reuters, July 15, 2014. [Page 144]

4. . . . *hundreds of kids, some traveling with their mothers, some traveling alone, are being put on airplanes and will be deported that*

same day back to Honduras. Source (among several): Associated Press, "Immigrants in New Mexico Deported to Central America," July 14, 2014. [Page 145]

5. *"Looking happy, the deported children exited the airport on an overcast and sweltering afternoon. One by one, they filed into a bus, playing with balloons they had been given."* Source: Gabriel Stargardter, "First US Flight Deports Honduran Kids Under Fast-Track Push," Reuters, San Pedro Sula, Honduras, July 15, 2014. [Page 146]

6. *. . . the freight trains that cross Mexico, on top of which as many as half a million Central American migrants ride annually.* Source: Rodrigo Dominguez Villegas, "Central American Migrants and 'La Bestia': The Route, Dangers, and Government Responses," Migration Policy Institute, September 10, 2014. [Page 147]

7. *Thousands have died or been gravely injured aboard La Bestia, either because of its constant derailments, or by falling off during the night, or by falling into the hands of smugglers, policemen, and thieves.* Source: Padre Alejandro Solalinde et al. *La Bestia* (Documentary). Miami: Venevision International, 2011. [Page 147]

8. *. . . we see a discreet trail of flags that volunteer groups tie to trees or fences, in order to indicate that there are tanks filled with water there for people to drink as they cross the desert.* Source: I wrote an e-mail to the translator Kevin Gerry Dunn, who has worked for volunteer groups, asking about this. He replied: "The water tanks with the flags are left by a group called Humane Borders. I believe that they have permission from the government to leave these tanks in designated spots. The problem is that they're big and unwieldy, so they have to be left near main roads, where migrants are much less likely to walk for fear of getting caught. Other groups (the two I know of in Arizona are No More Deaths and Samaritans, though there may be others) leave gallon jugs along migrant paths, where migrants are much more likely to find them. These gallons are regularly slashed by vigilantes and/or Border Patrol. In one instance

Border Patrol was caught on video vandalizing a drop (https://www.youtube.com/watch?v=za_Tmt9rSGI)." [Page 148]

9. . . . *eighty percent of the women and girls who cross Mexico to get to the US border are raped on the way. The situation is so common that most of them take contraceptive precautions as they begin the journey north.* Source: Eleanor Goldberg, "80% of Central American Women, Girls Are Raped Crossing into the US," *Huffington Post*, September 12, 2014. [Page 149]

10. *In 2010, the bodies of seventy-two Central American migrants were found piled up inside a ranch in Tamaulipas.* Source (among others): In 2010, the Mexican journalist Alma Guillermoprieto inquired further and also organized a discussion group of writers and journalists to write about the tragic event. A webpage and "altar" were created in memory of the seventy-two, containing information about the event and, when available, about the deceased: www.72migrantes.com/recorrido.php. [Page 149]

11. *That same year, a sixteen-year-old boy on the Mexican side of the border was shot to death by an American officer on the US side, who claimed the boy and other people had thrown rocks at him.* Source (most recent article on the matter): Nigel Duara, "Family of Mexican Boy Killed by Border Patrol Agent Can Sue, Judge Rules," *Los Angeles Times*, July 10, 2015. [Page 150]

12. *In 2013, the US Border Patrol found the remains of 463 migrants—most of whose deaths were unaccounted for, and most of whom were found near Tucson, on the US side of the border.* Source: Fernanda Santos and Rebekah Zemansky, "Arizona Desert Swallows Migrants on Riskier Paths," *New York Times*, May 20, 2013. [Page 150]

13. *Later, in the summer of 2015, it was known that between April 2014 and August 2015, more than 102,000 unaccompanied children had been detained at the border.* Source: Sarah Pierce, "Unaccompanied Child Migrants in US Communities, Immigration Court, and Schools," Migration Policy Institute, October 2015. [Page 152]

14. *They remain there for up to seventy-two hours, though many complaints have been made because children are kept for longer, subject not only to the inhuman temperatures, but also to verbal and physical mistreatment.* Sources: "A Guide to Children Arriving at the Border: Laws, Policies and Responses," American Immigration Council, June 26, 2015; Cindy Carcamo, "Judge Blasts ICE, Says Immigrant Children, Parents in Detention Centers Should Be Released," *Los Angeles Times*, July 25, 2015. [Page 154]

15. *In July 2015, for example, AILA filed a complaint after learning that in a detention center in Dilley, Texas, 250 children were mistakenly given adult-strength hepatitis A vaccinations, and became gravely ill.* Source: Wendy Feliz and George Tzamaras, "Vaccine Overdose of Detained Children Another Sign That Family Detention Must End," American Immigration Council and American Immigration Lawyers Association, July 4, 2015. [Page 154]

16. *The states with the highest number of children released to sponsors since the crises was declared are Texas (above 10,000 children), California (almost 9,000 children), and New York (above 8,000 children).* Source: Sarah Pierce, "Unaccompanied Child Migrants in US Communities, Immigration Court, and Schools," Migration Policy Institute, October 2015. [Page 155]

17. *But what are the charges, exactly? Fundamentally, that the child came to the United States without lawful permission. Admitting these charges alone would lead to deportation unless the child's attorney can find those potential avenues of relief that form a defense against deportation.* Source: In an e-mail exchange with immigration lawyer Rebecca Sosa, she explained: "Although the formal charges are uniform, a child's first hearing before the judge varies depending on factors such as whether the child has an attorney, and whether it is a case on the priority docket, which the government has fast-tracked and imposed short deadlines to move the cases along faster." [Page 158]

18. . . . *the majority of children who do find a lawyer do appear in court and are granted some form of relief. All the others are deported, either* in absentia *or in person.* Sarah Pierce, "Unaccompanied Child Migrants in US Communities, Immigration Court, and Schools," Migration Policy Institute, October 2015. [Page 160]

19. . . . *despite the creation of the priority docket, many cases filed between October 2013 and August 2015 (55,513) remain unresolved. That's, more than forty percent of them. There have been 14,024 removals* in absentia, *and 3,360 removal orders and "voluntary departures" in person. On the other hand, 11,610 children have been given "informal" relief, such as prosecutorial discretion; but only 313 cases have received formal relief.* Sarah Pierce, "Unaccompanied Child Migrants in US Communities, Immigration Court, and Schools," Migration Policy Institute, October 2015. Author note: These numbers may not be accepted by all, and the purported 11,610 "informal" reliefs have to be taken with a grain of salt. [Page 161]

20. *And without legal status, they are likely to live and work in the shadows, without access to social safety nets like health insurance and without legal representation to determine if they have any other routes to pursue lawful immigration status.* Source: In an e-mail, immigration lawyer Rebecca Sosa explains, "There is no right to legal representation in the immigration context because it is a civil proceeding, and the rights to counsel protections present in the criminal context do not apply. All immigrants seeking immigration benefits or defending their cases have a right to obtain counsel at no expense to the US government, meaning they have to find and pay for their own attorney or find an attorney who will work for free. Also, some undocumented immigrants are eligible for some limited health care benefits, but only until they reach age 19." [Page 162]

21. *Many school districts have reacted by creating more obstacles for newcomers. One of these is New York's Nassau County, which has the fifth-largest population of migrant children in the*

country. Sarah Pierce, "Unaccompanied Child Migrants in US Communities, Immigration Court, and Schools," *Migration Policy Institute,* October 2015. [Page 173]

22. *In the summer of 2015, the New York State Education Department held a compliance review and in the end determined that no public school was allowed to ask students for immigration documents of any type.* Source: Benjamin Mueller, "Immigrants' School Cases Spur Enrollment Review in New York," *New York Times,* October 22, 2014; and "Requirements Keep Young Immigrants Out of Long Island Classrooms," *New York Times,* October 21, 2014. [Page 173]

H. M. NAQVI is the award-winning author of *Home Boy*. Published by Random House in 2009, the debut was hailed as a "remarkably engaging novel that delights as it disturbs" by the *New York Times*. It has been translated into German, Italian, and Portuguese, and was awarded the DSC Prize for South Asian Literature at the Jaipur Literature Festival in 2011. Naqvi has worked in the financial services industry, taught creative writing at Boston University, and run a spoken-word venue. He resides in Karachi, where he is completing his second novel, "a big, bad comic epic"; working on a collection of nonfiction; and engaging in an initiative to revive the old city.

The Selected Works of Abdullah (The Cossack)

H. M. NAQVI

CRITICAL DIGRESSIONS
(OR THIS AND THAT & THE OTHER)

My head is like a rubbish heap: you have to sift through the muck to find a working toaster. When I was eleven, I overheard one of my brothers telling another that I am a bastard. They say if you scale the cliff at Shah Noorani (RA), you happen upon the clenched mouth of a cave; they say if you can manage to crawl in, you are your father's son. I do not patronize Shah Noorani (RA)—if I am a bastard, I am a bastard—but you might find me at the seaside shrine of Abdullah Shah Ghazi (RA) on a Thursday night, inhaling hashish among the malcontents who congregate on the rocky southern slant of the hill. It's always a carnival. There are fortune-tellers, bodybuilders, thugs, troubadours, transvestites, women & sweet, rowdy children. I am at home there.

When I enter the cool confines of Agha's Supermarket to purchase Smoked Gouda, however, shoppers part to give me way.[1] Those who knew me once turn to memorize the sodium content in shelved cans of French Onion Soup. The last time I was there dragging myself through the aisles, I called out to this busty, sixty-six-year-old Persian cat who just held her fifty-fifth birthday party. Although she is married to a portly patrician now, she would be at the Olympus in the old days, making eyes at the young men with carnations fixed in their lapels. When I hooted *Sweety!* she paused for a moment, as if recalling to cross off the loaf of bread from her list, before disappearing around the corner from the shoe polish and lighter fluid. Verily, decency is dead or dying.

I have been mulling some permutation of the Mythopoetic Legacy of Abdullah Shah Ghazi (RA) since the fateful day my father asked me to punctuate the following sentence: *That that is that is that and that that is not that is not.* Naturally, I retorted, "Comma after the sixth word, sir!" Papa could be difficult but I knew then that he had in an indirect way communicated to me his aspiration for me to be a phenomenologist even if he would deny it vehemently afterwards.

There is no doubt in my mind that my mother would have encouraged the project. A fine lady of Afghan blood and deportment, Mummy spoke Urdu like a native because her clan claims to have been settled in the Subcontinent since the Reign of Sher Shah of Bihar. When she entered a room, people squinted as if she were wrought of light. If I close my eyes I can recall hers: bright, blue, and sunny like the sea at Sonmiani. Married to a cousin at seventeen, the Khan of This or That Khanate, she ran away when she realized that he was only

---

1. Of course, one frequented Ghulam Mohammed Brothers for bread & butter in the old days, and Bliss & Co. for tonics & balms. Long after the proprietors, Mr. & Mrs. Black, sold the business & moved to the U.K., they wintered at the Olympus yearly. You can, by the way, still pick up a bottle of Bliss Carbonate or Calamine at pharmacies in the city, presumably even at Agha's.

interested in hunting partridge. She met Papa at the Olympus in '29 when visiting an aunt twice removed for high tea. She had five sons with rhyming names: Ataullah, Bakaullah, Abdullah, Fazlullah a.k.a. Tony & Rahimullah a.k.a. Babu. When Mummy passed, the family became unglued.

After retiring as a Major from the army in the seventies, Ataullah moved to a palatial residence in the suburbs featuring a diamond-shaped pool while Bakaullah, once a card-carrying communist, immigrated to some dusty corner of the Near East where he reportedly runs a logistics and transportation business. Tony, my favourite brother and boon companion,[2] left for college in the United States of America before squatting on our estate in Scinde where he cultivates women and produces wine—our very own vinos de la tierra.

I am certain I was Mummy's favourite. She raised me to be myself. I am not a bad man, not a particularly good one either, and am not good for much anymore. I am a fat man, and an anxious one. The insides of my thighs chafe when I climb down the stairs from my quarters. I avoid loitering downstairs because my youngest brother, Babu, lives on the mezzanine with his plain, moon-faced wife Nargis, a lass with all the charm of an opossum, and his twin boys. The arrangement poses a bit of a problem because I love the children, those two crazy little Childoos.

When they manage to break free, they sneak up on me like those Ninja Warriors[3] and clamber atop my domed belly. We sing, cavort, sneak up to the roof to observe the silently sundering clouds, the

2. I christened Tony Tony because as a child he could not pronounce his own name—like all our names, it is a mouthful—and because he resembled Tony Curtis circa *The Prince Who Was a Thief*.

3. You might recall that that Lee Van Cleef chap—a peer by age perhaps if not by distinction—played a Ninja Warrior in the eponymous serial in the early eighties. I am no Lee Van Cleef. I cannot scale walls or walk between raindrops. I would be happy if I could scratch my back without risking a herniated disk.

odd meteor. We startle the nesting crows to put the fear of God in their black hearts. When their rasping protests ring in the still of the evening, Nargis the Opossum comes bounding up the stairs. She does not approve. She changes the rules all the time:

1) No Taking the Children to the Roof at Night (or during the Day, the Afternoon or at Sunset)
2) No Feeding the Children Walnuts (or Custard Apples, Chili Chips, Sugar Wafers)
3) No Singing Tom Jones to the Children (or Cliff Richards, Boney M., the Benjamin Sisters)

And even though I cradled him in my arms, carried him on my shoulders, even though I taught him how to whistle, how to say thank you—*thunku*, he said—the aforementioned Babu is not an ally. Many years ago, he laughed when informed I am a bastard. Like many, like most, he quietly judged me then; he quietly judges me now. I don't care. I am not going anywhere. A fortune-teller named Sarbuland once told me, "Tum lambi race kay ghoray ho," or *You are the horse of the long race.*

But I am not the same man I was yesterday.

A NOTE ON ONTOLOGICAL PANIC

I wake feeling fraught and delicate like a soft-boiled egg for I have transformed into that dwindling subspecies, *Homo septuagenari*, overnight, and there are few conjunctures that stupefy, that jar the soul than the thought of a life misspent. Lying amid faded canvases, steamer trunks, rolled Turkish rugs, Mummy's cut-glass perfume bottle collection, China from the Olympus, a brass candelabra, a functioning clockwork gramophone, the cadaver of an exercise bicycle, several dusty Betamax recorders, I stare at the whirring fan with one open cataract-swept eye, dimly pitting reasons for and against remaining prone: *Nobody would care if you stayed in bed*, I tell myself. *You're a sad old man, an animal: you drool, stain your knickers*. It is a downpour of self-pity, a veritable monsoon of misery. Then the urge to relieve myself compels me to the commode. There is no doubt that there is reprieve if not respite in ritual, in bowel movements (even if the exercise has become trying on account of my piles), & in the pages of *The New Golden Treasury of English Verse*.[4] Oh, that golden crowd! What jocund company!

Slipping into Mummy's jungle-print robe de chambre, I take tea and insulin on the balcony. The sky is cloudless and blue, the air smoky and trilling with crickets. An old crow perches on the ledge above, cawing hoarsely, damnably, like the Angel Israfil. I won't get any work done today; I have the feeling that it will be a very long day, or a very short one. Draining the acrid lees, I hoist myself from the cane armchair, dentures rattling in pocket, and teeter purposefully towards the railing. As I consider the diagonally inclined potted cacti, the pansy bed below, I notice a pair of eyes peering at me over the horizon of the boundary wall as if I am on display—a primate shelling nuts. "Stop, Kookaburra, stop," I chunter, returning the gaze through the interstices of the evergreens, "That's not a monkey, it's me." But then I apprehend the manifest drama: I am brandishing my member, flush and bulbous and overrun with wild reddish hair. As usual, I have nothing to show for myself.

Uncannily, the eyes, fantastic obsidian eyes, follow me as I collect my genitalia in the teacup and nearly trip down the spiral staircase. I am curious, mortified, titillated. Imagine: a seraph, a siren, a sphinx!

---

4. A cursory survey of my lavatory library would reveal back issues of *She*, *MAG*, *The Civil & Military Gazette*, as well as *The Field Guide to Ocean Animals*, *Justine*, *Not Without My Daughter*, & *Freedom at Midnight*. The most entertaining of the lot, the lot that belongs in the loo, is Maulana Thanvi's *Heavenly Ornaments*. Did he not expire on the pot?

But mythology has long ceded to the mundane: it is, more likely, the usual transvestite, the maid's good-for-nothing locksmith husband or that swine Chambu,[5] the manager of my piddling garment-dyeing operation who fleeces me every quarter then demands Sundry Expenses. Sundry my foot! By the time I cross the lawn, fastening my robe, the eyes vanish like fireflies taking flight. There is the usual activity outside: buses lurching, rickshaws sputtering, the odd, laden donkey cart, and at the corner, the street-side dentist sits on his haunches, administering what might be a root canal. Barefoot & breathless, I stand unsteadily on the toasty asphalt, considering the gaze that bore into my soul—*Who did it belong to? Why was I being watched? Why today?*—but then I hear the distinct voices of the Childoos over the clamour of traffic.

"Chachajaan!" they cry, "Cha! Cha! Jaan!" they chant. They are single-pasli, suffer from unfortunate bowl cuts and wear white button-down half sleeves, navy blue knickers, white socks pulled up to their scratched knees. They waddle as they run, run as they waddle, backpacks flapping, maid straggling behind. I pick them up, peck them on flushed cheeks, and break into song: "There lived a certain man in Russia long ago!"

"He was bigs and strong," they chime, "and eyes flaming gold."

And together we bellow: "RA-RA-RASPUTIN / Lover of the Russian queen / There was a cat that really was gone / RA-RA-RASPUTIN / Russia's greatest love machine / It was a shame how he carried on!"

We make a spectacle of ourselves—several passersby gather and gape—and why shouldn't we? We are loud and gay—the Von Trapps of Currachee! We might break into "Do-Re-Mi" next—an admittedly more apropos number—but have attracted the jaundiced attention of the authorities. I feel the quick teardrop eyes of my dear sister-in-law

---

5. Chambu, a portmanteau, was coined by Barbarossa when he was lucid: Chutiya + Lambu = Chambu.

on my back. Not one for song and spectacle, Nargis the Opossum leans against the gate, wrist on hip, sucking her teeth, shaking her draped head from side to side like a broken doll. "Chalo, chalain, bacho," she bids. "Lunchtime!"

Setting the children down, I surreptitiously fit my dentures into my mouth then turn to greet Nargis but she has already marched in, trailed by the Childoos, waving shyly. I wonder when I will see them again, wonder if they would know to wish me. Not even my pal Tony has called, but then who remembers the birthdays of sad old men? I swear to God I could stand kerbside all day, watching the world go by, waiting for those haunting eyes to gaze upon my hairless, roly-poly, chicken-flesh chest—any witnesses are welcome—but the day has become hot and brackish like a belch. Shutting the gate behind me, I return unceremoniously to my perch amid the clutter, and certain ontological panic. I consider launching myself over the balcony for the second time but mercifully my man appears, sporting one of those red and white baseball caps & joggers.

A pensioner, my pensioner, Barbarossa has been yanked from de facto retirement even though he hears voices—reportedly, a chatty djinn[6]—since the couple who cooked & cleaned for us did not return from leave. (Nargis has difficulty retaining help.) Although he has become as weathered as a banyan, it was once said that he possessed "the jib of Clark Gable." In the old days he would deliver the paper but I have no interest in the news anymore; now he only bears my daily jug of bitter gourd juice. "I won't abide this poison!" I protest. I have been protesting for a quarter century—bitter gourd tastes like vegetal diesel—but Barbarossa insists it mitigates sugar, & I am beholden to him: he oft saves me from myself.

6. The story goes that Nargis' preacher instructed her to say "*salam*" before entering a room. When she entered the garret one afternoon, a voice replied & she yelled bloody murder. Barbarossa's known him since.

"Juice especial today," he says in English. He speaks English on occasion. He picked it up buttling at the Olympus. In recent history, however, he is only wont to mutter gibberish: *Yessur, nossur, cocklediddledosur.*

"What? You garnished it with hemlock?"

Stroking his freshly hennaed beard, Barbarossa announces, "Is haypy-buday-juice!"

I kiss him on the head then slip him a note folded in the pocket of my robe, a tip for the welcome wishes, the welcome wine. I take a swig then ask him how he remembered, for the old fox is not always compos mentis. "You friend calling," he says. "I have no friends!" I cry. "Pinto," he says.

By Jove! Pinto, good old Felix Pinto, the Last Trumpeter of Currachee! I have been summoned to the Currachee Goan Association. "Prepare my bath!" I holler. "Dust off my smoking jacket! Iron my kerchief!"

In all the excitement, I forget the obsidian eyes, myself, and almost tumble over the balcony again.

AN ANECDOTAL HISTORY OF THE JAZZ AGE OF CURRACHEE

According to my friend and former colleague, Byram Avari, proprietor of the world famous Beach Luxury Hotel, jazz came to Currachee in March '53. He told me that when his parents were away in Beirut or Mauritius or someplace like that, he "booked this Dutch quartet, called several hundred people, many of them friends. The musicians played all night. There was a traffic jam in the parking lot." When jazz came to the city, it caused traffic jams.

Old Goan rockers, however, will tell you that they were grooving to jazz even earlier. They will tell you that their forefathers had started trickling into Bombay, Calcutta and Currachee by the middle of the nineteenth century to escape the Portuguese—a dashed scourge. There were D'Souzas, Fernandeses, Rodrigueses, Lobos, Nazareths. They set up St. Patrick's Cathedral with the Irish Fusiliers in 1881, and the Currachee Goan Association five years later. They organized choirs at the former, staged Gilbert and Sullivan operettas at the latter, and jazz, they will tell you, was in their blood. They sang and danced at jam sessions at each other's houses, in the backyards of Cincinnatus Town: somebody would bring a guitar, somebody else the drums, and horns had become de rigueur by the late fifties. And of course, everyone would bring liquor—Murree, caju feni or Goan hooch, and the foreign sauce, if they could afford it: Dimple, Black & White, Vat 69.[7]

Of course, there were also bars, clubs and cabarets: the Taj and the Lido and the Anglos congregated at the Burt Institute of the Railway Club. While others were waltzing properly across ballroom floors, the Goans were swinging to the Lindy Hop or shuffling to the Cha-Cha-Cha, to the Carvalho Trio or the legendary Janu Vaz Band.[8] Then Eddie Carrapiett began hosting the weekly radio show *Hit Parade* on Radio Pakistan, injecting jazzy riffs into the bloodstream of the city. One fine day Dizzy Gillespie rolled into town, selling out the garden at the Metropole. Duke Ellington showed up as well. It was a marvelous time.

Run by my father, a Khoja, the Shadow Lounge at the Olympus was naturally tamer than establishments such as the Excelsior where the likes of Gul Pari bared all, or Roma Shabana, where you

---

7. Three Parsee brothers—technically speaking, two brothers and a cousin—had a virtual monopoly on distribution in the country by the middle of the century. They ran the Quetta Distillery Ltd., which along with the Murree Brewery remain the premier producers of liquor in the country. Nota bene: one should avoid the latter's Peach Vodka. One should also avoid the products of that more recent Scindee distillery as they taste like paint thinner.

8. Lynette Dias-Gouveia reminded me that the band comprised Alex Rodrigues & Dominic Gonsalves on saxophone; John Fernandes on trumpets; double-bassist, David William; and Basil and Rudy D'Souza on the drums.

would attend cabarets featuring the likes of the Stambuli Sisters, or "Carmen & Anita in French Can-Can." What you got at the Shadow Lounge were musicians who knew their Bird from their Beiderbecke. The stage was elevated and so spacious that you could fit a chamber orchestra on it. It faced a round, oak dance floor which was surrounded by round tables draped by crimson tablecloths. There was a solid oak bar at the entrance and ferns everywhere and on a good night, there would be close to a hundred jazz aficionados arranged around tables, smoking 555s, sipping cocktails, before cramming the dance floor.

I knew all the musicians of that time because they were all regulars at the Olympus. They wore thin black ties and their black hair swept back. That's where I met everyone—The Ay Jays, The Bluebirds, The Thunders, The Keynotes—and one night I met this crazy, trumpet-playing cat, Felix Pinto, the Caliph of Cool.

It was said that the Caliph had had a hand in the composition of the National Anthem though the stories were apocryphal even then.[9] When asked, Pinto would grin mysteriously and raise a toast to the prosperity and well-being of the country—a wily strategy. Some attribute the commission to the Caliph's doppelgänger, old Dominic Gonsalves, but I believe that it belongs to Tollentine, or Tolly, Fonseca, a celebrated bandmaster known for original compositions that include the famous Barcelona Waltz, Officers' March, and Diwan-e-Khaas. I never had the opportunity to meet the man—he expired soon after the anthem was completed[10]—but have come across his

9. The words, of course, were penned by the renowned poet Hafiz Jallandari, and the orchestra, reportedly a navy band, was conducted by one Ahmed Chagla.
10. Although he was known to frequent the Olympus, I was not allowed into the bar then. I was eighteen when permitted into the bar area but didn't drink until my turn as the Cossack. It should be noted here, however, that since Mummy treated my childhood colds with brandy (to Papa's chagrin), I have, in a way, been weaned on drink.

nieces at Currachee Goan Association. In any event, the Caliph of Cool was a legend in his time.

Although the Shadow Lounge was dim, smoky and leafy, you could always spot Felix Pinto: he possessed a slick bouffant, a boxer's jaw and the shiniest trumpet this side of the Suez. He was a dandy in a way that was only possible in Currachee in the Sixties. He always sported shaded, thick-rimmed glasses, whether it was at three in the afternoon at Café Grand, or at three on a moonless morning at Clifton beach. I would wager that he wore them while bathing and sleeping. Because they were glued to his nose, you would have never noticed his sunken, blue, vertiginous eyes. Ask me then: how do I know?

Pinto's trademark spectacles were knocked off his face once and only once, one night at Le Gourmet circa '59, when he was biffed in the face during a drunken bar brawl with a young landowner who sported two-toned patent leather shoes. There was a woman involved, a sexy Anglo named Eleanor or something like that, and a spilt glass of wine. Although Pinto sported a black eye that night, he got his opponent in the bird's nest. When the boy crumpled, I whisked the Caliph out via the kitchen. Otherwise he would have had to contend with the thuggish entourage of the landowner.

When the landowner became Prime Minister some years later, I helped Pinto escape to Australia.[11] My friend knocked about down under during the Disco Era before returning to Currachee but by then, the prime minister had imposed prohibition in a gutless attempt to gain currency with the excitable religiously inclined rabble. The clubs, bars and cabarets were shut down soon after. (Naturally, the Olympus also suffered during his disconsolate reign but that's another story.) Many Goans left. It was the end of an age.

11. The Australian Consul-General at the time, a certain His Excellency Darling, was a friend of ours.

A NIGHT AT THE CURRACHEE GOAN ASSOCIATION
WITH THE CALIPH OF COOL (OR TAKE FIVE)

The Currachee Goan Association is housed in an imposing double-storied stone edifice featuring arched windows and cornices and pilasters flanking the entrance. There is a library and wine shop downstairs typically manned by a ruddy tubby chap whose mouth is permanently fixed in a golden grin, and a vast hall upstairs where concerts and plays and marriages are staged with great foon faan—not to mention the annual Valentine's & Independence Day balls. It is always cool inside because the walls are thick and the ceiling is high and the doors open out. You pass sequential portraits of the presidents of the institution when you enter whose solemn expressions suggest a tale that is best not to broach with the members of the storied institution.

I find Felix in a tatty tuxedo and dark glasses towards the far end, leaning for effect, nursing one of those deadly bottles of feni. "I looked at him," he is saying, "he looked at me, then I said, 'Why don't you sit on the trumpet, mister!'" There is a roar of laughter from the audience, a cast of pirates arranged in a circle: there is the barkeep, the magnificently named Titus Gomes, and two others, a walnut of a fellow with bushy whiskers, and a pelican type who elbows Pinto upon my advent.

Waving his arms as if parting a stage curtain, Felix proclaims, "Ah, the Cossack cometh! Happy birthday, you rascal!" Turning to the trio, he adds, "He might be a Mussalman, but he's all right!" They all hoot and toot and raise empty glasses. "Get the birthday boy a chair, and some feni." Although I rarely partake on account of sugar and gout, I cannot refuse my old friend. I down a Patiala peg[12] and wince. It feels warm going down, feels like the old days.

---

12. Recall that the Maharaja of the Princely State of Patiala invented the measurement to beat the team of visiting Irishmen on the field. They, of course, fell for it.

"I was going to hold a party for you, man," Felix begins, "but you don't have any friends anymore, and mine are dead or in Australia—which is the same thing. You know, I've been everywhere in that penal colony of a country—Perth, Sydney, Melbourne, Adelaide, I've even been to that big rock in the outback—and I tell you I'm happy in this godforsaken place any day. *How ya goin? What tribe ya from?* they ask. 'Goan, man,' I'd say, 'Pakistani,' and they think I'm saying Papua New Guinea. *G'day, mate, good on ya.* Sure, I played gigs there, good gigs, or good enough, but here I've got a name, a place—"

"Context—"

"Exactly, man, exactly! You have a way with words, Cossack."

"That's what I do—"

"You know, I walk into any hotel in this city and somebody comes running, *Good afternoon, sir, good evening*, sir, because they know I'm an old-timer. I've survived. The other day, I was at the Intercon, and who do I see? Do you remember that bachcha Yusuf? He'd say, call me Joseph, Mr. Pinto, and I'd say, Joseph, help me carry the equipment back to the Foxy. Now he's a seth. He owns buildings on the beachfront. *Anything you need*, he said, *you call me.* He palms me his card but what do I need? I need a drink, I need my trumpet. I need people to know that I am the best bloody trumpet player in the country."

"They need to know you knocked out the prime minister—"

"Exactly, man, exactly!"

"Aun-houn," Titus chimes in.

"Enough jib-jab!" Pinto proclaims. "Time to jam!"

As he bites his trumpet, the others conjure a double bass and an accordion, and Titus Gomes joins in, dhol in tow. (The snare drum, I learn, is torn.) "I know what you want to hear, Cossack," Pinto says, tapping his foot. "Happy birthday, old friend."

What follows is an awesome rendition of "Take Five," more Puente than Brubeck, more technically marching band perhaps than jazz:

197

Titus beats the edge of the dhol tentatively with a bamboo stick, reproducing the sensation of the introductory movement of the number, that peculiarly syncopated 5/4 beat—duddud-duddud -da-da-da, duddud- duddud-da-da-da—while the walnut strums the double bass as if this was the moment he was preparing for since the Dawn of Time. When the trumpet enters the medley, I shut my eyes. You have to shut your eyes.

"Take Five" is like you are flying, arms extended, inhaling the beach at Seaview on a cool December evening, duddud- duddud-da-da-da, duddud-duddudda-da-da. You see floodlights lighting up loping camels, and miniature families huddled around miniature stalls roasting corn on charcoal. If you are lucky, you see a lass dancing in the surf, her wispy aquamarine dupatta fluttering in the breeze. If you are lucky you see the silver-grey fin of a dolphin cutting the silver-grey waves, duddud-daada-da-da-da, duddud-daada-da-da-da.

The Felix Pinto Quartet play into the night. They play Armstrong and Getz. They play selections from the ragtime canon and even a couple of Bollywood numbers, including that modern classic, "Shadmani."[13] They play until they are tired and sottish and can play no more. When they are done, the walnut dozes in a corner, squeaking through his nose. Then Pinto, clutching his drooling trumpet, puts an arm around me and takes me aside. "I need a favor, Cossack."

There was a time when I could extend favors, when I had resources, succor. I was a different man then, a known man, a scion of a respected family. Although I have nothing, am nothing, the Caliph of Cool still believes I can help. "Of course, old friend," I slur. I do not want to disappoint, or disappoint immediately.

13. Recall the lyrics of said song: "Aaj to nasha aisa charha, puchon na yaron / Mein to aasmon pe, mujhay neechay utaro," or, "Don't ask me how drunk I am tonight, friend/ Can you help me get down from the clouds?" The number was de rigueur at weddings once. Now it's all just dances I don't dance and dish-dish boom-boom.

198

"Is my grandson, man, Bosco. My daughter's in a pickle and her husband's a doper so you need to put him up for some time. Teach him whatever the hell you do. It'll be good for him. It'll build character."

When I say I do not think I have had the pleasure of meeting said Bosco, a dark, gangly lad of twelve or thirteen emerges from the shadows. He has a long face, a parenthesis of a moustache, and wears a checkered shirt too big for his frame. For all I know, he might have been standing there all night. "Say hello to Uncle Cossack," instructs Pinto. "Hello, Uncle Cossack."

Lo and behold, a ward is thrust upon me. It is the damndest development.

THOUGHTS ON MEMORY (& THE MAKING OF MAN)

Verily memory is a tricky wench.[14] It catalogues images, episodes, reifies yesterday today, but recent research suggests yesterday's memory might change tomorrow or the day after. When I rake through the soil of memory, however, there are certain episodes impressed in my consciousness like pebbles: I remember a fearsome cat with a severed tail stalking me in the garden, remember waddling inside the Lodge, teary; remember my grandfather setting me on his bony lap, cooing in Gujarati, "Tamay kaim cho?" or *You okay?* Although he never completed school—he dropped out in seventh form—he could just negotiate the Queen's English because he had to: like his contemporaries—Messrs. Merchant, Mistry, Ebrahimji Sulemanji—he had business with the Britishers. When I would shove my foot in his shoe, for instance, he chided, "No naughty-pun!" I was six when he passed. I bawled when I beheld his shrouded corpse,

---

14. The opening sentence of fellow Khoja Badr-ud-Din Tyabji's *Memoirs of an Egoist* comes to mind.

bawled louder when I was told that he was going to Heaven. *There are rivers of milk there!* "But he didn't even drink milk," I sobbed in English. "He only took black tea!"

My father spoke English to me (so I have little Gujarati), and generally cultivated an English air about him: he sported hats and used the word "pardon" as a threat. One of my earliest memories features a smart young man in seersucker,[15] pulling into the driveway in a cool blue Impala as the staff stood in rapt attention. Of course, I also remember the wraith curled on an untidy bed in a striped sweater and lunghi one cold January night in '78. Whenever somebody else speaks of him—*Your father used to say*, or, *If only your father was alive*—some other face emerges from the Miasma of Memory. The canonical Papa, however, resides in the parlour downstairs (just as the canonical Mummy graces my chamber): rendered by a family friend,[16] the portrait betrays little: clad in a Jinnah cap, a black buttoned sherwani, he stares back, stands tall, fist on hip, at once commanding & indifferent. We all aspired to be like that figure. Perhaps that's why we all fell short.

When one thinks about it, my eldest brother Ataullah, looked most like him, down to the aquiline nose, though he was a breed apart: he was loud and even as a boy, somewhat louche. Fair and lean, Bakaullah, the next in line, looked more like Mummy, and though always temperamentally sober, he would become severe. Neither took interest in the flagship business, the Olympus. Ataullah did spend time in other hotels, carousing with the scions of the

15. Unbeknownst to most, "seersucker" is derived from the Urdu *khir* and *shukar*, or "pudding" and "sugar." Pudding! Sugar! Hoo! Ha!
16. Said friend was the late great Pakistani Jewish painter Samuel Fyzee Rahamin, protégé of one John Singer Sargent. The latter is often neglected by Western art critics while the former has been all but forgotten here though in recent years, I managed to sneak into a secret room in the Mohatta Palace Museum seven years back to see many a canvas.

established families, while Bakaullah, Comrade Bakaullah, frater-
nized with the Communists or Soorkhas who populated Zelin's &
Café George on Preedy. Later he organized discussions on rooftops
or street corners (attended by the likes of Syed Sibte Hassan) and
rallies supporting farmers, the labour movement, but his career
in activism came to an abrupt end when he was nabbed by the
authorities outside the Volk's House, the Soviet "cultural centre,"
for "subversive and suspicious activities." After spending seven
months in jail—Ataullah, a major in the army by then, lobbied the
IG police for an early release—Comrade Bakaullah left for points
West, or rather the Near or Middle West, to become a dyed-in-the-
wool capitalist. In his new incarnation, he hounded me because he
believed I was running the family into the ground. That is slander,
libel, bovine fecal matter.

It is true that unlike the Major or Comrade Bakaullah, I was
not a sportsman or academically accomplished.[17] I was a sensitive
child, a curious soul: I talked to myself, lolled in the garden. When
the neighbourhood children congregated to play tennikoit or gulli
danda in the vacant plot adjacent to Apollo House, I made figurines,
squatting in the flowerbed—the variety of local sphinxes featured
at fairs and mud-men recalling the Priest King of Mohenjo-daro.
Although the zoo was around the corner—you could hear the lions
roaring at night—I had a fetish for ants, beetles, dragonflies, creatures that conduct themselves with quiet resolve. While the others
waited for the tun-tun-wallah, I waited for the cycling librarian to
deliver *Reader's Digest*. Mummy called me "Anokhay Mian," or
Master Unusual.

---

17. Ataullah was tennis champion at the Gymkhana and then at St. Lawrence.
He was also a swimmer, runner—he ran the fifty metres—and later, took up
skeet-shooting. On the other hand, Bakaullah topped in Senior Cambridge
and then again at NED—the famous Nadirshaw Eduljee Dinshaw University of
Engineering & Technology.

Papa attempted to draw me out, taking me on excursions, mano a mano:[18] there were jaunts to Empress Market and Gandhi Garden and a memorable trip to the shabby shrine of Mungho Pir—patron saint of the Sheedis, the Afro-Pakistani community.[19] Gawking at the crocodiles lazing in a murky pool, I remember Papa telling me that the frightful reptiles were "just big lizards," said to be the "lice shaken loose from the saint's head." "He must have been a giant," I noted. ("Primusinterpares," he remarked cryptically.) When Papa narrated a story of how the mighty Sheedi general fought the British, losing ten thousand men to the machine gun, a leathery old man within earshot invited me to bang on a sheepskin drum—dhug-dhug, dhuga-dhug—a rare honour. I can also remember quarterly pilgrimages to the Toy Trading Agency where I once picked up a locomotive labeled, *Made in Occupied Japan*, but as I grew older, Papa made me put away childish things. Circa nineteen hundred & fifty four, he took it upon himself to make a man out of me.

During oppressive Currachee summers,[20] when families we knew made their way to hill stations up north—Murree, Ziarat or the emerald abode of that Fairy Queen—Papa put me to work in the kitchens of the Olympus. I remember peeling potatoes until my fingers bled & chopping onions until I bawled. Although it was trial by fire, burn by burn & by & by I learnt to negotiate the involute

---

18. Typically, however, excursions were en famille. I remember when the entire clan was stuffed into the Impala to visit the expansive Ranikot Fort. We camped in the open under a powdery spread of stars, attended to by a sizeable staff. I also remember relieving myself in the bushes and spying Badbakht Begum's ras malai buttocks.

19. Sheedis maintain *sheedi* is a variation of the Arabic *Sahabi*, or "companion." Some claim descent from the Prophet's associate, Bilal (RA) while some, the Qambranis, claim descent from Ali's (AS) coterie.

20. The summer lasts from April to July. August & September is the Monsoon. Then there's the Indian Summer.

ecosystem. It helped that the chef, a jolly Goan named Pereira, took a shine to me. He had been recruited from Agha's Tavern, the finest steakhouse in Currachee, on the condition that he had absolute dominion over the kitchen, & there was truth to it: I remember him telling Papa once, "You do your work, man, I do mine." Nobody dared confront Papa, save Pereira. I also recall him telling Papa, "Boy's a natural"—I could, after all, prepare beef bourguignon and coq-au-vin—but I doubt my father was impressed. He was hard to please.

Consequently, save the two years I spent at the American University in Cairo after the Suez Crisis—I read political science—I devoted myself to become Papa's Aaron (AS) or Ali (AS). After all, if I could not become Papa, I could become his man. Politics or science had nothing to do with it. At the tender age of twenty-two then, I was virtually running the Olympus. I had a card printed on ivory paper that read: Executive Manager. I wore spotted kerchiefs, felt important. Papa could be proud.

I remember it all as if it were yesterday. But yesterday is no more.

ON THE HAZARD OF SPIRITS (& HIGH TEA)

There is a proverb in Gujarati, "Jagya tya thi savar," which translates to, *It's morning whenever you wake*, in the Queen's English. I am uncertain of its import but the day after my anniversary festivities, I wake to find myself beside my bed, marinating in my smoking jacket. There is a pounding in my head, and a pounding on the door, *dhas-dhas-dhas*, but I am like a fly on flypaper. At my age, of course, every gesture requires Herculean stamina: it takes four swings to peel myself from a sofa; my knees crack like biscuits, and I have dispensed with socks because I have not been able to touch my ankles since the Fall of the Berlin Wall. Somehow, I manage to hoist myself up; I traverse the expanse of the room as if braving a sandstorm. Although a patina of crust glues my eyes shut, I perceive a disembodied visage when I turn the knob. "Who is this?" it squeals.

"This is who?" I reply through my fingers, chuffed that even in a state of raw, gut-churning lassitude, my capacity for inductive logic remains functional. Stepping aside, Nargis reveals a bony, rabbit-faced boy regarding his joggers. *I don't know him*, I begin to say, *Don't know why I've been lying around like a beached whale for that matter*—but instead, I find myself mouthing the curious appellation: *Bosco*.

"Bosco?" Nargis repeats.

"Bosco," Bosco confirms.

"I found him wandering around downstairs. I was so frightened. You know, I'm alone in the morning after Babu and the children leave—"

"Bully for you!"

"Really, Bhai-Jan!"

"Come on, lad."

"What's wrong with you?" she asks with earnest exasperation.

Shutting the door on her, I mumble, "Hungover, and not well hung," before falling, face-first, into a coma on the bed.When I come to, I find my trousers around my knees, a syringe lying next to my pulpy, pallid thigh, and Bosco sitting on his haunches beside me, chin balancing on palms, mumbling Memorare or some esoteric supplication.[21] "Cheers," I say. The boy—God bless his heart—extends a stringy hand as I attempt to stand but I am a sack of potatoes. It is only the cordial whiff of the alloo bharay parathay,[22]

---

21. It might have been the Guardian Angel or Miraculous Medal Prayer, prayers we all learnt as children due to our rigorous Catholic schooling. I enjoy the pomp and circumstance of Catholicism.

22. In case Bosco was unfamiliar with the dish—who knew if his mother made alloo bharay parathay—I volunteered an explanation: "Think of these as pancakes filled with mashed potatoes sautéed in cumin and chili powder."

204

pickled mangoes & yogurt that finally gets me to my feet. The March of History attests to the fact there is nothing like hunger to transform a thinking man to a man of action. And one can attest to the fact there is nothing that sates the soul like Barbarossa's luncheon spread.

Bosco and I sit under the fan in the veranda and eat like kings. Although I would like to ascertain the nature of the boy's familial problems, apprehend the boy's familiarity with the scourge of diabetes, he keeps stuffing his mouth as if he has led a life of privation, weaned, as it were, on a diet of grass and shrubs. I ought to lecture him on the Protocols of the Sunset Lodge—First Things First: Stay Clear of Nargis the Opossum—but I just enjoy watching him eat; his entire being informs the act. I offer him paratha after greasy paratha and he keeps tucking in. The only request he makes is for a napkin—I wear my old striped plastic apron as a bib—and a bottle of pop, Pakola. "Ah," I proclaim, "a man after my own heart!"

I am compelled afterward to contend with that classic problem in the Life of Man: what the dickens do you do with a ward? Not quite the Boswellian type, was he Watson to my Shaukat? Aflatoon to my Socrates? The trajectory of the query reminds me that the library requires attention: there are pamphlets, gazettes in indiscrete stacks on the floor, yellowing articles cut out from magazines dating back a half century,[23] a decalogy on the Intellectual History of the Ancient World strewn by my feet. "Your grandfather," I say, "told

---

23. In Burney Sahab's excellent *Outlook*, for example, articles such as "An Exposé on the American Role in the Dismemberment of Pakistan" have as much resonance today as yesterday. Another project I initiated but failed to complete was an anthology of my friend Badruddin Ahmed's brilliant "Gardening Notes" in the *Mirror*. One should note in passing here that Mohammad Aslam Mian's *Flower Gardening in the Plains of Pakistan* is also an invaluable resource though the prose is somewhat flat. W. Firminger, Woodrow, & Johnston have also made meaningful contributions to the field even though they were Brits.

me to build your character, and they say there's no better place to begin than Greece."

It's a swampy afternoon, and I am feeling low on account of BP so I retire to my chamber for a snooze, what the Spanish term a Siesta, but before being swept far from the shores of consciousness, I am roused by the housemaid, the slate-faced, iron-haired dame known universally as Bua, who informs me that I have been summoned downstairs for tea. It is a decidedly odd development: the family dines together Sundays but seldom fraternizes otherwise.

Anticipating a dressing-down, I don my tomato-red silk shirt (one ought to look the part of an elder even if one does not behave like one), comb my kinky hair to the side for good measure (though it will spring back in time), buff my crisp nails (though my nails require clipping not buffing) & glance at the mirror to assess whether a shave is required (though I have never been capable of whiskers). I tell Bosco to hold the fort. There is no reason to subject him to the Opossum again. I pick up a couple of finger-shaped balloons on the way out. The Childoos always expect a gift. An egg crate would do. Oh, if only realizing joy were so easy!

As I lumber down the staircase, suddenly, uncannily, halfway up, halfway down, I have the sensation of being observed again. I am admittedly lightheaded—blowing those balloons requires great lung capacity—but sense that it's that Phantom Firefly who has been haunting me since my birthday. I pause to collect my wits, my breath, survey the gate, the length of boundary wall, but my cataract eye renders me practically blind in weak light. I can only hear the cartoon voices of those crazy little Childoos, playing Train-Train. Verily they have the power to banish ghosts! When I enter flinging balloons in the air, they run to me chanting, *Cha! Cha! Jan! Cha! Cha Jan!* as if welcoming a politician.

"You must let Cha-cha-Jan sit!" Nargis cries. "You're in his way!"

"Not in my way," I say, "they're never in my way."

Palming my cantaloupe knees, I tell the three-year-olds, "I want a kiss on this cheek, a kiss on the other." Toto, a famously inept kisser, immediately licks my cheek as if licking ice cream. He is also known for speaking with a Teutonic intonation and conspiring against Guddu, his elder brother by a few minutes. It's not difficult. Guddu aspires to be a mailman. After delivering a pithy exposition on the phenomenology of balloons that concludes *phew-phew, pop-pop*! Toto marches off with his confrere, hollering *Choo-choo-chuk-chuck*!

Babu suddenly embraces me, blurting "Happy birthday"—an awkward gesture partly because he is not the embracing sort, and partly because I am in medias res. *When they were up they were up*, I chunter to myself, *and when they were down they were down—*

"Sir?"

"Cheers, partner."

"Happy birthday!"

Drawing my attention towards a wreath with the proportions of a tractor tyre, the sort that embellishes the grave of a bureaucrat or brigadier, he says, "It's special, isn't it?" as if he has fashioned it himself. "It's for you." He claims he had sent a message the day before via Barbarossa to join the family for tea, a claim that cannot be corroborated because the old man oft cannot recall the number of toes on his feet. I play along: I say I was out with a friend but do not mention the friend or venue because Nargis is the sort who consults the Holy Book to make the most mundane decisions. I can swear I once observed her flipping to determine whether they ought to serve Polka ice cream during the holy month of Ramzan.

A cake arrives—the spongy, saccharine sort, the sort that can kill a diabetic. *Good God!* I think; "Good job!" I say. "My Nargis organized it," Babu declaims. Although she and I do not have an equation, she is probably a good girl, or good enough: she takes care of her family & unlike me, is integral to the household even if she does not appreciate the Lodge. She bemoans the seepage, broken tiles, weedy backyard. There is no doubt that she would immigrate to the suburban wasteland of Defense if she could afford it. She should go if she likes. Man's been searching for suitable habitats since the Dawn of Time.

When seven candles are lit, I call out to the Childoos, knife in hand, like Abraham (PBUH) at Moriah. They storm in, hop on either knee, howling *Hay-pee Baad-deh Too-yoo*! like drunks. They take mousy bites, chew with mouths agape. During the commotion, I fold the deathly collops into a napkin & shove them into the recesses of my trouser pockets. You do not want to die with cake on your face.

Babu and I sit facing each other afterward, contemplating the walls for a few moments. What do you discuss with an IT manager at a Shariah-compliant leasing firm? "Say," I begin, "why don't you play table tennis anymore? If I recall correctly, partner, you excelled at it. You won that trophy—"

"It was for third place, in class six."

"I was never any good at it myself but you could have become world class if you continued, a champ—"

"I wanted to talk to you about something, Bhai-Jan."

"There is no doubt in my mind that there is an international conspiracy to deride the noble sport of table tennis by characterizing it as ping-pong—"

"You know this house, it's like a clock," Babu blurts.

As he wipes his flat forehead with a gesture that calls attention to the hair plugs pocking the gleaming surface of his scalp, I shift my weight from one cheek to another, wondering how I fit: Am I a hand? Spring? Tourbillion? I know this much: Whatever my role, function, purpose, I possess agency like everyone else: Babu, Nargis, those crazy little Childoos. Why do I have to solicit permission for taking on the thankless responsibility for mentoring a ward? Do they solicit my permission to hire a sweeper? "What are you getting at, partner?"

"Let me start again," Babu says, changing tack. "When Papa, God grant him Heaven, was alive, things were different. And now things are different. Wouldn't you agree, Bhai-Jan?"

"You have quite ably stated the obvious."

"There's so much upkeep required, you know, and we can't expect —"

Before the conversation can scrape further, I'm saved by the proverbial bell. But respite or reprieve is not on the cards: the *thak-a-thak-a-thak-a* of a Derby cane against the floor heralds another brother, the eldest, Ataullah, *Major Sahab to you.* Sweeping in like a gust, he booms, "Happy birthday, shehzaday!"

I sit dumbstruck for a moment, gaping at the unexpected guest. The Major possesses a white mane, an enviable Hungarian moustache, and large gesticulating hands. He only wears starched white kurtas and jackets adorned with filigreed gold-plated buttons. After "retiring" from the army—the Major was eased out due to insubordination—he reinvented himself as a "real estate baron." Although success has eluded him in recent times, he became President of the Rotary Club and has influential friends in the capital and hinterland. He is not known to frequent these parts. "It's the spondylosis," he claims though the condition doesn't stop him from playing bridge at the Gymkhana or gallivanting around town for lunches with local consul-generals. "How old are you now?" he asks.

Peeling myself from the sofa, yanking the waist of my sagging trousers, I mumble, "Seventy, sir."

"Seventy my foot!"

"Does he look seventy?" Babu chimes in. Nargis shakes her head like a new bride.

I have oft been told that I do not look my age—it is, perhaps, one of the few benedictions of corpulence—but I sense conspiracy in the easy effusion. "I am flattered—"

"I remember," the Major continues, "he would be messing about in the house and lawn in the afternoon, nanga patang—"

"I wore nappies—"

"I remember you trapped worms and beetles and made those little muddy mud-men. Where did they go?"

"In the sweat of thy face shalt thou eatest bread," I mutter, "till thou return unto the ground."

"You've finally started reciting the Koran, shehzaday?"

"Will you have cake, Bhai Sahab," Nargis interjects, "and biscuits?" Nobody has offered me any biscuits & I like biscuits, a splendid genus, incorporating everything from the modest saltine to the vanilla wafer. "Please sit," she adds, "please sit."

As the confections are passed around the room, the Major inquires, "What are you doing these days?"

"Me? Oh. Well, sir, I'm working on several urgent projects, essays, articles, monographs mainly, one concerning historiographical sensibilities, one on culinary anthropology, and the mythopoetic legacy of —"

"I have always said that raw talent is like sewage: it needs to be treated."

"Sir?"

"When will we see the fruits of your labor?"

"It's a matter of time." I notice my red silk shirt is wet in twin crescents under my chest. "I'm ironing out some didactic tics—"

"I'll be dead soon, shehzaday."

"Then avoid the cake," I mutter.

As we sit around like a family, discussing this, that, the other, the trade deficit, foreign policy, the flower show, I find myself speculating about the purpose of the Major's visit. Although we gather at marriages, funerals, during Muhurram and on the second day of Eid, after Mummy's death, the family has become fundamentally unglued. The Major's third wife, a Kashmiri who wears too much rouge, has been to the house three, four times in the last decade, usually for the Childoos' joint annual birthday, but I cannot remember when the Major visited last. "We have to think about the future," he suddenly announces, digging into the chair.

"What about the future?"

"The past is the past but the future belongs to them," he says with a vague nod towards his audience, and conspirators. "We have to think about acreage and equity. We have to think about the Lodge."

And suddenly it all makes sense. Suddenly, I pass gas. When vexed, I can pass gas. It sounds like a bleat and smells like French Onion Soup. I glance at the painting on the wall facing me—a landscape featuring a winding stream cutting through a forest bordered by twin peaks—study the adjacent Dutch tapestry depicting cherubs feting a gracefully voluptuous dame, Athena perhaps, that has been in our possession for at least seventy years; and the porcelain plates besides my arm featuring round-faced Chinese women of an arguably homosexual bent inhaling a plucked flower. I notice two heirlooms—the Bohemian cut-glass stallion, the ivory horn—are missing. They, presumably, have been sold. I will not allow myself to be sold.

Rising in a huff, I announce, "There was a Certain Man in Russia Long Ago! He was Big and Strong and his Eyes were Flaming Gold!"

The audience, aghast, is rendered speechless. I am out the door, however, when I hear Nargis whisper, "Is that cake in his pocket?"

ON HISTORIOGRAPHICAL SENSIBILITIES
(OR ON THE POLITICS OF PRESERVATION)

It is said that on the continent of Europe and in certain swaths of the Americas, the Trajectory of History is considered linear. It has not always been this way—Homer, old Pliny the Elder & that curmudgeon Marx posited other paradigms—but since the Enlightenment and the Colonial Conquest, the Caucasian tribes have broadly believed that history chronicles progress. The Chinese, on the other hand, maintain that History is Cyclical. After occupying the centre of the world for an epoch, they experienced an epoch of profound turmoil, of barbarism, bloodshed, war.[24] After inventing bells, noodles, and printing, plastromancy, metallurgy and fireworks,[25] they were swept by insidious opiate winds, a brutal occupation. After Great Leaps Forward and falling flat on their rumps, they generated muscular economic growth that is expected to eclipse (what the Caucasians call) the West (but the Chinese consider the East). The motto of the Chinese could be: *We Might Be Eating Grass Now, But Wait a Millennium. Things Change. Things Will Change.*

Then there are the Mussalmans. It is said that Mussalmans subscribe to a third historical paradigm, the paradigm of The Golden Age. We hearken to different times, different eras, whether the Caliphate of the Pious (termed CP4 hereafter) or the Splendour That Was Andalusia. Of course, the period of the Caliphate was not

24. There was even a period that is known as the "Warring States Period." It went on for two hundred years! Imagine that! That's as if the America Civil War had continued to this day!
25. While researching acupuncture when my back gave way several years ago, I compiled a list of the following Chinese inventions at the Currachee Club Library: animal zodiac, cannonballs, coffins, golf, football, high-alcohol beer (the regular variety was invented in Iraq), landmines, pinhole camera, lavatory paper, toothbrush.

particularly rosy: Omar the Caliph (RA) biffed the elected successor to the Prophet (PBUH)[26] circa 632 CE then instituted severe punishment for inebriation; Usman the Caliph (RA) was knocked off by protestors protesting his good-for-nothing governor; and the Mighty Ali (AS) defeated the armies led by the Prophet's feisty widow before being felled by the first bona fide fundamentalists of Islam.[27] In our collective memory, however, CP4 is an oasis in the Sahara of history.[28]

One would think that the Mussalmans' predilection of looking back would compel them to preserve the past but that is nary the case. Like children with dynamite, the Bedouins running the Hijaz have been tearing down monuments testifying to history. In 1924, the graveyard that housed the Prophet's first wife was razed, then two years later, the mausoleums of the Prophet's daughter and grandson were leveled as well. When we did not protest, the Bedouins blasted the Seven Famous Mosques.[29] In their place, they constructed shopping complexes, retail banking outlets, those currency dispensing machines, and public toilets on the Prophet's wife's house![30] Then they began wholesale demolition in earnest.

26. And Saad bin Ubayda (RA) never recovered. For a comprehensive account of the events subsequent to the Prophet's death, Madelung's brilliant *Succession to Muhammad* is an essential tract, and will make a Shia out of you.

27. It is no secret that the Khariji Imperative has returned with a vengeance today. Many Kharijis, by the way, settled in Beloochistan. Go figure.

28. Of course, our notions of history are more complicated than the three above paragraphs would suggest: the Great Ibn Khaldun articulated the most sophisticated historiographical analysis known to civilization; Marx was fundamentally, a cyclicalist; and we have not even touched the Buddhist or, for that matter, the Papuan conception of history. According to the Hindoos, incidentally, we have entered the Age of Kali.

29. Said mosques belonged to Salman Farsi (RA), Abu B. (RA), Omar the Caliph (RA), the mighty Ali (AS), and his wife, among others.

30. The tragedy is that there wasn't a peep out of the faithful.

Verily Islam became better the further it moved away from the desert. The drop of water drips down from some secret glacier, flows into a stream that gushes into a river which irrigates land, only nourishes communities, culture, civilization, when it picks up momentum. The Torrent of Islam thusly ran through Syria, Persia, Anatolia, North Africa then widened into a sea, & the sea touched the rest of the world. Unbeknownst to most, Islam first reached the Subcontinent not on horseback but via the coast.

Although there has not been any wholesale destruction of the Bedouin variety in the Subcontinent, historical preservation has been wanting.[31] Once upon a time my brother Tony told me that his childhood policeman friend, Hur a.k.a Hawkeye, told him the following story: "You know I've been stationed in the Garden several times. So Yahoodi Masjid, Magen Shalome, as it was known, came under my watch. When I heard that the land mafia was eyeing the property I went to investigate. The caretaker, this genial old lady named Rachel, said that most of her kind had left—mind you, not all, and mind you, due to persecution not before but after the creation of Israel. She furnished various documents from the title deed to expense reports.[32] Since everything was in order, I tried to secure the site but my superior resisted. If I were a better man, I'd have stood up for it." The synagogue was razed in the summer of '88. That's not even yesterday.

Secular constructions, broadly speaking, do not command much interest or attention—Mohenjo-daro, Makli, Rohtas Fort or, for that matter, the Sunset Lodge. Built by my grandfather in 1912,[33] the

31. We preserve Sufi tombs but the hundreds of stupas spanning the land are rotting like carcasses under the sun.
32. He told me he also came across a card that read Circumcisions: 4 annas Bar Mitzvahs: 8 annas.
33. Although he originally resided in the Preedy Quarters, he bought property in Garden at the turn of the century.

Lodge is constructed of yellow limestone masonry, quarried in Gizri. The architect,[34] the renowned Moses Somake, a local Jew, also designed Uncle Jinnah's residence, Flagstaff House. The Lodge is symmetrically arranged around the veranda in what they call the Indo-Gothic mode. (It should be noted that Sunset Lodge was named thusly because the vista of dusk from the veranda was said to be spectacular.) The central structure is flanked by semicircular turret-like structures featuring narrow windows. A stairway ribbons down one side and another at the back. The garage was constructed by Papa in 1949, as well as the annex that once housed the domestic staff quarters.[35] There are three bedrooms downstairs, three and a half upstairs. Bosco inhabits Tony's tiny old room which remains plastered with posters of Elvis Presley and sixties pinups that include Jean Seberg wearing not much more than a hat and Jane Fonda in an animal-skin miniskirt. My parents' erstwhile abode serves as my bedroom & library, drawing & dining room.

I would like to believe that the Lodge will remain when I am gone, rearing successive generations of the clan. But I might be mistaken. Although I inhabit the Master Bedroom, I am reminded that I am not Lord of the Manor.

34. The architects of renown of the time included J.A. Shiveshankar, Jamsedji P. Mistry, Durgas Advani, M. Nazareth, Gulshan Jalal, & Khemji.
35. I will note in passing that I believe that the bungalow was initially conceived as single storied but plans were revised in light of the prosperity of the business spanning the mercantile belt of the late Raj: Currachee, Gujarat, Bombay.

ATHENA FARROKHZAD was born in 1983 and lives in Stockholm. She is a poet, literary critic, translator, playwright, and teacher of creative writing. Her first volume of poetry, *Vitsvit* (*White Blight*, Argos Books, translation: Jennifer Hayashida), was published in 2013 by Albert Bonniers Förlag. In 2016, her second volume of poetry, *Trado*, written together with the Romanian poet Svetlana Cârstean, was published.

JENNIFER HAYASHIDA is a writer, translator, and visual artist. Her most recent projects include translation from the Swedish of Athena Farrokhzad's *White Blight* (Argos Books, 2015) and Karl Larsson's *Form/ Force* (Black Square Editions, 2015), named one of the ten best books of 2015 by *Partisan*. She is director of the Asian American Studies Program at Hunter College, CUNY, and serves on the board of the Asian American Writers' Workshop.

Letter to a Warrior

ATHENA FARROKHZAD
TRANSLATED FROM THE SWEDISH BY JENNIFER HAYASHIDA

My child, kicking warrior, little life inside my stomach.
In a few months you will finally arrive in the world.
If the contractions began now there would be a chance to save
    you.
I feel your movements reproduced inside me.
Like a wave that flows and as quickly ebbs again.
Like the fin of a fish suddenly breaking a calm surface.

Opposite the bed I have mounted pictures of you.
The first thing I see when I wake is your black and white
    silhouette.
The last thing I see when I fall asleep is you resting inside me like
    a half-moon.

Packages for you arrive in the mail from other continents.
That someone can be so loved before their birth.
That someone can change me before they have begun to exist.
That someone can occupy so much space before they intervene in
    the world.

I don't know what you will look like.
I don't know with what pain I will deliver you.
I don't know who you will become or what you will make me.
I don't know what our days together will be like.
I don't know when our nights will drive me insane.

I wonder if you will be born with hair on your head.
I wonder if your heart will beat with a rhythm that worries me.
I wonder if you will begin your life silently or with a scream.
I wonder if the umbilical cord will be coiled as a sign around your
        body.
I wonder if your gaze will see through me from the beginning.
I wonder if my conception of mothers will change when I become
        one.

I have no inheritance for you.
No china, no paintings, no lace cloth, no jewelry.
I have nothing that has been passed between generations.
For you belong to families that have abandoned everything.
That have left with nothing.
Neither of your parents grew up in the same place as their
        parents.
We have nothing to pass on, since nothing has been passed on to us.
Nothing except stories about decisive hands.

We have stories about the fight that precedes you.
We have stories about the struggles that enabled us to survive.
So we one day could give you life.
We have stories about where we come from.
We have stories about which battlefields brought us here.
Here to the place that will soon be yours.

I traveled with your father to your grandmother's hometown.
We went to a park where the names of the dead are written.
There were thirty thousand.
They were arranged alphabetically.
When the same last name was repeated I understood.
An entire group of siblings had been annihilated.
I held your father's hand when he threw roses into the river.
In the park I understood something about your aunt's poems.
When she writes about carrying the names of the dead as
        talismans it is not a symbol.
Your grandmother pointed out the names to us in the park.

She named her children after all her dead.
She named them after sweethearts and comrades.
She gave them the names of the dead because something was
    already lost.
Because death in all its futility would at least serve as protection.
Your father said his ashes should be scattered in the park one day.
To be reunited with all the dead.
For his death will remain tied to theirs.
For it will belong to the place they were forced to leave.
It was when I saw your father cry in the park that I understood
    you were possible.

For a love that does not contain such grief cannot give rise to life.
For a desire that does not know history can break us cannot be
    dwelled in.
For a future that does not tend to such defeats I have no faith in.

I wonder if you will be the first who is allowed to remain.
If you will end your life in the same place as it begins.
If you will call a place home and not see it devastated.
If you will bury us in a place you can return to.
Or if you must also bid a hasty farewell that turns out to be final.
If you must also stand by prison gates and wait.
If someone will stand outside and wait for you.
If someone will search for your name in lists of the dead.
If all suffering one day will be placed in relation to a freedom gained.

My child, kicking warrior, little life inside my stomach.
I will teach you the language of the dead so you will remember
    why they disappeared.
I will sing you lullabies I barely master.
If you do not understand your grandmother's chants she will have
    fought for nothing.
If you do not know your aunts' songs their struggle will end with you.

I am afraid something will end with you.
If it ends with you I don't know how we will recognize ourselves in
    each other.

I hope something will end with you.
If it does not end with you I don't know how long it will continue.

There are so many ways to be annihilated.
One way is to die of bullets and lashes of the whip.
Another is to destroy yourself because you didn't.
Like your uncle who against all odds evaded the hands of
    repression.
He who fled and told me how escape routes became dead ends.
He who told me who had gotten married and who had been
    unfaithful.
He who showed me where I should place my feet not to slip down
    the mountain.
Then he took one pill too many and never woke again.
I who promised him that one day we would return and make
    victory signs.
I who imagined how we would lean back and toast each other.
I know that grief is the price of love.
I know that even the earth will go someday.
I know that one either buries or is buried by those one loves.
But his shoes still stand in the hallway waiting for him to awaken.
It was when I kissed his cold forehead that I understood you were
    necessary.

Because love lives in flesh and not in stone.
Because if someone disappears someone else must become.
Because death is so inexplicable that it can only be soothed by
    the inexplicability of life.
Because if we do not increase in any other way we must do so
    through you.

Can there be lullabies that are not songs of struggle.
Can there be children's hands not taught to form fists.
Can there be daughters not named after warriors.
Can there be fireworks that do not evoke memories of gunshots.
Can there be games of tag that do not recall escape routes.

I am afraid I have nothing to offer you.
I am afraid the only thing I can console you with is stories of our
	defeats.
I am afraid the only hope I can convey is about our delayed
	victories.
I am afraid you will reject the stories, as I have rejected them.
I am afraid they are told in too many versions.
I am afraid the guilt is the same regardless if the stories are
	swaddled or undressed.
I am afraid loss defines us even though we cannot remember what
	we have lost.
I am afraid our lives are conditioned by experiences inaccessible
	to us.
I am afraid this is why we must continue to tell.
I am afraid you will not want to listen.
I am afraid freedom will make you a stranger.

My child, kicking warrior, little life inside my stomach.
I push home a stroller and think that the next time you will be
	asleep in it.
I assemble a crib and see you hoist yourself out of it.
I fold a onesie and imagine you crawling around in it.
I match socks and try to understand that this is the measure of
	your feet.

I will dress you in our stories as mothers have dressed their
	children for an eternity.
I will place your arms in our victories as a mail.
I will wrap your legs in our defeats as a shield.
I will arm you with stories to bear you when the ground gives
	way.

Your grandmother joined the guerrillas when she was fifteen.
When she went underground she was carrying her first child.
When her mother knew the military was searching for her
	daughter she cleaned the apartment.

She said that she didn't want to give them the satisfaction of
 seeing it dirty.
From her window she saw the helicopters going to dump the
 corpses in the river.
In the square the mothers gathered to demand the return of their
 disappeared children.
When your mother had crossed the border her father brought the
 passport home.
So that someone else's child could also be saved.
He continued to dream that there would be enough champagne
 for everyone.
It was when I heard about the price of his exuberance that I
 understood you were essential.

For there are traumas so defining that to move on would be a
 betrayal.
For there are damages so decisive that they can only be left as
 inheritance.
For there is grief so dumbfounding that it can only be told in
 fragments.

We who consist of all these stories.
We who spoke with our cousins on crackling phone lines.
We who cried in airports during the summers.
We who knew what was concealed in the lining of the suitcase.
We who called our parents different names depending on who
 wanted to know.
We who longed for a place that had never been ours.
We who were nostalgic for a time we had never experienced.
We who armed ourselves for battlefields already abandoned.
We who bandaged the wound before it had occurred.
Our only inheritance is stories we hope will exist when we no
 longer do.

Your grandmother distributed flyers and agitated at the factories.
Your grandmother delivered babies during bombings until it was
 her turn to give birth.

When she got married the taxi driver was a witness since
    everyone had gone underground.
When she returned she packed her suitcase full of bananas for her
    nieces and nephews.
Her brother remained even though everyone else had left.
He did not want to live anywhere other than the place that had
    robbed him of life.
They planted weapons in his office so he would be unable to
    prosecute his cases.
Thirty years later he said that he should also have left.
That he had hidden hope deep in his closet until it withered like
    a plant.
Your grandfather spent nine years in a prison cell.
When I was a child he said that he was fed and didn't have to pay
    rent.
When I became older I read about the mock executions.
Your grandfather will never be the same and I don't know who he
    could have become.
It was when I realized he could not tell that I understood you
    were critical.

For I wonder what it feels like to see oneself in a face regarded as
    precious.
For I wonder what the changing seasons are like for someone who
    is not in a place temporarily.
For I wonder what it feels like to have a body shaped by the earth
    one treads on.
For I wonder what death means for someone with a grave to
    visit.

My child, kicking warrior, little life inside my stomach.
I rub my skin so the sheath that surrounds you will stretch.
I practice breathing so I can bear the contractions when you rush
    forth.
I learn that the pain is not dangerous so I should not be overcome
    with fear.
I dismiss the thought that one of us will not make it.

I will kiss your feet and hope they will never have to cross a border.
I will wash your skin and imagine it will never be scarred.
I will speak your name and think of what its vowels will let you
     bear.
I will tousle your hair and wonder where its blackness will take
     you.
I will brush your teeth and hope they will never be knocked out.

What is quaking in the future erupts at the thought of your
     stomach's smallness.
What is baffling in the present appears when I see myself caress
     your back.
What is cyclical in history blooms when I imagine your earlobes'
     softness.

I will tell you about all your aunts.
Those who fought so I could decide it is now that I want you.
Those who struggled so we would both survive your arrival in the
     world.
So the sheets would be clean.
So the midwife would be rested.
So no one would hurt you without punishment.
So I would have time to get to know you.
I will tell you about your aunts with their strollers leading the
     demonstration.
Those who continued when police ordered them to stop.
Those who had bandages in their backpacks and lemon wedges in
     their pockets.
Those who did things I cannot recount.
Those who dreamed of fields of flowers and awoke in prison cells.
Those whose experiences were never recognized as knowledge.
Those who survived even though they weren't meant to.
I will tell you about your aunts who fostered the hatred that is in
     service to love.

My child, kicking warrior, little life inside my stomach.
I will tell you about everyone who precedes you.

I will tell you why your life is connected to theirs.
I will tell you why they are not here to greet you when you
    arrive.
I will tell you why you receive packages from other continents.
I will tell you about the walls that hold them hostage.

I will tell you about self-defense that cannot be punished.
I will tell you about movements that transform us into many.
I will tell you about history that will not be repeated.
I will tell you about abilities that give according to need.
I will tell you about victories that do not make us heroes.

I will tell you about the places you come from.
Where you come from the tanks cross the squares like
    combines.
Where you come from escape routes become dead ends.
Where you come from the dying reach for each other with a
    prayer for remembrance.
Where you come from the ambulances drive directly to the
    morgues.
Where you come from the living are worth less than what their
    hands have made.
Where you come from the present rhymes with history like
    syllables in a poem.
Where you come from the rivers are cemeteries.
Where you come from the cobblestones are memorials.
Where you come from the profits are individual and the debt
    collective.

Where you come from we have supported what has destroyed us
    for too long.
Where you come from we have left our mothers' houses.
Where you come from we have realized that the road leads to our
    executioners' houses.
Where you come from we have thrown gravel into the machinery.
Where you come from we have discovered that the factory turns
    gravel into grease.
Where you come from no courtroom can give us restitution.

Where you come from even we have taken our testimony as
   perjury.

My child, kicking warrior, little life inside my stomach.
You have a face that resembles mine, one I have not yet seen.
You are the future present here.
You are an unknown promise.
You come into being independently of me, a condition for your
   creation.
You are foreign and my continuation by other means.
You renegotiate my dependence.
You displace my limit.
The frailty that is life appears through you.
The connection between us grows with every movement.
The body I have been alone in I share with you.
But I have never been alone in this body.
It has always been connected to other bodies.
To other stories that you will hear when you arrive.

When Living Is a Protest

RUDDY ROYE

Most of the people I photograph are from the lower rung of society. I recall growing up on this same rung and realizing that nothing I did outside of going to school would change my status in life. I get the feeling that the folks I've photographed here see their lives in the same way. Almost nothing they do from one day to the next presents them with a door to improving their lives. Maybe they can buy a bigger television set, buy more clothes, the newest gadgets—but owning their own home, opening a business, accomplishing something that will truly shift their position and expectations? There is no hope for that. Yet like me they are hopeful that from day to day they will be able to eat, to pay rent (albeit late).

I am shooting a series of portraits called "When Living Is a Protest," which chronicles how black men go about their daily lives. I am intrigued by the psyches of black men who constantly face, and have to negotiate, spaces where they are demeaned, demoralized, or rendered invisible. I am concerned with the psyche of a people who see their kind sleeping on the street, begging or panhandling, stinking on the subway, covered in their own feces, homeless, picking through trash as a means of support, labeled welfare recipients, labeled thugs and shot down in the streets just for being of a different hue.

I look into the eyes of black men and I see their fear and their anger. I see the self-hate and I see how they hate to see anyone who looks like them succeed. I see whom they aspire to be and how they live vicariously through the stories rap songs project. I don't know if there has ever been a time when a black man has ceased to be a commodity—from slaves to ball players and rappers, from artists to convicts.

Ema

CÉSAR AIRA
TRANSLATED FROM THE SPANISH BY CHRIS ANDREWS

E ma ate just one piece of the fowl and drank a glass of wine; then she got up from the table.

"Don't you want any more? You should keep your strength up."

She shook her head and sat down in the rocking chair, at the edge of the lamplight, half closing her eyes. She put her hands on her belly.

"So restless!"

Gombo went over to feel for himself. She showed him where to place his hands, and he waited; eventually there was a big thump and a tumble, so unexpected that they burst out laughing.

"He's stretching as if he'd just woken up. Do you think he sleeps like we do?"

"He sleeps when you're asleep."

Gombo passed Ema an apple, which she nibbled half-heartedly, while he disposed of the rest of the guinea fowl and the bottle of wine. Then he leaned back in the chair and looked at her again. She had closed her eyes.

"Are you sleepy?"

"No, I don't think so. I slept all day."

Gombo produced a bottle of cognac and two glasses, which he warmed slightly over the candle before filling them. He took just a sip and got up again, to make the coffee.

"On a night like this," he said, "there's no rush to get to bed because you know that sooner or later you'll fall asleep anyway."

"Some people can't get to sleep when there's a storm."

"But we're not like that, are we? No one has trouble sleeping in Pringles. Sometimes I wonder . . . if sleep doesn't form a part of the landscape and the society we live in. But how could we quantify it?"

For a while he pondered this question. Ema had begun to roll two little cigarettes, and as her husband watched, captivated by the sure movements of her fingers, his meditation took a turn.

"Why is it . . ." he said in a dreamy voice, leaving the question incomplete.

Ema looked up.

"Why is it," he repeated, "that women roll men's cigarettes?"

Ema was accustomed to these interrogative epiphanies. Her husband seemed to have a gift for coming up with the most unexpected questions, distilling them from any situation, even the most trivial.

"Why, indeed?" she said, but he was too absorbed to notice her mocking tone, and simply repeated:

"Why?"

Ema slipped a rolled mulberry leaf into the lamp and used it to light the cigarettes. They began to smoke.

Gombo hadn't finished. After the first puff he went on talking.

"Just then, when I was looking at you, something occurred to me that actually has nothing to do with the cigarettes: why do pregnant women take up so much space? I don't understand."

"Space?"

"It's incomprehensible. What I mean is, they *become* space," said Gombo.

"They say that pregnant women are always seeing other pregnant women wherever they go. Does that answer your question?"

"No."

"Anyhow, there'd be no way to test it here."

"True. All the women are gestating. What else is there for them to do? At least it's a way of passing the time. Besides, that's why they've been sent to the desert. To populate it."

These were old liberal jokes, which Gombo repeated out of habit, but his mind was elsewhere.

"When I said space, I meant something else. Where do children come from? When will the world be totally populated?"

"There are answers to all these questions."

"I know, my girl . . . But . . . sexual things are invisible. They don't show."

Gombo concluded with a vague gesture, wreathing himself in smoke. But the water was already boiling, so he slowly filtered the coffee. Its aroma made him chuckle: he had remembered something.

"My grandmother used to say: 'Nothing smells more gossipy than coffee.'"

They filled the cups and drank in silence. Then they poured themselves more cognac. The cigarettes had gone out; Ema rolled another two. How distant the storm was beginning to seem! And yet how close! All they had to do was reach out and touch it . . . But they preferred not to.

"I wonder what happens to the storm in the forest."

CLAIRE VAYE WATKINS is the author of *Gold Fame Citrus* and *Battleborn,* which won the Story Prize, the Dylan Thomas Prize, the New York Public Library Young Lions Fiction Award, the Rosenthal Family Foundation Award from the American Academy of Arts and Letters, and a Silver Pen Award from the Nevada Writers Hall of Fame. A Guggenheim Fellow, Claire is on the faculty of the Helen Zell Writers' Program at the University of Michigan. She is also the codirector, with Derek Palacio, of the Mojave School, a free creative writing workshop for teenagers in rural Nevada.

10-Item Edinburgh Postpartum Depression Scale

CLAIRE VAYE WATKINS

1. *Since my baby was born, I have been able to laugh and see the funny side of things.*
   - As much as I ever did.
   - ○ Not quite as much now.
   - ○ Not so much now.
   - ○ Not at all.

2. *I have looked forward with enjoyment to things.*
   - As much as I ever did.
   - ○ Not quite as much now.
   - ○ Not so much now.
   - ○ Not at all.

My husband beside me in the waiting room, reading over my shoulder, frowning. "That's rather evasive, isn't it? 'As much as I ever did.'"

"You think I'm being dishonest?"

"No, but."

"But what?"

"This should be short answer, not multiple choice." He rocks the car seat with his foot. "Short answer or essay. Don't you think?"

"As much as I ever did."

It becomes our inside joke, the answer to the questions we're afraid to ask.

1. *Since my baby was born, I have been able to laugh and see the funny side of things.*

We try to find you a nickname in utero but nothing fit so well as the ones we have for your father's scrotum and penis, your brothers Krang and Wangston Hughes.

An app dings weekly developmental progress and fruit analogies. Every week we write our own:

This week your baby is the size of a genetically modified micro-peach, which itself is about the size of a red globe grape. Your baby's ear holes are migrating this week. Your baby can hear you and may already be disappointed by what it hears.

This week your baby is the size of a medjool date knocked from the palm and left to soften in the dust. Your baby is now developing reflexes like lashing out and protecting its soft places. It is also developing paradoxes, and an attraction to the things that harm it.

This week your baby is the size of a navel orange spiked with cloves and hung by a blue ribbon on the doorknob of a friend's guest bathroom. Your baby is developing the self-defeating emotions this week, among them doubt, boredom, self-consciousness, and nostalgia. It may even be besieged by ennui!

This week your baby is the size of a large, thick-skinned, inedible grapefruit. Your baby has begun to dream, though it dreams only of steady heartbeats and briny fluids.

2. *I have looked forward with enjoyment to things.*

Sushi, beer, pot brownies, daycare, pain-free BMs, getting HBO, my in-laws going home.

Erica visits and asks, Does a person really need a doula? No, I tell her, not if you have an older woman in your life who is helpful, trusted, up-to-date on the latest evidence-based best practices and shares your birth politics, someone who is nonjudgmental, won't project her insecurities onto you, is respectful of your boundaries and your beliefs and those of your spouse, carries no emotional baggage or unresolved tensions, no submerged resentment, no open wounds, no hovering, no neglect, no library of backhanded compliments, no bequeathed body issues, no treadmill of jealousy and ingratitude, no debt of apology, no I'm sorry you feel that way, I'm sorry you misunderstood me, no beauty must suffer, no don't eat with your eyes, no I cut the ends off the roast because you did, I did it to fit the pan.

Erica says, So it's basically $750 for the mother you wish you had.

3. *I have felt scared or panicky for no good reason.*

There are little moths drifting twitchy through our apartment, sprinkling their mothdust everywhere. I cannot find what they are eating. I brace myself each time I take a towel or a pillowcase from the linen closet.

235

Our baby is born runty and jaundiced. We wrap her in a hot, stiff so-called blanket of LEDs, to get her levels right. She's at twelve, they inform us, without saying whether the goal is fifteen or zero or a hundred—not telling us whether we are trying to bring them up or down. I don't know which way to pray, your dad says. Little glowworm baby, spooky blue light-up baby in the bassinet, hugged by this machine instead of us, a gnarly intestine-looking tube coming out the bottom. Jaundiced and skinny skinny though neither of us is. *Failure to thrive*, the diagnosis. In the car we agree that a ridiculously lofty standard. Haven't we every advantage—health insurance and advanced degrees, study abroad and strong female role models? Aren't we gainfully employed, and doing work we do not hate, no less? Didn't we do everything right and in the right order? And yet, can either of us say we are *thriving*? We remind ourselves it's not so bad, the jaundice, the smallness. Erica says, I was little and look at me! We remind ourselves of the Nick U and pediatric oncology, which we walk past on the way to our appointments. I remember the apparatus we learned about in breastfeeding class that lactation consultants can rig up for a man: a tube from a sack at his back taped up over his shoulder and to his pectoral, to deliver imitation milk to the baby as though through his nipple. I comfort myself with the dark, unmentioned scenarios wherein that would be necessary.

A box on the birth certificate paperwork says *I wish to list another man as the baby's father (See reverse)*. I see reverse, curious what wisdom the hospital has for such a situation, what policies the board has come up with to solve a clusterfuck of such magnitude, but the reverse is blank.

My husband has hymns and spirituals, but when I sing to the baby I can only remember the most desperate lines from pop songs.

If you want better things, I want you to have them. My girl, my
girl, don't lie to me. Tell me, where did you sleep last night?

Q: Do you think having a baby was a good idea?
A: As much as I ever did.

4. *I have been anxious or worried for no good reason.*

Erica says, Your phone is ringing.
What's the area code? There are certain area codes I categori-
cally avoid.
What about home?
Especially home.

In my Percocet dreams our blankets are meringue but quicksand
thick, suffocation heavy, and the baby somewhere in them. From
the toilet I shout it out.
She's not in the bed, my husband says from the hallway.
How do you know?
Because she's in the bassinet.
But how do you know she's in the bassinet?
Because I'm looking at the bassinet and I see her in there.
But, I want to know, how do you know that you are really seeing?

5. *I have blamed myself unnecessarily when things went wrong.*

A postcard arrives addressed to both of us but meant only for my
husband: *Funny how some people feel like home.*

Q: Do you still want to be married?
A: As much as I ever did.

The world slips out from under us approximately every hour and a half.

6. *I have been so unhappy that I have had difficulty sleeping.*

Over Skype people say things about the baby I don't like—she seems small, she seems quiet, she's a princess, she will be gone before we know it—and I slam the computer closed. After, I send them pictures of the baby and small loops of video, to prove I am not a banshee. I am a banshee, but cannot get comfortable with being one, am always swinging from bansheeism to playacting sweetness and back. I cannot play nice and don't want to, but want to want to, some days.

7. *I have felt sad or miserable.*

I can hear the whispers of my own future outbursts: I wiped your ass, I suctioned boogers from your nose, I caught your vomit in my cupped hand and it was hot! I cut the tiny sleep dreads from your hair and blew stray eyelashes off your cheeks. I can feel the seeds of my resentment as I swallow them. When you couldn't sleep I lay beside you with my nipple in your mouth. For hours I did this!

I can feel lifelong narratives zipping together like DNA, creation myths ossifying. You would smile but only if you thought no one was looking. Your hands were always cold, little icicles, but pink and wrinkly as a man's, little bat claws, little possum hands. Your dad cut the teensiest tip of your finger off trying to cut your nails, and after that we let them grow. That's why you have socks on your hands in all your pictures, to keep you from scratching yourself.

When we took the socks off you had little wooly worms of lint in your palms, from clenching and unclenching your fists all day. We had a machine that rocked you and another that vibrated you and another that made the noises from the world you'd never seen—breakers and birds, rain on a tin roof—but they soothed you anyway. Robo-baby, I worried you'd become, since you liked the machines so much more than me.

8. *I have been so unhappy that I have been crying.*

Ours is not even a bad baby. She sleeps so much I have to lie to the other moms, pretend to be tired when I'm not, commiserate lest they turn on me. In truth ours sleeps through anything, even two adults screaming at each other, crying, saying things they can't take back, making up, and screaming again—our baby sleeps through all of it, waking only when we stagger into our own bed.

When her cord stump falls off I put it in the pocket of my bathrobe. I don't cry until the robe is put in the wash.

Creation myth (his):
He broke his collarbone falling off a fence. He was trying to get to the neighbor girl.

Creation myth (hers):
When they brought her baby sister home from the hospital she tried to deposit the bundle in the trash.

Q: Do you still love me?
A: As much as I ever did.

9. *The thought of harming myself has occurred to me.*

And also the profound pleasure of sitting in the backyard on the
last warm day of fall, the baby and her dad on a bedsheet on the
grass, me in a lawn chair because I cannot yet bend in the ways
that would get me to and from the ground, in my lap a beer and
a bowl of strawberries.

Q: Do you appreciate being alive?
A: As much as I ever did.

10. *Things have been too much for me.*

On Christmas Eve the upper-class grocery store is a teeming
jingle bell hellscape. I decide to play nice for once, an exercise,
my Christmas gift to the universe. I strap the baby to me and
do not pretend not to notice when strangers gape at her there.
I stop and let them say oh how cute and even oh how precious
and when they ask if the baby is a boy or a girl I do not say, Does
it really matter? nor A little bit of both! nor You know, I'm not
sure, how do I check? And when they ask how old I do not say,
Two thousand eight hundred and eighty hours, nor A lady never
tells. Instead I round up and say four months today! I wag the
baby's hand and make the baby say hi and bye-bye. I spend too
much money on stinky cheeses and chocolate coins, stovetop
popcorn, armfuls of cut flowers, muffin tins I will never use,
pomegranates that remind me of home. I do not use self-checkout,
the misanthrope's favorite invention, and when the nosy checker
asks me to sign my name on the electronic pad I do not write
666 nor draw a big cock and balls and instead I sign in elegant
cursive the baby's name. And outside I do not look away when
more lonely people ask me with their eyes to stop so that they

240

might see the baby and touch her and instead I do stop, in the fresh snow falling and padding the parking lot, let them hold the baby's hand and let them tell me how I will feel in five years or ten years or twenty years or at this time next year, let them tell me where I will be and what will be happening and how I will cherish every minute.

Wild

TRACY K. SMITH

But I want her to be tame.
I know. I know. Different game.

I see her from a distance.
The loud high squeal that spills,

How she stomps, leaps, runs.
It pleases almost everyone.

What small gear slows in me,
Stalls? Is it a matter of damage (mine)—

The way my mother made me
whisper ma'am and sir, conquer my hands

their animal urge? I never ran wild.
Obedient child. It took me years—Oh, the pleasure

Was slow, secret, rich—to discover night's
Cold black anesthetizing air. I'm older,

Feraler, and wrong—I suspect—
To want the same for her.

JOANNA KAVENNA is the author of several works of fiction and nonfiction including *Inglorious, The Birth of Love,* and, most recently, *A Field Guide to Reality.* Her writing has appeared in the *New Yorker, London Review of Books, Guardian,* and the *New York Times,* among other publications. In 2008 she won the Orange Prize for New Writing and in 2013 she was named as one of *Granta*'s Best Young British Novelists.

If There Was No Moon

JOANNA KAVENNA

This morning I woke and my father wasn't there. This was plainly disturbing. In the time I have lived with my father, his routines have been consistent. Usually he rises before me. In recent months he hasn't been sleeping much. I hear him often during the night, as he clatters around downstairs. He moves laboriously, and often he stumbles or nearly falls. Because of the condition of his internal organs, his limbs are inadequately supplied with blood and his muscles are atrophying. And yet, he is civilized and loquacious. He possesses opinions about everything, from cosmology to military history to contemporary fiction. If you ask him, *What would happen if there was no moon*, he might say, well, of course there would be no eclipses anymore. The moon's shadow is almost exactly equal in length to the earth-moon distance and so if there were no moon (he would firmly advocate the use of the subjunctive), there would be no shadow and no disc to block the disc of the sun. It would also be much darker at night. The tides would also be much less significant, he might add. Tides from the sun are only about 40 percent as strong as tides from the moon. When the sun and moon line up in the new or full moon phases then we have spring tides, which are 140 percent as strong as a typical tide, and when they're at right angles we get neap tides, only 60 percent as strong. And the days would be shorter, about 6 to 8 hours, if we had never had a moon and didn't have one now, so there would be 1100 to 1400 days each year. Our axial tilt would vary significantly over time. My father would explain all these elements at some length and with recourse to cutting-edge theories of cosmology. Then he would move on to something else. You might ask him, *What would happen if there were no sun*, now adhering to his advised grammatical protocols, and he would continue. There would be nothing, no one, and you would not be asking the question.

This morning, my father was nowhere to be found. I went upstairs and his bedroom was empty, sheets strewn across the floor, the window open. I could see the cold river beyond and the skeletal forms of the trees. There were bloodstains around the bed, as was usual—my father's condition has caused his skin to split, and he always has open sores on his ankles and feet. His alarm rested on the bedside table. He has another alarm, which he wears around his wrist. I looked in the bathroom, and in my bedroom, further along the corridor. Then I ran downstairs again, calling his name. No answer.

Every room was empty. I became quite panicked, my heart pounding, and then I thought it was unreal, because of course—people don't just vanish! It was so absurd, and it made me feel as if everything else might suddenly vanish as well. I felt as if there was a cloud, a dark cloud, a shadow, chasing across the skies towards the house, so I recoiled—

I went to the door, I had to get out. Besides my heart was constricted, it fluttered weakly as if it might stop and I had this dreadful gouging pain in my chest, I cried again—'Father? Father?' The words bounced meaninglessly around in space. Five clocks ticked on the wall, all set to different times. He was nowhere to be seen.

My vision was blurred, I went outside, I tried to breathe slowly. Calm and quiet—I kept telling myself, it's alright. Just fine. And so—I made myself focus on these ordinary aspects of the day—the grass, blown gently by the breeze, the river silver-white beyond the path. The sky, like hammered steel, and the cry of birds, these undulations of sound, always beautiful, so many cries. And the oily sliding ripples of the water, and the gathering hum of traffic from a road somewhere. A man was walking quickly into town, speaking into a phone, and a V-shaped flock of birds reeled across the silver sky.

My father would return I thought. Of course—wherever—he had gone—it wasn't—far . . .

No wind, no leaf stirring. Only the soft splash of distant oars on the river. I shivered as if I might be sick and there were strange dark spots, they moved, like flying insects, or something that could crawl through the air. I tried to blink, I rubbed my eyes, but when I opened them again these weird patterns blocked out regions of the sky, I kept blinking hard and trying to disperse them. Then I thought that such minor hallucinations could of course be attributed to fatigue. I really hadn't slept much, not for a long time. Each night was disturbed. Cries and then—sudden alarms. I had bad dreams. The sound of ambulance men banging on the door. I gathered myself, I wondered, where had my father gone anyway? It was much better, outside, with the cold air calming me down. It was much better outside, in the air. I repeated this a few more times, how the air was soothing, how the days were long. The broad sky slamming onto the fields. Winter had bleached the colours, turning everything monochrome. The skeletal forms of trees were reflected in the still water.

I watched a pair of swans gliding along, and I thought, he'll come back. Wherever he has gone, I'll wait here and he'll return. He's not going to board a plane and disappear to the Far East, to Australia, to Uruguay, as he did in the past. My father, the great and unpredictable traveller, who would phone my mother abruptly from the airport, and explain that his research made it impossible for him to stay. He loved the absolution of a long-haul flight. He procured objects for collectors and galleries. He collected significant detritus and this is why his house, for example, is so ornate. The many pasts, of others, and his own, arranged on shelves and in glass cabinets.

My father's house stands on the banks of the Dyfi, as it flows through the Welsh town of Machynlleth, and continues to Aberdyfi and the ocean. I have lived here for twelve months, maybe slightly more, since my father's predicament became so unfortunate and Dr Samuels became so patient and serious. A low wall divides his garden from the river path, at the front, and the fields behind. This was a neglected area, for decades—the sketchy pastures behind the workers' cottages and industrial estates. In the medieval era you would have been set upon by cut-throats, robbed and tossed into the river. Even now, we reside in a strange and silent terrain, an unlikely realm of unkempt pastures, with horses rustling through the grass, and in front the silvery winding river, winding onwards to the sea.

I stood for a moment, looking at the trees reflected in the water; I noticed how constantly the water moved, how the reflections of the scrawny trees were dispersed and then re-formed. I was wearing pyjamas and trainers, a coat and a hat. I rubbed my arms, puffed out white air. A man rowed past in a small boat, and I glanced towards him, noticing that he had dark, curly hair, pale skin, high cheekbones. His head was down, he had thin arms and thin legs barely contained within the small boat; he wore thin white shorts, a thin white vest. He looked familiar, there was something about him as he rowed along, that—somehow—I wasn't sure—so I dismissed that thought and gradually he moved onwards—until he went around the bend in the river and towards the sea.

Now the doctor arrived, cycling along the path. Another thing I like about my father's house is that you can't reach it by road. Responses vary when you explain this detail to prospective visitors. Some people simply never come to visit you again! They think you're some kind of reactionary lunatic, growing your own cabbages and refusing all contemporary forms of society. It's surprising more people don't travel by water in this town. The roads are clogged each morning with wild-eyed, harried people trapped in their cars and yet the river is almost empty. Dr Samuels had come along by bicycle and he looked reasonably irritated, but that was his habitual mode. He was wearing a grey trench coat, and thick-weave cords. He nodded to me and asked how I was doing. I nearly told him that my father had vanished but I didn't want to worry him. Besides, people make such a fuss about these things. There would be a hue and cry! Benevolent officials, all of them running up and down the bank, flapping their coat-tails and wringing their hands and searching for my father who had probably just gathered his waning strength to go for a walk. The doctor asked if I had the bag he had asked me to put together, some old medicines that my father no longer needed. Then I was uncertain.

'But what if—we need them—later?' I asked.

He looked at me with his customary patient air and said, 'I'm very sorry but of course they can't be used again. They were specific to your father's condition.'

He kept going in and out of focus. I wanted to tell him that everything was clouded, the day completely indistinct. Instead, I said, 'Oh yes, of course.' I really didn't want to get into some sort of protracted debate. The man wanted the medicines! Of course, he could have them. 'Yes, yes,' I said, 'I have them inside.'

I found the bag inside the front door. I must have put it there the night before. Lapses of memory are caused by fatigue, of course. So we should all be reassured. When we forget our names, when we forget—even where our fathers have gone—we should be reassured because—we are just a little tired and overwrought. We just need a quick nap and then everything will be clear and pristine again. The fact I was finding—that at times reality was—somehow—elided with things that were plainly unreal—that was just exhaustion. When the edges of reality become blurred, when they start to merge into something we suspect can't be real at all, then we can all assume that we need an extra hour of sleep a night and perhaps some sleeping pills, or another analgesic. Antidepressants, said the doctor, furrowing his brow. Why not just try them? Like a drug-pusher, trying to get me addicted to something in the end. But antidepressants? I wasn't remotely depressed. I wanted him to be completely aware of that! I was if anything more alert to this weird thing about reality—that it just isn't actually very real! If you stopped rigidly adhering to this general fixed notion of how reality should be, then suddenly it started to slip, and slide, and morph into something that you couldn't even define. The doctor nodded politely on the rare occasions when I had the nerve to tell him what I thought about his foolish notion of reality. He nodded like a nodding dog my father once brought back from a trip to Cairo. It sat on the dashboard of his car, for years, agreeing with everything. I wanted to tell Dr Samuels how much he resembled this acquiescent plastic animal. But, of course, that would be exceptionally rude. You can't tell a virtuous and kindly medic that he resembles a piece of novelty plastic, a souvenir! So I kept quiet and handed the medicines over to him.

Dr Samuels has a reassuring air and this counteracts his prevailing resemblance to a fox. When he was young he must have been beautiful, in a vulpine way. Now he is quite grey, his brow ravaged with lines. He has furrowed it so many times, confronted by the dying and their relatives, and this has permanently creased his face. He's been tending to my father for a decade at least, and for the last year I have seen a great deal of Dr Samuels. Now he was leaning against the gate, looking thin and gaunt and generally as if he would like to help, but of course he couldn't. He kept talking about shock and how it was inevitable, that things hadn't quite sunk in. I had a sudden urge to punch him, I really wanted to smack him hard and pummel him to the ground, but I handed him the medicines instead.

Of course, you really can't go around punching doctors. It's simply not allowed. I was adrift but I understood that, at least.

Something to cling onto, I thought.

'Thank you,' said Dr Samuels, about the medicines. He put them into the basket of his bicycle. This made me incredibly angry too.

'Appalling events in the Middle East,' he said. I agreed, it was insane. 'I have no belief in God, do you?' he added. Then he looked really stricken, as if he had said something terrible. I hadn't even had a chance to answer, when he started saying, 'I mean, it's not my business to say such things.' We paused because it was uncertain whether it was his business or not.

'You'll need to bring back the wheelchairs, the walking frames, those sorts of things. When you're ready, of course,' he said, still looking sorry. 'No hurry.'

The sun glistened behind him and it illuminated his grey hair, so it shone like silver. This shining silvery man was about to go and because I didn't want him to leave I said that, while I could not be remotely certain there was a god, or goddess, or any other variety of divine being, I could also not be absolutely certain that there was not.

'Well, that's right, many people feel there may well be a spiritual aspect to the world,' he said. 'I tend to a materialistic worldview.' Then he was preparing to cycle off, but I said, 'What do you even mean by spiritual? Or materialistic? What the hell do those words mean?' I was brimming with questions! How did he classify the spiritual? Did it mean anything invisible? And if so, what about nanoparticles, or dark matter, or anything that we did not fully apprehend and understand? Where was it not, if it was definitively and constitutionally not? Had Dr Samuels somehow apprehended the absolute parameters of reality and decided what was categorically and what was not?

'I mean, that the world is matter, and reality is matter, or prob-ably.' He had furrowed his brow again, creased his face in this

251

expression of earnest penitence, because he mainly didn't want to offend me. That was more important for him than any expression of belief, one way or the other. He was saying, with virtuoso kindness, 'But I appreciate, and I'm sorry, this is not the right time for this sort of conversation.'

'When is the right time?' I actually wanted to stamp my foot. I wanted then to jump up and down screaming, and beating my chest and tearing at my hair. It made me savage with frustration. The words, he thought they were so solid and I didn't believe in their solidity at all. Matter! This word *matter*! What was it, anyway? 'All you mean,' I said, 'is that you think my opinions are insignificant, and you have more important things to do, you assume, than listen to them. So, why bother?' Now I wanted to shout at him, my father isn't even here, you idiot! And you're pedaling off, with your fox-face and your former beauty now sunken into something grey and less definitive—you see, Dr Samuels, even your former beauty is sliding into the nebulous realm—and the river—the river is so cold!

A flock of those free as hell birds went above our heads and flew away, to wherever they were going. In their creepy telepathic way they turned and turned again, all in synch, and I thought—is that matter? Or spirit? Or something else? How do those birds know when the others are preparing to change course again? All the way to wherever they're going? The south, far below?

'I'm sorry,' Dr Samuels said. He looked almost frantic. He rubbed his hand across his dwindling features, and tousled his hair. With that, he suddenly looked like an embarrassed boy, a teenager who had been handed some formal garb and told he was playing the doctor and pillar of society. He was trying his best to be convincing. 'Of course, it's awful,' he kept saying. 'I'm just so sorry. We take consolation from whatever we can, don't you think?'

He teetered on his bike, he suddenly looked quite clumsy, as if he was going to fall to the towpath and brain himself and discover abruptly whether there was a spiritual dimension to reality or not. The medicine bag was rustling in his basket, as the wind swirled around us. As if that mattered! And now I wanted to tell him about the slip-sliding, this thing, the edge of vision, but then I knew he would just start offering me drugs again. It would be fair enough. He had a lot to contend with. House after house, and all these eager people, with their bags of redundant medicines, and their expectations, and their tearful greetings, because they were trying so hard to forget—what was real, and yet impossible.

I had to remember: my father was dead. I had to remember. I had to stop arguing with random strangers. Of late, it had become a worrying tendency. I really had to make a resolution about that and abide by it.

For a moment I stood there, and I tried so hard not to cry, it was a horrible possibility, and Dr Samuels looked desperate, and said, 'Well.' That was it. All his former eloquence, compressed into this one word. He was trying to use it as a stopper, to stem the flow of my tears, but it was just this one little word. He couldn't think of anything else.

'You have everything you need?' I said, finally. I'd got it back, the mode of self-regulating adulthood. I had slammed myself back into that again. Brisk and amiable. We both kept saying sorry for a while and then he said there was no need to apologise. Nothing at all was the matter. Except everything was the matter. Then I wondered why we both kept saying the word *matter*.

'Do give me a call, if you need anything, if I can help,' he said.

'Are you taking—your father—to Aberdyfi today?'

'Oh yes,' I said. I wondered how I had forgotten that as well. 'Yes, of course, that's right. I thought I might walk.'

He smiled, as if this was a joke. I tried to explain that I didn't feel like taking the train, that it seemed wildly inappropriate, though actually my father has always liked—he always liked—trains, but anyway—I was going to walk.

He gave me an awkward wave, then cycled away along the path. He was heading downstream. I thought of the water, this water that is never the same, ushered from the depths of the earth and the constant flow of moisture through the land, and how the rivers meander to the sea. And I thought of how I was poised, just here, on the bank—and this river came from the mountains above my father's childhood home. I thought how strange it was, that my father's life charted a movement precisely down this river—of course, this was a mere conceit, and he had roamed widely across the world and only settled in Machynlleth in his declining years. But, from the moment of his birth to the moment of his death, he had gone from one end of a river to the other, and this seemed strange to me.

When I went inside I got an incredible shock, because I thought my father was in his chair again. Just for a moment, I thought he was poring over a book. I was so pleased to see him, and then I was angry with him, too, for vanishing without telling me where he had gone. For being here and then not here at all and then—I was trying to move towards him but I started to cry. When I looked directly at him I couldn't assemble his features, so I had to look at him from the side. I was so tired, I was weary beyond measure. After I rubbed my eyes and looked up again I realised my father wasn't in the chair at all. I had arranged his coat on the chair, and a waterproof hat he always wore, I was going to wear them today. Of course he wasn't there, it was absurd! I was speaking to nothingness, I felt the sky had become heavy and tangible and was bearing down on me so I almost fell to the ground—

I was really late by then. I made a cup of coffee and then ran around in that quotidian ritual way, getting dressed, finding my boots. My father—was not here—and yet reality continued. Today I had forgotten everything that was important. I had become confused. I simply had to go; I put on my backpack and noted how heavy it felt. This was insane, but real. I tried to remember—nothing else

254

remained. If my father was only matter, only his material bodily self, then nothing else remained. Except memory. To walk and to remember. Today I was walking downstream with my father in an urn, in a backpack, my father's dust, ashes, and then I would drop him in the ocean.

That was what I was doing today.

The sky was rucked like a curtain. It was so beautiful, I stood at the window for a moment, watching the trees swaying against the white sky. There were some questions even my father couldn't answer. I picked up my bag, which was so heavy. I walked up the towpath thinking I must separate reality from unreality. I must really start remembering things. But that's a risky business!

You Better Not Put Me in a Poem

SANDRA CISNEROS

To All the Boys, Give or Take a Few

One had a long curved scimitar like a Turkish moon.

One had a fat tamale plug.

One had a baby pacifier.

One had a lightbulb he was proud of.
    It gave me the creeps.
    I can never forget it.
    I could never pick it out in a police lineup.
    Not in a million years.
    Not even with an AK-47 to the side of my head.

One liked to pull it out like a switchblade when least expected.
    At his mother's.
    Standing in the bathroom, the door open.
    His ma in the kitchen talking on the phone.
    Me on the couch trying to read.
    He thought this was sexy.

One liked to skim *Playboy* magazines when we were making love.
    I found this humiliating.

One liked to put his hands on his hips like he was Mr. Big Stuff.
    This pissed me off.

One liked to dip his fingers in his semen and lick them.
    He drove me wild.

One slept in my bed, but never touched me.
    This was my choice.

One drew a spiral on the envelopes of all his letters.
    Translation: Your back door is mine alone.

One lived with a woman.

One lived alone, but refused to let me see where he lived
    Like a serial killer with something to hide.

One liked to whack me with his dong like a cop's baton.
    He had issues.

One liked to dress me as a boy and take me from behind.
    He had issues.

One was an alcoholic and would go on endless riffs.
    The war.
    The women who left.
    The wife he wouldn't.
    One night he called from a bar and left seventeen messages
        on my machine.
    Did I mention he was an alcoholic?

One never touched the stuff. It made him vomit.
    He was always home.

One drove a nervous car with too many miles and not enough
    insurance.

But every weekend he drove two hundred miles in frantic
 traffic to see me.

One never came even when I offered to pay the airfare.

One was married to somebody. A string of somebodies.

We saw each other off and on/in between/during/above and below/
 over

A quarter of a century.

When he divorced the last time, I realized finally:
 He was the father almighty's approval.
 I would never get his approval.
 I didn't need his approval anymore.
 I had made him up.

When he came, he:
 Hiccupped like a dolphin.
 Snorted like a horse.
 Embarrassed me hollering like a girl.
 Was strangely silent like a deer.
 Panted like a little dog and planted a kiss on my butt.

Each and every time.

Never. And afterward he:
 Laughed a little.
 Wheezed.
 Hacked up a furry cough.
 Sprinted off to the shower like I was the plague.
 Lit up a smoke.

Never smoked.

Had a collapsed lung.

Had only one lung and was a percussionist.
After our good-bye I sent him
Pawnshop bongo drums and marshmallows from Texas
All the way to an address in Athens.
A year later the bongo drums and marshmallows came back
    unopened.
Across how many oceans?
A package stamped in Greek letters: "Address Unknown."
But I read it as: "Undress Alone."

I sent a hundred-dollar bouquet of parrot
Tulips to a restaurant where one worked as a bartender
Even though he was terrible in bed because:
    I was grateful.
    I was needy.
    I was young.
    (See above.)

    I was/am/always will be a romantic.

Which is the same as saying: I fall in love all by myself.

I sent one a poem.
I never saw him again.

I sent one a twenty-seven-page letter wrapped around a brick for
    dramatic effect.

I sent one postcards from Trieste, Sarajevo, Sparta, Sienna,
    Perpignan,
Describing my other lovers.
All he did was laugh.

One was a Tejano fitness freak from Austin.
    Tremendous.
    A lottery prize.

I'm not kidding.

Until he opened his mouth and spoke:
    Like a guitar.
    Like a white man.
    Like a white Texan.
Once when I was making *licuados* for breakfast, he said,
    Great, I love smoothies!

One knew what a woman wants above all else is words.
    To be told he loves her.
    To be told how he is going to love her as he is loving her.
    To be told there is no woman like her.
I can't forget him.

I don't remember his name.

He is not my ex,
Nor my y, nor even my z.
He is my *eterno*.

One night on a bed of sand, under a canopy of falling stars,
One, who wanted to make love to him,
Made love to me.
He to him. I to they.

And afterward I concluded a ménage à trois is useless because:
    I need love.
    A semblance of love at least.
    Eternity.
And how can you ignite eternity if preoccupied with—*How do I
    look?*

One didn't care what he looked like, and this was precisely why:
    He was sexy.
    He was as impeccable and godly as *GQ*.
    But the more exquisite he grew, the more I turned into a rodent.
    He was my own height and weight.

261

It was easy to flip him over in bed, and the fact that I could
Made me feel powerful.
And I liked this power.

One was big as a redwood, and when he lay on top
Of me, I felt like hollering:
Timberrrrrrrrrrrr!

One was violet like the ink from a sea creature, beautiful but
    deadly.
    The skin beneath his clothes glowed from within like a lamp
        of alabaster.
    His thing was a blue baby born without air.
    His thing was pink like an angry child holding its breath.

I don't remember his thing. I don't remember anything.

One confessed, after making love to me, he was still in love
With a ballerina who had moved away to Kansas. Then,
He bought me pancakes.

One confessed he was still in love with an actress he'd dumped
    when
She was an unknown, but was now celebrated in Cannes
And Paris. And this was killing
Him.

One bought me a five-pound typewriter,
    A white Izod polo shirt I never wore because it was too
        Dallas.
    A bag of *pan dulce*, and put me to bed as if I was his only
        child.
    But,

I was in love with a sex-*puto* who made
Love like a water-hose drowning a riot.

One took pictures of me nude when I was too shy to be nude.

I took pictures of me nude when I was too old to be nude.

It was obvious one had an Oedipus complex.
I was forty. He was twenty-one.

I lost interest in one, because I thought he looked like an old man.
He was forty. I was twenty-eight.

Pee on me, one demanded, and I knew I had to get out of there.

I came to bed wearing nothing but a belt of bells like a flock of
    sheep.

I came to bed wearing nothing but a mink coat.

I came to bed wearing a granny gown and long underwear.

I came to bed the moment one called, because he had to get up
    early and go to work,

And if I didn't, he said I wasn't going to get any.
And his love is the sweetest memory.

We made love on a train in Genoa in a restroom that smelled of
    pee.
I hated/adored/was terrified of him because:
    I was poor, and worse, ashamed of being poor.
    I knew he would eventually leave me.
    I wanted him to destroy me.
    I thought pain was necessary.
    I wanted to be him.
    (All of the above.)

One was a pre-med student, and after making love would:
    Ask me to cough.

263

Tap on my back.
Thump me like a drum.
Read my body as if I was a well-tuned machine.

I had a crush on one until he appeared at my door
One night with a mustache exactly like my brother's.

I met one in Tenejapa when he rose
From the Mayan jungle like a plumed serpent.

I met one across a boardroom table where he licked my nipples
    with his eyes.

I met one at a bar where a gay friend and I both wanted him, but
I was the only one brave enough to ask,
        Are you gay or are you straight?
Silence. *Why?*
        Because I don't have a lot of time.

One shook like a little tree when I left him.
    There were no tears from me.

I shook like a little tree when one left me.
    There were no tears from him.

Subsequently I learned this emotional equation:
    The first one to cry robs the other of the need to.

One was a sham shaman, and when we first made love he

Smudged me with copal and let me place my tongue on his scars.

One became famous, and they make movies about his books.

One is a loser. He teaches at a university where they don't care
    he's a hustler.

One got married to Hello Kitty, though I suspect he's in the closet.

One was Opus Dei. He dumped me for a Catholic he knocked up.

One wanted to knock me up just so he could say he knocked me up.

One was an anarchist, and I can't forget the sex.

I don't remember the sex. I remember him, and that was sexy
    enough.

One was bi, and now he's gay.

One was straight, and now he's celibate.

One had teeth like a rat, and now he can afford to have them
    fixed.

One was in love with a man, and when they kissed each other
    once
In front of me, slowly, deliberately, a cigarette burning flesh,
I was neither jealous nor sad, but
Fascinated like a fleck of glitter somersaulting
In a globe of snow.

I was Cinderella searching for the perfect fit,
And when I tried his on for size, I knew.

It was the opposite of childbirth. One was born in my life
When he slid in with a grunt, and it was then, I knew.

One was soft as a custard cone. I always felt it was my fault.
Once I dreamed I was carrying his penis through an airport
When, without warning, it sputtered a geyser of shit.
I rushed it to the ladies'. Hesitated.
Decided the men's room. Then paused.
I wasn't sure where to go, but one thing I knew.
Over and over I said to aghast bystanders,
But it's not mine, it's not mine.

You better not, he said kicking
Off cowboy boots, unzipping his tight
Jeans, *Put me in a poem.*

And the arrogance at first
When I had no such intent. Well,
I just knew

That would be the first,
If not the last,

Thing I would do.

CLAIRE MESSUD's most recent novel is *The Woman Upstairs*. She teaches at Harvard University and lives in Cambridge, Massachusetts, with her family.

Going to the Dogs

CLAIRE MESSUD

People react differently to our canine situation. From what they say, I glean information about their natures. Of course, one way or another, they judge us—our dogs provide a morality play all their own.

We're a family of four, or of six: two adults and two kids (ages fourteen and eleven), with two dogs. They're relatively small dogs, although not (we like to believe) obscenely so. Myshkin is a standard-sized, red, short-haired dachshund whose antiquity is in some dispute: she came to us as a puppy in the fall either of 1998 or of 1999, so long ago we can't remember. Her junior consort, Bear, a rescue mutt, joined the family back in 2009, at which point he was said to be about eighteen months old. Part terrier and part min-pin, he's toffee-colored, scruffy and professorial in aspect, with wiry legs and, once upon a time, amazing speed and agility. (Myshkin, incidentally, means "little mouse" in Russian, so we have, in name at least, two non-canine creatures; though only the first was named after the protagonist of *The Idiot*.)

At this point, Myshkin the matriarch, still silky and fine-featured, is deaf, blind, intermittently incontinent and increasingly weak on her pins. Her sturdy front legs splay and slide with the effort of standing, and her back legs have a way of collapsing. She ends up

269

reclining—like the Queen of Sheba or a beached whale, depending on your perspective—in unlikely places, occasionally almost in her own excrement, which makes constant vigilance imperative. She's so demented that half the time when you take her outside, she remains immobile but for her wagging tail, apparently unclear why she's there.

Oh, and did I mention that she reeks? Not just a bit of dog-breath, or even the comparatively pleasant scent of wet dog. It's a holistic foulness, emanating not just from her mouth, which smells like the garbage can behind the fishmonger's (hence her nickname: Fishbin), but at this point from her entire body, which, in spite of frequent bathing, carries about it the odor of a dung-heap in hot weather. Her stench precedes her, and lingers in a room after she's left. It's hard to sit next to her, let alone take her on your lap, without gasping at the fecal, fishy gusts.

The worst of it, though, is her constant state of existential crisis, which has her either moaning or, more unnervingly, barking, for hours at a stretch. Dachshunds, though small dogs, have big dog barks: they bark loudly, deeply and resonantly, in a way that can't be ignored. Our house isn't big, so we're never far from her barking. She's barking right now, in fact. If the phone rings, you can't hear what the caller says. If the radio or television is on, you won't catch that either. But you can't stop the barking: lift her onto the sofa; take her off again; check her water dish; take her outside; through it all, with but a few minutes' respite, she will bark, and bark, and bark. And bark. Like a metronome. Sometimes, when we have dinner guests, we stash her, barking, in the car.

She was supercute as a puppy. We chose her from the litter because she was the first to run to us and nuzzle our ankles; though we quickly came to understand that food is her first and abiding passion, and she may simply have thought we had some to offer. Scent is the one sense really left to her, and she can still sniff out a candy bar in a closed handbag, or a cookie crumb underneath the fridge. It pleases her enormously to do so—the thrill of the hunt! And she can still thump her tail magnificently when caressed. We have adored her, and made much of her, lo these many years, and have overlooked some significant disadvantages (e.g., a lamentable penchant for coprophagia). Before we had kids, she slept on our bed; and latterly, in her great age, as she has taken up existential barking in the dead of night, she sleeps on our bed all over again, although now on a special (smelly) blanket at its foot, with a towel over her head. Myshkin rules the roost; but Bear, too, has his ways. He was, when first he came to us, runty but beautiful, and restless. He could run like a gazelle, and, in the early months, skittish, took any chance to do so: he chomped through leashes and harnesses, he opened doors with his snout, he darted and feinted and fled. Half a dozen times we had to enlist bands of strangers—at the reservoir; on our block; in the parking lot at Target—to help catch him. You felt you got him in the end only because he let you. He could jump, too: one leap up onto the kitchen table, if you weren't looking, to eat a stick of butter. A single bound onto a wall, or down again. He was fearless.

I loved to walk him. I'll confess: I was vain about it. He was so dapper and elegant, so handsome and swift. After years of plodding along beside the plump-breasted dowager Myshkin, whose little legs and long body have dignity and power but not much élan (I've always maintained that dachshunds really do understand the absurdity of life), I was delighted to dash around the block in minutes, witness to his graceful sashays. And I loved the compliments—he got so many compliments! A certain type of person loves a dachshund ("My grandmother used to have one of those; his name was Fritzie"); but anyone who tolerates dogs was taken by Bear. He had something about him, a star quality.

One late January evening in 2009, when my husband was out of town and a cousin was visiting, when I was in charge of the kids (then eight and five), the dinner, the dogs and life, I took Bear for his twilight round. (It should be said that we've never been able to walk both dogs simultaneously, because their ideas of "a walk" differ so vastly.) Regrettably, I was multitasking: I had the dog, the bag of poo, and some letters to mail, and I was on the phone to my parents, who were then alive but ailing, and to whom I spoke every evening without fail. I'd almost finished the round of the block, was up on the main road at the mailbox, when, while trying to manipulate the leash, the poo, the phone, the letters and the handle to the mailbox, I dropped the leash. It was the stretchy kind, its handle a large slab of red plastic; it made a noisy thud on the icy pavement.

Bear panicked, and bolted. I slammed my foot down on the leash. I was wearing clogs with ridged soles; the icy ground was uneven; and the leash, being the stretchy kind, was thin as a wire. I didn't catch it with my shoe. I stomped again, and again: too late. Bear dashed out into the rush hour traffic. All my parents could hear down the dropped cell phone line was my long wail.

Being small, he was treated by Fate like a tumbleweed: having made it halfway across unscathed, he banged headlong into the bumper of a moving car on the far side of traffic, then rolled beneath it and out the other side. I recall only the headlights, made blurry by my tears, and the noise, in the encroaching dark; and seeing him, then, against the far curb, and hearing him howl.

I took him in my arms; his left eye protruded from his head as if on a stalk, or a spring—I thought, "How do cartoonists know this?"— and I cradled his little bloody head against my chest. I carried him down to our front porch, and sat with him on the step.

A woman, a stranger, whose car had been behind the one that hit Bear, had driven down my street. She had her two kids and her own dog in the car. She pulled over, and offered to help: she knew the way to the nearest veterinary hospital, whereas the one we'd used for Myshkin's gold-plated back operation several years before was forty-five minutes away, on the other side of town. She'd lead me there; I could follow in my car. I gestured at poor Bear—how could I simply put him on the seat beside me? He was shaking, almost convulsing. She, nameless Samaritan, offered me the company of her son.

That amazing child—a boy of perhaps eleven or so—sat in my car (a stranger's car) with Bear upon his lap (a pulpy, bloody thing, with an eye upon a stalk), and stroked the dog and whispered quietly to him as we crawled up the highway behind his mother in the rush-hour darkness to the hospital. (I had to leave my young cousin in charge of the kids. Thank goodness he was there. He was very amiable and unfussed about it, but I think supper was a bowl of cereal that night.)

The eye that had burst out couldn't be saved. The other they retained, though purely for cosmetic purposes: Bear can't see a thing. In the early days, he'd try to leap onto a piece of furniture that wasn't there—a wonderful sight in its way, to see him bounce high into the air and plop right back down—or he'd sit patiently facing a wall, his head slightly cocked, as if gazing upon a beautiful vista. Now, he navigates the house as if he could see it all perfectly; unless we drop a suitcase in the hall, or move a chair. The vet assured us that for a dog, sight is like taste or smell for humans, a secondary sense; and that Bear could lead a full and happy life without his eyes. Asked about the possibility of brain damage, she gave a wry smile: "Even if there is some, you won't be able to tell. It's not like he won't be able to do algebra anymore."

Tiresias-like, Bear is an inspiration, a teacher of how to make the best of things, how to enjoy what you have and not lament what you've lost. He has an aura of patient wisdom. No longer skittish, he no longer leaps; most painfully, he no longer runs. He tried, in the beginning, but a few sharp knocks subdued the urge. He's biddable, patient, and very sweet, largely content to let Myshkin order him about. (The only time they cuddle together is at the cageless kennel: we've seen photos, so we know it's true. At home, if he approaches her sofa, she'll growl at him.) I suffered grief and guilt after the accident; some part of me felt, too, that I was being punished for my vanity, for having been so proud of Bear's superficial charms.

I didn't mention earlier that the handsome Bear came to us with a fatal flaw. We suspect it may be why he ended up in that kill shelter in Georgia in the first place, when someone had clearly bothered to teach him to sit, to stay, even to stand on his hind legs. Bear is a widdler. When the postman comes—or the UPS guy, or the FedEx truck; and because we're book people, they, too, come almost daily—Bear erupts: he dashes to the door, hopping up and down in a fury; the hair on the back of his neck stands up; he roars for all he's worth and bares his tiny fangs. Unlike Myshkin, who has a grown-up bark, Bear has an awful, little-dog shriek, an indignity. And then, when he's danced around in his rage for a while, he all too often lifts his leg against a chair or sofa leg and sprinkles a few rebellious drops, just to make a point, sort of like flipping the finger at the guy at the door.

He did this from the first. We were working on training him out of it—a passionate young man came to the house to teach us how to think like a dog: re: the stick of butter: "Correction! He knows he's not supposed to do it *when you're in the room*. That's all"—but the training went down the tubes after the accident, apparently along with any memory of it. A bit of brain damage after all. We put a plastic sheet under the sofa nearest the front door, and that's been an improvement. Dismayingly, the vet has no other suggestions, though she shakes her head in sympathy. So in addition to the walking room-desanitizer that is Myshkin, we live, and our children are growing up, in a faint but persistent ammoniac fug.

So, to recap: we have the obstreperous, incessantly barking, stinky old deaf and blind dog who can't really stand up; and the completely blind pisser. Whenever we travel anywhere, they stay in a wonderful (spectacularly smelly) old house in Reading, where dogs are free to roam and a bevy of loving young women tend to their needs. It's like paying for a spa vacation for two extra kids. But we couldn't ask anyone else to take care of them: one animal virtually can't walk, the other ambles at his own sniffy pace (where once he looked always ahead and darted onward, Bear can now take half an hour to circle the block). One risks incontinence at unforeseen moments; the other, highly predictable in his incontinence, is virtually unstoppable. Myshkin needs to sleep with humans at night; Bear needs to go outside every three hours in the daytime. Who, we say, *who* could possibly put up with them?

As you can tell, we complain about our dogs. We berate the barking, perorate about the pissing, lament our enslavement, and throw up our hands at the bad smells. We curse when on our knees cleaning carpets; we curse when trying to quell the crazed barking at four in the morning; we curse when one or other of the dogs vomits yet again. My husband always jokes that a true vacation is when the dogs are in the kennel and we're at home without them. But we also stroke them and kiss them and hug them and worry about them. (My husband is always concerned that they're bored. Bear has grown quite stout from the snacks provided to alleviate his boredom, a beneficence I can't condone.) When we're in the house without them, we're baffled by the silence, and amazed by the free space and time (separate walks amount to seven or eight outings a day). We have, it's fair to say, a love-hate relationship with the animals.

This is where people have opinions. When you tell people about our canine situation, many can't believe it. They see it as our moral failing that the dogs are still alive. "Get rid of them," they urge scornfully. "What are you thinking?" We've been told that the dogs' behavior is a reflection upon our characters, that were we better alpha dogs ourselves, our pack wouldn't misbehave as they do. We've been told that we are weak, and that we owe it to our children to have these dogs put down. One friend even suggested that we're heartless to keep Myshkin going when she's lost so many of her faculties; although the vet, whom we visit repeatedly in hopes that she'll tell us when it's time, will give us divine dispensation, assures us that Myshkin is doing just great.

Then there are those on the other side. They don't just forgive us, they pat us gently on the back, offer quiet encouragement—"Good for you" or "It must be tough." Or they see it as hilarious, part of life's wondrous absurdity. Sometimes people even see it as an act of Christian charity. Or as a case of do-as-you-would-be-done-by. Or just plain old love. We prefer this, needless to say, to contempt and derision.

Really, of course, the difference is between those who believe that each of us controls our destiny and has a right to freedom; and those who don't. The former contend that we have the right, even the responsibility, to exert our wills, certainly over dumb animals, in order to maintain order and keep healthy boundaries. It's the only path to sanity, righteousness and good action; and keeping these dogs in our lives is just sentimental claptrap. On the other hand are those who feel that life is a mucky muddle, in which unforeseen situations arise, and possibly endure; and that we must care as best we can for those around us, whatever befalls them, with faith that a similar mercy may be shown us in due course.

Before Myshkin was lame and foul and intolerable, she gave us years of affection and happiness. Even in her dotage, she's shown her love by inching ever closer, or by pushing her damp nose under our hands for a caress. For God's sake, she's shown it even by her barking. She waits up for her master to come home; she wakens us at dawn to start the day. And Bear: he's sweetness itself, except with the deliverymen and the sofa leg. If he can't prance or dart the way he did once; if he's no longer the most handsome dog in town;

how, knowing what he suffered—and having caused that suffering, indeed—can I not love him the more?

We're torn, hoping for a deus ex machina that might liberate us from the discomforts they inflict upon us—my parents' dogs never barked obsessively, or peed in the house, which would give credence to those who say it's about our failure properly to lead the pack—but all the while we love their loyalty and generosity and, well, love. The dogs, after all, are the only people who are *always* glad to see us. Who are we to be anything but grateful for their affection and trust? Who are we to play God over them? And yet, what have we done all along but play God?

Or again: how does our strife with the dogs differ from our general strife: could it not be said that our canine situation is simply our life situation? From deep in the doghouse, that's what it looks like to me.

ALEXANDER CHEE is the author of the novels *Edinburgh* and *The Queen of the Night.* He is a contributing editor at the *New Republic* and *Literary Hub* and an editor-at-large at *VQR.* His essays and stories have appeared in the *New York Times Book Review, Tin House, Slate, Guernica,* and *Out,* among other publications. He lives in New York City.

Rich Children

ALEXANDER CHEE

"Early Hanukkah Party," the instructions for the party said in my voice mail. "Tuxedo. Plain collar shirt. You'll be answering the door mostly and doing coat check."

The year was probably 1997, and it was not quite winter, perhaps just barely fall, and the family's son was leaving for a new job running the offices of an American company in China, and his proud parents hoped to have a holiday with him before he left. Friends and family were coming, about eighty to a hundred people. Very simple buffet.

Everything about this catering job sounded like easy money to me until I was there, the captain waving me in through the double doors at the entrance to an apartment where the wealth of the family involved was so apparent, in every detail, that even just the cleanliness of the place, as the doors closed behind me on the hall, left me feeling I had left a contaminated area for the insular world this family commanded.

The floors were what I noticed first: a pale grey marble, smooth and loud to my first step—every sound echoed. I felt as if I were in a museum after hours, a museum with a view of Kips Bay from the twenty-fifth floor. We entered the butler's kitchen, where the hostess appeared, and the captain introduced her as she glided by, nodding her head at me while holding out a pair of slacks, shouting, "Marga! Can you press these?" The slacks looked alarmingly smooth already, already pressed, as she held them out to Marga, who had appeared almost by magic, her long dark hair carefully bound back in a bun, her mouth flat. She took them out of her employer's hands and vanished again.

The captain gave me a short tour of the area assigned to me. I was to open the door to guests, take their coats, and guide them toward the food and drink. After the arrivals had concluded, I was to then focus on bussing the party and also making sure the children invited to the party did not climb on the art. In particular, the host had asked us to protect a life-size, fully articulated statue of a nude woman in the living room, complete with realistic pubic hair. We came to a stop in front of her.

She was positioned by some sort of lacquered cabinet, kneeling beneath a signed print of an Andy Warhol *Dollar Sign*.

"There will be children," the captain said. "And they will probably try to touch the statue. But these are rich children, so you must be very careful not to overreact or, say, to grab them. Just keep them from touching the statue."

"And it can't be moved?" I asked. The captain looked at me darkly and shook his head heavily.

"It's worth too much to touch it. It's worth more than you."

You're doomed, I thought, looking at the statue. But then, the faint study of misery on her face seemed to suggest she knew.

Whoever she was modeled on was a woman of uncertain age—no longer young exactly. The statue was not erotica, or at least, not any conventional sort of erotica—her hands and feet showed red, as if she had run on her hands and knees to get to this position.

I had become used to this by now in this line of work—what I thought of then as the elaborate pornography of the rich. Artwork, technically avant-garde, of relative obscenity and with varying degrees of nudity and social challenges, displayed in their studies and living rooms. I had often worked the awkward parties they had in front of these images, so at odds with their lives, or seemingly so. But it seemed to me they all liked it—they all did it.

This statue at least was something I could imagine as technically innocent in front of children. She was not making any kind of erotic display, unless submissive misery is erotic to you. She looked as if you could have left her on any beach, anywhere. Her nudity was unadorned, as it were.

"You can change upstairs in the study, some of the other waiters are already there," my captain said to me, and as I looked around for a staircase, he gave me another apartment number one floor up, and directions to go back out to the elevator. I left, tuxedo on my shoulder, and knocked on the door when I arrived. Another waiter peeked out and, seeing my tux, let me in.

This apartment was the opposite of the other, though done in the same pale grey. The floors were carpeted, the walls lined in grey flannel, as was the modern furniture, and the windows all had a mottled glass, so that it was impossible to look in. It was like the lair of a James Bond villain. "What is this place?" I asked the waiter who let me in.

"I think it's Daddy's playroom," another of the waiters said. "Frosted windows so no one can snap a photo. Daddy brings his ladies here." He pointed to a stack of *Penthouse* magazines in the bathroom.

"Who would snap a photo?" I asked.

"Mommy's PI."

Not quite an hour later, the doorbell began to ring every few minutes as guests arrived. I had practiced my greeting by the time I opened the door to see a beautiful Korean woman in a Nancy Reagan red Chanel suit smiling at me with that air of waiting so specific to waiting for someone to notice something. It was then I looked down to see she was pushing a wheelchair, in which a tiny elderly white woman in a mink coat sat, her hands holding her coat shut, her knuckles covered in diamonds. Her curly hair was pulled back into a bun that was already in disarray.

"Hel-*lo*," I said. "Welcome!" And I was about to repeat some sort of instructions on coats and the like when I became aware that the look of confused suspicion on the woman's face had become fierce determination—and that this was all directed behind me.

I turned.

The hostess, now dressed elegantly, and her sister, who had arrived earlier, stood there, legs akimbo, arms crossed on their chests.

"Ma, you can't wear that coat," the sister said.

"You're not getting this coat off me."

"Ma, you can't wear the coat. Come on," the hostess said.

"You're not getting this coat off me."

The hostess's sister was a former beauty, tanned and fit, who'd had one of those bad face-lifts, her mouth now a strange asymmetrical line across her face, and one she couldn't quite close, her mouth open with her face at rest. Everything she said sounded as though it was said in a cave before it hit the marble floors. She had dressed and done her hair sort of along the lines of Charo—but an Upper East Side Charo—wearing the very best in platform cork wedges. "You're not wearing that coat, Ma." She took the handles from her mother's aide and wheeled her mother into the bedroom to the left of the foyer, her sister close behind. They positioned the chair at the end of the bed and hoisted its passenger from it, pulling her onto the bed until she was flat out on her back, elbows close to her sides, her fists of diamond gleaming as she continued to hold the mink coat shut.

Together, as practiced as a circus act, the sisters began to shake her up and down, trying to loosen her grip, raising her up off the bed and slamming her down. But her grip was firm. She was like the hero in the cave facing monsters, her face full of victory, her eyes on the ceiling.

"You're not . . ."

slam
"getting . . ."
slam
"this coat . . ."
slam
"off me!!! . . ."
slam

Her curly grey hair shook in the wind of her passing, the coat's elegant brown fur moving heavily around her thin frame. Her shoes flapped.

I was, by now, simply standing in the foyer, watching all of this from where I stood by the door. The door may even have been open. I didn't know what to do. Did I call the police? Was this elder abuse? It seemed like it. If the mother hadn't looked so fierce I would have been even more afraid, but she seemed as hard as her diamonds, as if wearing them conferred mythic powers. Who knew the power then in the coat?

From behind me now appeared the host, the man with the mysterious room, wearing the impeccably smooth pants, a shirt with the sleeves rolled up, and in his hand, an orange popsicle, the wrapper peeled back. "Ma! Ma! Look! I got your favorite!"

The sisters let her go as he approached the bed, as if he held some magical sword they feared.

"Creamsicle!" he shouted, all knowledge.

With that, the hero on the bed smiled for the first time since arriving. Her daughters released her and she sat up to take it from his hand.

When the last of the guests had arrived, I made my way to my other post cautiously.

The party was now in full swing. The son had arrived with his fiancée, and a brother appeared also, with a date, and together the family and their friends toasted the son on his success. It was as if the scene by the door had never happened.

The children I was warned about were also here, and as the host seemed to have known, not only did they want to touch the statue of the woman, they wanted to sit on her lap. The youngest ones seemed afraid of her, the older ones, cautious, as if she were a real woman, another of the employees around them—and someone they could test, by touching or sitting on her. I used my most careful uncle voice. "Please look, don't touch," a refrain in my mouth, careful not to touch any of the children as their parents wandered with buffet plates and the noise thundered around us.

At some point I noticed the grandmother, still in the coat, Creamsicle in her hand, her aide behind her, carefully swabbing as the Creamsicle melted down her wrist. They had put her in front of the statue in the living room.

She wore the mink as easily as a housecoat, her face serene, lost in the cold flavor in her mouth. The coat had fallen open to reveal an elegant if ordinary dress. She watched either the children or the statue or both, or none of it, something else maybe, I couldn't tell. I only knew she had won another victory.

DAVID KIRBY's collection *The House on Boulevard St.: New and Selected Poems* was a finalist for the National Book Award in 2007. Kirby is the author of *Little Richard: The Birth of Rock 'n' Roll*, which the *Times Literary Supplement* (UK) called "a hymn of praise to the emancipatory power of nonsense." His latest poetry collection is *Get Up, Please.*

Inside Voices

DAVID KIRBY

American tourists. American tourists! Hold it down, will you?
Nobody wants to hear about your bills, boils, blisters, backaches,
    and dysfunctional relatives, especially the last: they weren't
even here in the restaurant until you invited them, and now
    they're eating off our plates, tipping over our wineglasses,
telling racist jokes as the food falls from their mouths.
    Now you're shouting, "Hola!" when you want to get the waiter's

attention, even though we're in Italy. You like the rain.
Wait, you don't like the rain. Oh, I get it: you like the rain
    when you're at home, you just don't like it when you're here
in Italy. Maybe I can do something about that,
    or if not me, then maybe the waiter can. Hola! I agree,
your mother's a bitch for retiring; she wants to travel
    the world, and that means there won't be a thing left

"for Alex and I." Greed aside, darling, it's "Alex and
me," unless you're from Jamaica, which you're so
    not. And just listen to the couple one table over: they've
called the chef out and are telling him they are
    to have "no tomatoes, nothing too acid-y, no cheese,
no cream, nothing spicy, no seafood," and then have him
    go through the menu line by line while the rest of us

wait. Some days I feel as though I should print up a card
that says, "I'm a poet, motherfucker—don't you know

you're going to end up in a poem?" You tell the waiter
you want "a Jack Daniels and ginger ale," and when
    he looks up at the hundreds of bottles that line the walls
of this trattoria as though to determine which might
    contain that sublime combination and then down at you

in confusion, you shout, "Jack and ginger! Jack and ginger!"
as though these words might cast a spell that would turn
    this beautiful restaurant into an Applebee's and him into
a college kid named Tripp or Jordan. Hola! We Americans
    are notoriously monolingual. If only you spoke some
other language—then you could say whatever you wanted to,
    and I wouldn't understand you. Or if only you'd had

ESL classes! Then you'd know your mother wouldn't
be leaving anything to "Alex and I." Mothers, retire now.
    Retire and tour the world. Stay in the best hotels and dine
in the finest restaurants. Spend everything! And give the rest
    to charity: I recommend Kiva, a nonprofit that lets people
make microloans to women in third-world countries so
    they can start their own businesses and not spend all their time

at home caring for ungrateful children with bad grammar.
No, Louis Armstrong was not the first astronaut on the moon.
    No, Louis Armstrong was not the first *black* astronaut on the moon.
Actually, thank you for making this poem possible.
    In fact, thank you for making the world possible: if everybody
were quiet and polite and stayed home, nobody'd ever get out
    and spend money, thus creating a tax base that pays for

the protection and renovation of such national treasures
as the diary museum in Pieve San Stefano and Horace's
    villa at Licenza. At first they thought it wasn't Horace's villa
at all because it was too grand a domicile for a poet,
    but then they figured that, since Horace died childless,
the villa was left to the state and was eventually replaced
    by a much fancier edifice erected by Vespasian as a resting

place on his journey to, oh, never mind. I wonder if
Horace ever wished he had a gaggle of little Horaces
to cheer him up in his old age and bring him wine
and cheese and olives. Probably not. Probably he figured
the odes were enough. Love, friendship, religion, morality,
patriotism: everything's in those odes. The uncertainty
of life. The pursuit of tranquility and contentment.

The habit of moderation or the "golden mean."
Allegro ma non troppo. See? It works! You're happy now.
Not too much. I know you're not a bad person,
just loud. Yes, I will have one of your cookies. The waiter
brought you too many, didn't he? Here's to your hometown
and your favorite sports team. Here's to noise, to silence,
to the gift of life. Here's to poems, always, more poems.

HELEN GARNER is an Australian writer who started out in 1977 as a novelist and since then has published ten books of fiction, essays, and long-form nonfiction. Her most recent work, *This House of Grief*, is an account of a murder trial in Melbourne, Victoria, where she lives.

This Old Self

HELEN GARNER

For the first time, on our bike ride to school, Ted and Ambrose thrash along in front of me with their noses in the air, and sail through the gate without saying goodbye. I retire injured to the nearest café. At a corner table I find four of my daughter's friends, mothers from the school. They greet me and I take the empty chair. First one of them, then another, pulls a bundle of yarn out of her bag and begins to crochet. Their wrists and fingers make movements no bigger than they need to be, looping and plunging, drawing the yarn firm, flicking the tail of it out of the way. A tattooed girl in a pretty apron brings the coffee. For a while no one speaks. They too seem to be recovering from something.

In the low voice of shame I say, 'I think I've just been given my marching orders.'

The mothers look up, dreamy with craft. I tell my sorry tale. They click their tongues and puff out air. One of them bursts out, 'Where do they get off! Yesterday I got out of the car to speak to the teacher. And Charlie told me not to come in! He said, "Do NOT come in!" I was furious! I said, "Back off! This has got nothing to *do* with you!"' In a fit of weary laughter they lower their heads over their work. The silence of their industry begins to comfort me. Then another one's needle stops dead: 'Oh my God. I've just realized. You're another generation. You're going through this *for the second time*.' On their faces dawns an emotion I have never seen before, outside the movies: the pitying respect of the soldier for the grizzled veteran.

F orty years ago I had a little blouse. It was white and floppy with panels of lace at the neck. One summer day I stored it carefully in a metal locker at the Fitzroy Baths while I had my swim. When I came back and opened the locker with the key, the blouse was gone. This is one of the impenetrable mysteries of my life.

W hile I'm lying in bed weakened by pneumonia, my friend texts me that when he went to hospital for spinal surgery he took CDs and DVDs, imagining he'd have time to amuse himself. 'Eventually I looked almost with bitterness at these things, and my stupid self.'
    I reply, 'I've been and still am like that. Disgust and boredom with this old self. Are we supposed to do something about it?'
    Just as it's getting interesting, he falls silent.

I n my car outside the analyst's, early as usual, I hear someone on the radio describing a self-portrait by the painter Sidney Nolan: 'A bleak smudge of a head . . . a blue veil of self-doubt.' Yes, that's why I'm here.

B efore dinner Ambrose, whose parents had forbidden him any screen for the rest of the evening, brought his copy of *The Hobbit* to my house. He lay on the dark blue couch, I lay on the light blue one, and for an hour, while we waited to be called to eat, we read in companionable silence, taking comfort from each other's presence.

I had a pain in my jaw, on the right side. In the early hours of the morning I lay unnaturally on my back, full of a dull anxiety, remembering my mother sitting by the fire after all her teeth had been pulled out. Holding a hanky to her face. A bowl beside her to spit blood into. The smiling, eating, drinking, expressing part of her face hollowed out and made weak. Spare me that: the secret oldness of the toothless person. In your private room you take out your teeth, and your face in the mirror becomes that of a corpse.

She sat down opposite me in the cocktail bar, turned her face up to me and confessed that she had fallen in love. I had never seen her look so beautiful. Her eyes had moved out to the extreme edges of her face. They were like brown pebbles at the bottom of a pool. An intense, golden-brown glow came off her. She was a character out of Homer—a mortal clothed by a god in a miraculous disguise. And I dropped a ton of bricks on her. I clapped my hands in her face, I shouted, I banged the table. By main force I dragged her back to this world, where there is no magic and nowhere to hide. I will not be forgiven for this.

The guy who shampooed my hair had a lot of tats and a bright white T-shirt. When he crossed the salon he leaned forward and broke into a trot. In other chairs sat young girls with thick hair that hung down heavy and glorious. But he treated me as if he didn't find me any less worthy of his care than they were. He gave me a head massage and handled my hair with a tender solicitude. When I was leaving he called out goodbye and gave me a look of such sweet courtesy and kindness that I floated out the door.

There wasn't much to do at my friend's place, just light housework and resting, waiting for her cancer to make its next move. I lay on my bed and reread a novel by Colm Tóibín. I love the respectful, patient, unflashy way his thoughts move along. An adult daughter estranged from her mother. The refusal of the mother to show her pain or accept comfort. Blow after blow he knows me.

At a famous shrine in the centre of Bangkok a young man in a yellow T-shirt puts down his backpack and walks away, looking at his phone. Three minutes later the place is blown sky-high. What's the connection between this madness and the intense longing my grandsons have for explosions? Why do boys and men love to blow things to smithereens? My friend the old German professor tells me of his boyhood passion for the Wild West novels of Karl May. One of his teachers had the full set of sixty-five. 'I remember reading the last one when I was fifteen, near the end of the war,' says the professor, 'just before I had to go into the army. I read it quickly, in the days I had left. And after that they didn't interest me any more. Because I had to shoot real guns.'

At a sensitive moment in my sister's life I did something that made her very angry. She pulled rank, and rapped my knuckles in a headmistressy text. I would have to swallow my pride. It took me a day. Between clenched teeth I texted: 'I was in the wrong. I am sorry. With love.' She replied: 'Thank you for your apology and your understanding. And for your love. With my love.' Love, love. We're always talking about love. 'Love' is a thin membrane over a bottomless chasm of violent feelings—rivalry, envy, hatred, even simple dislike. The war between siblings never ends, even when one of them dies. But the laughter. Where does the saving laughter come from, where does it fit in?

'Fresh fragrant garden flowers.' Hand-lettered sign outside a collapsing house in the valley. But we were going to catch a plane, and we had to keep driving.

Late on a dry and scorching afternoon I step out my front door, heading for the station and a drink with a friend downtown. I can smell something burning. The cool change has come: the wind has swung to the south, and thick white smoke is billowing out of the railway cutting at the bottom of the street. A grass fire! In our suburb! Thrilled, I jog towards it. No one in sight but a young woman staring blankly into the whiteness. Without looking at me she strolls into her front garden, stowing her phone. 'Wow!' I say in an excited, neighborly tone. 'Have you got a hose? Or will I run back and get mine?' As if I had not spoken, she fills a small plastic bowl at her garden tap and carries it across the road. Hobbled by her business suit and heels, she leans over the cyclone fence of the railway line and flips a pint of water at the flames, which are close to the ground and running sideways fast and nasty on the wind that's funneling north up the cutting. A young man appears on the veranda holding a little red kitchen fire extinguisher. He passes me without a glance, climbs the wire fence and with a superb disdain points his feeble weapon at the fire. The blast of chemicals snuffs out a square inch of the swift-running sheet of flame, and is engulfed. The fire engine's siren sounds, streets away. 'Hurray!' I cry. 'Here they come!' Still they refuse to meet my eye, or speak. What is the matter with these people? It's a citizens' adventure! Why won't they let me play? Disgusted, I trudge away. On the overpass, choking in the smoke that's streaming north up the track, I hear the sirens and the bells. Two big trucks full of blokes come keeling round the corner. I leap out of the way and watch them lumber past. Before I can wave a warning they turn left too soon, and rush down the wrong side of the tracks. Oh, for God's sake. Fuck the lot of them, if they don't know east from west. With my hand over my nose and mouth I strike out on foot for the Gin Palace.

Contributor Notes

Nominated for a Neustadt Prize and the Man Booker International Prize, **César Aira** was born in Coronel Pringles, Argentina, in 1949. He has published at least ninety books.

Chris Andrews is a poet and teaches at Western Sydney University in Australia, where he is a member of the Writing and Society Research Center. He has translated books by Roberto Bolaño and César Aira for New Directions.

Garnette Cadogan is editor-at-large of *Nonstop Metropolis: A New York City Atlas* (coedited by Rebecca Solnit and Joshua Jelly-Schapiro). He is currently a visiting fellow at the Institute for Advanced Studies in Culture at the University of Virginia, and a visiting scholar at the Institute for Public Knowledge at New York University.

Alexander Chee is the author of the novels *Edinburgh* and *The Queen of the Night*. He is a contributing editor at the *New Republic* and *Literary Hub* and an editor-at-large at *VQR*. His essays and stories have appeared in the *New York Times Book Review*, *Tin House*, *Slate*, *Guernica*, and *Out*, among other publications. He lives in New York City.

Sandra Cisneros is the author of novels, short stories, poetry, and children's books. Her most recent works are *Have You Seen Marie?*— an illustrated book for adults, with artist Ester Hernández—and *A House of My Own: Stories from My Life*.

Linda Coverdale has a PhD in French studies and has translated more than seventy-five books. A Chevalier de l'Ordre des Arts et des Lettres, she has won the 2004 International IMPAC Dublin Literary Award, the 2006 Scott Moncrieff Prize, and the 1997 and 2008 French–American Foundation Translation Prize. She lives in Brooklyn.

Athena Farrokhzad was born in 1983 and lives in Stockholm. She is a poet, literary critic, translator, playwright, and teacher of creative writing. Her first volume of poetry, *Vitsvit* (*White Blight*, Argos Books, translation: Jennifer Hayashida), was published in 2013 by Albert Bonniers Förlag. In 2016, her second volume of poetry, *Trado*, written together with the Romanian poet Svetlana Cârstean, was published.

Angela Flournoy is the author of *The Turner House*, which was a finalist for the National Book Award and a *New York Times* Notable Book of the Year. Her writing has appeared in the *Paris Review*, *New York Times*, *New Republic*, and *Los Angeles Times*.

Aminatta Forna is a writer of fiction, memoir, and essays. She is currently the Lannan Visiting Chair of Poetics at Georgetown University.

Helen Garner is an Australian writer who started out in 1977 as a novelist and since then has published ten books of fiction, essays, and long-form nonfiction. Her most recent work, *This House of Grief*, is an account of a murder trial in Melbourne, Victoria, where she lives.

Howard Goldblatt translates fiction from China and Taiwan, including the novels of Nobelist Mo Yan, for which he received a Guggenheim Fellowship and grants from the National Endowment for the Arts. He lives, works, and cycles in Boulder, Colorado.

Jennifer Hayashida is a writer, translator, and visual artist. Her most recent projects include translation from the Swedish of Athena Farrokhzad's *White Blight* (Argos Books, 2015) and Karl Larsson's *Form/Force* (Black Square Editions, 2015), named one of the ten best books of 2015 by *Partisan*. She is director of the Asian American Studies Program at Hunter College, CUNY, and serves on the board of the Asian American Writers' Workshop.

Aleksandar Hemon is the author of *The Question of Bruno, Nowhere Man*, and *The Lazarus Project*. His latest short story collection, *Love and Obstacles*, was published in May 2009. His collection of autobiographical essays, *The Book of My Lives*, was published by Farrar Straus and Giroux in March 2013. He was awarded a Guggenheim Fellowship in 2003 and a "genius" grant from the MacArthur Foundation in 2004. His latest novel, *The Making of Zombie Wars,* was published by FSG in 2015. His book on the United Nations, *Behind the Glass Wall*, is forthcoming from FSG Originals. From 2010 to 2013 he served as editor of the *Best European Fiction* anthologies, published by Dalkey Archive Press. He is currently the Distinguished Writer-in-Residence at Columbia College Chicago. He lives in Chicago with his wife and daughters.

Penny Hueston is an editor and translator. Most recently she has translated novels by Marie Darrieussecq.

Marlon James was born in Jamaica in 1970 and is the author of three novels. His most recent, *A Brief History of Seven Killings*, was the winner of the 2015 Man Booker Prize, the American Book Award, the Anisfield-Wolf Book Prize for Fiction, the Green Carnation Prize, and the Minnesota Book Award. His first novel, *John Crow's Devil*, was published in 2005 and his second, *The Book of Night Women*, was published in 2008. His short fiction and nonfiction have appeared in *Esquire*, *New York Times Magazine*, *Granta*, and *Harper's*. He lives in Minnesota and teaches at Macalester College.

Honorée Fanonne Jeffers is a poet, a fiction writer, a critic, and the author of four books of poetry, most recently *The Glory Gets* (2015). She is the recipient of fellowships from the National Endowment for the Arts and the Witter Bynner Foundation through the Library of Congress, and she is an elected member of the American Antiquarian Society. Honorée teaches at the University of Oklahoma.

Joanna Kavenna is the author of several works of fiction and nonfiction including *Inglorious*, *The Birth of Love*, and, most recently, *A Field Guide to Reality*. Her writing has appeared in the *New Yorker*, *London Review of Books*, *Guardian*, and the *New York Times*, among other publications. In 2008 she won the Orange Prize for New Writing and in 2013 she was named as one of *Granta*'s Best Young British Novelists.

David Kirby's collection *The House on Boulevard St.: New and Selected Poems* was a finalist for the National Book Award in 2007. Kirby is the author of *Little Richard: The Birth of Rock 'n' Roll*, which the *Times Literary Supplement* (UK) called "a hymn of praise to the emancipatory power of nonsense." His latest poetry collection is *Get Up, Please*.

Édouard Louis is a French writer, born in 1992. He has published two novels—*Finishing Off Eddy Bellegueule* and *History of*

Violence—and an essay on Pierre Bourdieu. His first novel will be released by Penguin (US) and Harvill Secker (UK) in 2017.

Valeria Luiselli was born in Mexico City and grew up in South Africa. She is the author of *Sidewalks*, a book of essays; and two novels, *Faces in the Crowd* and *The Story of My Teeth*. The latter novel, which was written in installments for workers in a juice factory, won the *Los Angeles Times* Book Prize and was a finalist for the National Book Critics Circle Award. She lives in Harlem.

Claire Messud's most recent novel is *The Woman Upstairs*. She teaches at Harvard University and lives in Cambridge, Massachusetts, with her family.

Patrick Modiano was born in 1945 in Boulogne-Billancourt. He has published over thirty novels, as well as the screenplay for Louis Malle's film *Lacombe Lucien*, and a number of children's books. His works have been translated into more than thirty languages and his many prizes include the Prix Goncourt, the Grand prix du roman de l'Académie française, and the 2014 Nobel Prize for Literature.

Nadifa Mohamed was born in Hargeisa in 1981 and moved to London with her family in 1986. Her first novel, *Black Mamba Boy*, was short-listed for the Guardian First Book Award, the John Llewellyn Rhys Prize, the Dylan Thomas Prize, and the PEN Open Book Award; and won the Betty Trask Prize. Her second novel, *The Orchard of Lost Souls*, was published in 2013 and Mohamed was selected as one of *Granta*'s Best Young British Novelists in the same year. She is the winner of the Somerset Maugham Prize and lives in London, where she is working on her third novel.

Mo Yan is the pen name of the Chinese novelist Guan Moye, who is one of the most celebrated writers in the Chinese language. His best-known novels in the West include *Red Sorghum*, which was made into an award-winning film; *The Garlic Ballads*; *Shifu, You'll Do Anything for a Laugh*; and *Big Breasts and Wide Hips*. He was awarded the 2012 Nobel Prize in Literature, the first resident of mainland China to win the award.

H. M. Naqvi is the award-winning author of *Home Boy*. Published by Random House in 2009, the debut was hailed as a "remarkably engaging novel that delights as it disturbs" by the *New York Times*. It has been translated into German, Italian, and Portuguese, and was awarded the DSC Prize for South Asian Literature at the Jaipur Literature Festival in 2011. Naqvi has worked in the financial services industry, taught creative writing at Boston University, and run a spoken-word venue. He resides in Karachi, where he is completing his second novel, "a big, bad comic epic"; working on a collection of nonfiction; and engaging in an initiative to revive the old city.

The twelve collections published by poet **Sharon Olds** include *Satan Says* (1980), *The Dead and The Living* (1984), *The Wellspring* (1996), and *Stag's Leap* (2012), which won both the Pulitzer and the T. S. Eliot prizes. Olds was New York State poet laureate from 1998 to 2000 and is currently a professor at New York University. Her newest book, *Odes*, will be out in fall 2016.

Heather O'Neill is the author of the novels *Lullabies for Little Criminals* and *The Girl Who Was Saturday Night*, as well as the short story collection *Daydreams of Angels*. Her books have been nominated for the Giller Prize, the Governor General's Award for Fiction, the Orange Prize, and the IMPAC Dublin Literary Award, among others. She lives in Montreal and her new novel, *The Lonely Hearts Hotel*, is forthcoming in February 2017.

Amanda Rea is the recipient of a 2015 Rona Jaffe Foundation Writers' Award. Her fiction and nonfiction have appeared in *Electric Literature's Recommended Reading*, *Kenyon Review*, *Missouri Review*, the *Pushcart Prize* anthology, and elsewhere. She lives in Colorado.

Colin Robinson is copublisher at OR Books. He was previously a senior editor at Scribner, publisher of the New Press, and managing director of Verso. Among the authors he has worked with are Tariq Ali, Julian Assange, Noam Chomsky, Patrick Cockburn, Mike Davis, Norman Finkelstein, Doug Henwood, Christopher Hitchens, Lewis Lapham, Mike Marqusee, Yoko Ono, and Matt Taibbi. He has written for publications including the *New York Times*, *London Review of Books*, *Sunday Times* (London), *Granta, New Statesman,* and the *Guardian*.

Radcliffe "Ruddy" Roye is a Brooklyn-based portrait and documentary photographer. Roye was born in Montego Bay, Jamaica, and studied English Literature at Goucher College. Roye is part of the Kamoinge black photography collective, was featured in the 2014 documentary *Through a Lens Darkly: Black Photographers and the Emergence of a People,* and was recently named one of the "50 Greatest Street Photographers Right Now" by *Complex.* Through Instagram (@ruddyroye), he is able to engage with over a quarter of a million followers, collapsing the space between artist and audience to facilitate deeper engagement and understanding.

Sunjeev Sahota was born in 1981 and lives in Yorkshire with his wife and children. His first novel, *Ours Are the Streets*, was published in 2011. His second, *The Year of the Runaways*, was short-listed for the 2015 Man Booker Prize. He is a *Granta* Best Young British Novelist.

Adania Shibli (Palestine, b. 1974) has written novels, plays, short stories, and narrative essays. She has been awarded the Young

Writer's Award-Palestine, by the A M Qattan Foundation in 2001 and in 2003. In addition to writing fiction, Shibli is engaged in academic research.

Tracy K. Smith is the author of three volumes of poetry, most recently *Life on Mars*, which won the Pulitzer Prize. Her memoir, *Ordinary Light*, was a finalist for the National Book Award.

Wiam El-Tamami is a writer and literary translator. Her work has been featured in *Granta, Jadaliyya, Banipal, Alif,* and in anthologies, including *Road Stories* and *Translating Dissent: Voices from the Egyptian Revolution*. She has lived in Egypt, Vietnam, England, and Kuwait, and is currently based on the Princes' Islands of Istanbul.

Claire Vaye Watkins is the author of *Gold Fame Citrus* and *Battleborn,* which won the Story Prize, the Dylan Thomas Prize, the New York Public Library Young Lions Fiction Award, the Rosenthal Family Foundation Award from the American Academy of Arts and Letters, and a Silver Pen Award from the Nevada Writers Hall of Fame. A Guggenheim Fellow, Claire is on the faculty of the Helen Zell Writers' Program at the University of Michigan. She is also the codirector, with Derek Palacio, of the Mojave School, a free creative writing workshop for teenagers in rural Nevada.

About the Editor

John Freeman was the editor of *Granta* until 2013. His books include *How to Read a Novelist* and *Tales of Two Cities: The Best and Worst of Times in Today's New York*. He is executive editor at the Literary Hub and teaches at the New School and New York University. His work has appeared in the *New Yorker*, the *New York Times*, and the *Paris Review*.